Palmetto Sunrise

Jim Lee

DocUmeant *Publishing*
244 5th Avenue
Suite G-200
NY, NY 10001
646-233-4366
www.DocUmeantPublishing.com

Published by
DocUmeant Publishing
244 5th Avenue, Suite G-200
NY, NY 10001

646-233-4366

Disclaimer: This is a work of fiction based loosely on the lives of Frank and Martha O'Berry, James Adolphus and Elizabeth Lanier O'Berry, with James W. and James Brian Lee. All other characters and events are fictitious.

Editor: Philip S. Marks

Cover Design & Format : Ginger Marks
DocUmeant Designs
DocUmeantDesigns.com

Publisher's Cataloging-In-Publication Data
(Prepared by The Donohue Group, Inc.)

Names: Lee, Jim, 1936-.

Title: Palmetto sunrise / Jim Lee.

Description: NY, NY : DocUmeant Publishing, [2019]

Identifiers: ISBN 9781937801939 (15.75)

Library of Congress Control Number: 2018956968

Subjects: LCSH: Families--Florida--History--19th century--Fiction.
  | Tomato growers--Florida--History--19th century--Fiction. |
  Florida East Coast Railway--Design and construction--Fiction.
  | Railroads--Florida--History--19th century--Fiction. | LCGFT:
  Historical fiction.

Classification: LCC PS3612.E34297 P35 2019 | DDC 813/.6--dc23

Dedication

This book is dedicated to my grandfather, James A. O'Berry, who was very influential in my life. As a young boy, he once told me that I had something no one could ever take away from me, but that I could lose it in a simple phrase or sentence. It was *my word*. For once you lie, deceive, or mislead, you will forever be judged as a liar, a cheat or dishonest.

Much of the material in this book are seen through the eyes of history and some of it experienced by the footprints of my grandfather, James A. O'Berry.

Jim Lee

The Old Hotel

It was November 25, 1984. James Brian Lee was quail hunting with his dad, James. They were a few miles south of U.S. Highway 60, just below River Ranch, Florida. They stopped their four-wheel drive Scout II beside the winding banks of the Kissimmee River, got out and started walking. Ahead, Brian could see the ruins of an old building's foundation.

Approaching the ruins, James stopped, squatted down, and removed his old Stetson hat. It was the last hat his grandfather, James A. O'Berry had given him before he died ten years prior. James, a fourth-generation Floridian, rested his shotgun on one leg and gazed out over the river covered in dark green hyacinths and bordered with grey-green cypress trees.

In his mind's eye, James could see an old paddle-wheel, flat bottom ferry boat, beached at an angle, with its bow resting on the sandy bank. The gangplank slanting down to the shore, just like his grandfather had described it to him. He could imagine the passengers as they walked down the gangplank carrying their bags and bundles toward the two-story, five-room hotel. The hotel was run by Jim and Elizabeth, Brian Lee's great-grandfather and great-grandmother.

The small hotel was the overnight stop for the crew and passengers of the stern driven, wood-fired paddle wheel ferry boat. The passengers were headed down river to the great Lake Okeechobee and Okeechobee city. This was their overnight stop, in the middle of nowhere, during those adventurous bygone days.

James could visualize his grandfather and grandmother, standing on the porch waiting to greet the passengers. Lizzy, as she was called, was a tall, handsome, full-figured woman, dressed in a long, pale blue, white-dotted dress, her blonde hair piled high, with a few stray wisps breaking free to blow in the breeze. Jim O'Berry was about 5'10", dressed in high boots, the tan trousers stuffed inside his boots. His suspenders stretched over a long sleeve grey shirt, tucked onto his trousers. On top of his tousled blonde hair he wore an old brown felt hat. Beside them lay an old Tennessee blue tick hound that never moved as long as he was in the shade. He answered to the name Sears. This hotel represented just one of Jim Adolpus O'Berry's many lives.

"What's up, dad?" Brian asked as he carefully leaned his shotgun against the foundation as a buzzard circled lazily overhead in the clear blue sky. Brian was 14 years old, dressed in jeans, snake boots, a camouflage jacket, and an old army boonie hat. He moved quickly and was a typical 14-year-old who enjoyed the outdoors.

"I was just daydreaming about your great-grandfather and grandmother Son."

"Why were you thinking of them, Dad?" Brian asked.

"I suppose, it's because we are standing on hallowed ground Son."

"What do you mean?"

"This place was once a hotel, run by your great-grandfather and grandmother,"

"You're kidding!" Brian exclaimed.

"Nope; I'm sure this is the very place where some of the best meals were dished out to travelers who came downriver on the ferry boat. Granddaddy O'Berry hunted deer and turkeys and raised pigs and chickens for meat. Grandmother would cook meals for the travelers with the meats he butchered and vegetables they grew. But, there was nothing like Grandma O'Berry's black eyed peas with a ham bone in the pot, or a piece of venison backstrap, wrapped in bacon and cooked in butter. Once in a while, the captain of the ferry boat would bring them some ice and Grandmother would get out the old hand crank ice cream churn and they would have ice cream for desert. They charged 50¢ for a meal and 50¢ for a cot to sleep on. That was darn expensive in those days, so they were doing pretty well back then.

"How long did they do this, Dad?"

"They worked the hotel for about three years. Then a drought set in and dried up the river, so Jim and Lizzy had to move on. This place, Son, is a piece of history—and part of your ancestry," Jim finished.

"Where did they go after that, Dad?'

"They went back to Kissimmee to visit his father, Frank O'Berry, Jr., then on to south Florida to farm tomatoes again and raise your grandmother, Kathleen.

"But, the real story was how your great, great-grandfather, Frank James O'Berry, carved out a dynasty here in central Florida."

"Tell me more about my great-great-grandfather, Frank," Brian entreated.

"Well Son, I only met him once. I was about five years old. It was 1941. He was very tall, and your great-great-grandmother was very short and a little plump by then. As a cattleman and truck farmer, he led an interesting and dangerous life. Your great-great-grandparents, Frank and Martha, migrated from Lake City, which, back then, was called Alligator Town, to the Kissimmee area. They traveled on horseback with a pair of oxen pulling their wagon. Over the years they were besieged by highwaymen, rustlers, killers, con men, snakes, alligators, panthers, bears, and wolves. But, it's getting late. Let's crawl into our sleeping bags now and I'll tell you more tomorrow.

Reedy Creek Trail, 1880

Frank O'Berry was making as much noise as possible to draw any potential thieves out of the woods.

"Let's go Lightnin', get up Speedy Boy, pull hard now, ya'll hear?"

The two oxen paid him no mind. He was about to break out into the palmettos and flatwoods.

There they were. He saw two riders in the middle of the trail, apparently waiting for him to get to them. There was no question what they were there for. He stopped about thirty-five yards away.

"What do you boys have those rifles pointed at me for? You think an ox driver is a danger to you?" Frank shouted.

Both Wolf and Martha were alerted. Wolf Johnson was riding out on the flank through the woods. Martha was about fifty yards behind the wagon. When she heard Frank, she moved up closer.

"This here is a toll road mister, and you're going to have to pay the toll," the taller hold-up man said.

"So, you two fellers are planning to rob me, is that it?" Frank shouted.

"You catch on quick farmer."

Frank slowly eased down off the wagon, thinking of his rifle in the back.

"Okay mister I'll get you what you want," he said as he casually stepped back until he was even with the back of the wagon.

"Hold it right their farmer or you won't be able to take another step."

"I understand mister, I'm just going to get my pocketbook so's I can pay your toll, that is what you want isn't it?"

But just then, a shot rang out from Frank's right, taking their attention away from him for a split second.

Frank darted behind the wagon, pulled his rifle out, and fired a snap shot that went over their heads. Wolf's shot was wide by about three inches as he was a good 100 yards away. Meanwhile, Martha had moved in closer and was behind a big cypress and also fired a shot in their direction.

The pair, realizing the three shots had come from three directions, wheeled and rode off as fast as they could.

"Ride, Zeke boy, ride! They got us in a crossfire," said the tall hold-up man, as they disappeared into an oak grove.

The three gathered up together to discuss what to do next.

"Well, I don't need any more excitement," Martha said.

"Now Red, I told you when we got married we would have a good time."

"That's not exactly the kind of good time you promised me Mister Joker Man."

The trail through the swamp looming ahead and was dark and foreboding in the fading light of a warm Florida evening. The crew of three needed to cross before dark. This was the time in the evening when alligators move to feed. They will snap at anything that wanders too close. Gators were more plentiful and more aggressive in those days. Both dogs with the group had been known to worry gators on land. So far, both dogs survived. But in the swamp water, the dogs could have a bad time of it—and even a horse could get a leg snapped at. Martha O'Berry, a petite, attractive young redhead, was wearing an old felt hat and a gingham dress. She used a small leafy branch to brush the mosquitos away.

Overhead, an owl flew silently down the trail in the failing light, heading for its hunting grounds.

Frank and Martha O'Berry, along with their friend, Joshua "Wolf" Johnson, were migrating to central Florida to start a ranch. They planned to round up wild cattle that roamed the woods, which were originally brought over by the Spanish.

Frank pulled their swaying wagon up beside Wolf's horse. In the stillness, Wolf Johnson's saddle creaked as he turned to ask. "Want me to scout ahead and see how deep it gets and see if there are any big gators or anything else to worry about on the other side?"

"I reckon that might be a wise move."

Wolf moved off through the gloom of the swamp and came back half an hour later.

"Well, Mr. Johnson, why are you frowning?" Martha asked.

"It looked peaceful enough at first glance on the other side, but I did notice some horse tracks—but they were old. Both dogs, Matilda and Blue, took off for the woods."

"We'd best call the dogs, don't want to lose them to the gators," said Frank.

"Gators!" exclaimed Martha. "Why, what self-respecting gator would have the likes of ole Blue, or Matilda for that matter, even to chew on?"

"Now Martha, ole Blue might hear you and think you don't love him anymore. But you're most likely right; those gators might be the ones in trouble."

"Blue," Frank called sharply. There was a distant rustling in the palmettos which grew closer and finally Blue appeared—wet, muddy, and panting but with a distinct look of canine accomplishment.

"We'd better put the dogs in the wagon," Frank said.

"Up here boy," Frank called and then slapped the seat with his hand. Blue leaped into the wagon and took his position between Martha and Frank.

"Where did Matilda go?"

"He'll be along directly when he hears me in the water."

"Matilda!" Wolf shouted and whistled as he headed off into the swamp. The grey trunks of the cypress trees were thick at the bottom and then slimed up into the thin pale green leaves of the overhead branches. There they almost covered the trail like a canopy, making it even darker. Wolf was gone about forty-five minutes.

"It looks as if the trail through this cypress stand is just about wide enough for the wagon and not too deep folks," Wolf commented. "It's also clear enough to see well out into the swamp on both sides. That will help us keep a lookout for varmints, so I'll lead out."

Matilda came romping through the reddish black swamp water until it got too deep and then paddled himself up behind Wolf's horse that was already belly deep.

"Wolf, there's a good size gator moving up behind Matilda."

"Here boy," Wolf called. "Come on Matilda!" Wolf yelled as he turned in the saddle, jerking his cow whip off the saddle tie. He let out about six feet of it and smacked the handle down on top of the gators head. The gator snapped at the handle but missed and sank into the murky water. Wolf grabbed Matilda by the nape of his neck and dragged him across the saddle in front of him.

Now ole Blue had never been known to miss out on a good fight. The gator reappeared and Blue leaped, sailing through the air right at the gator.

"Blue!" Frank bellowed.

But the dog hit the water with a huge splash, bobbed to the surface, and began swimming toward the confused reptile as it submerged again.

"Look out Frank, I think the gator's going after Blue!" Martha shouted. They saw the gator come back up, off to one side of the dog. Blue, unable to find the gator, had turned around and was swimming back to the wagon. It was apparent that the alligator would get the dog before he reached the wagon. Frank, sitting in a crouched position on the wagon, sprang off the wagon straight at the gator. As he hit the dark water, his huge hands grappled for the gators snout. They thrashed in the waist deep water for a few tense moments before both man and beast went under the murky depths. The splashing and hollering by Wolf and Martha, and Matilda's barking, created a totally chaotic scene.

Martha pulled out her 25/20 lever-action rifle from under the cowhide cover and levered a shell into the chamber as she stood up. Frank surfaced, standing, red-faced and with the six-foot gator under one arm, while the other held its snout shut. The gator thrashed wildly with its tail, splashing swamp water all over Wolf and his horse. That spooked Wolf's horse, which reared up nearly putting wolf and Matilda in the water, with Wolf hollering, "Hold him, Frank, hold him!"

"What in tarnation do you think I'm trying to do? What I want to know is, how do I let this dang thing go?"

Blue jumped off the wagon again to get back into the fray and grabbed the gator by a back leg.

"Blue's got him by the foot Frank, you're safe now." Wolf howled and began to laugh.

"Funniest thing I ever seen Frank, you trying to skin a live gator, while a dog is trying to take it away from you; Wooeee, what a sight. Eat 'em up Blue!"

Frank growled.

"Get back Blue! Down! Get away or so help me I'll let him have you!" Frank's tone was all Blue needed, so he let go and paddled back to the wagon.

"You want the loan of my skinning knife so's you can skin out that big lizard Frank?" Wolf laughingly taunted.

Frank, holding the gator by one rear leg and the snout, swung the beast up over his head, intending to heave it bodily back into the water. Suddenly a shot rang out, blowing a very large hole in the head of the reptile.

"Ain't you two a pair?" Martha called out, as she lowered the rifle. "One jumps on wild cattle for fun and the other wrestles alligators. What happens to us if one of you gets a broke leg or has your hand chawed off, Frank James O'Berry?"

They both knew she was seriously mad when she used Frank's full name.

"Now Miss Martha," Wolf pleaded, "he couldn't very well let that gator have Blue for lunch, now could he?"

Wolf, still amused by it all took one last parting shot.

"Frank, now don't that beat all? Blue's back in the wagon just awaiting for you. There he sits, tail a-waggin', just dying to lick your hand. Why he must be right proud of you."

"Alright," Frank said, "you all know the rule. If we kill it, we eat it. I'll cut off the tail for supper, since I'm already wet and off the wagon, and you can make all the jokes you want Wolf man, but I'd be obliged if you butcher the critter when we make camp."

"Fair enough, Mr. O'Berry," Wolf chuckled under his breath. Frank put the gator on a big cypress log and hacked off the tail with his trail knife. He handed it to Martha, who put it in a sack in the wagon. Frank turned toward the wagon and Blue barked at him.

Dripping wet, Frank glared at the dog and mumbled, "You'd best hush boy, while you still can."

Frank climbed back into the wagon and Blue lay down quickly. Frank addressed the dog. "Now Blue, it's a good thing you're a good cow dog, or I would have given you to that gator. Marthie, you're a good woman, and a good shot."

Martha didn't reply, but looked the other way, smiling, for she knew that was about as big a compliment Frank could give. They started off through the swamp again, Matilda across Wolf's saddle in front of him with Blue looking for more gators.

"Well, Frankie, that was quite a sight. A lot more excitement than we had at our church and dinners on the ground on Sundays isn't it?"

"Yes, but not as much as we had at the flowing well that time, Red."

"Believe me, husband, that was a different kind of thrill."

Martha added, "Well, let's just hope there are no crooks or robbers in these parts. We've made enough noise to wake up the dead. Besides, I've experienced all the thrills I need for one day."

Alligator Town, 1878

(TWO YEARS EARLIER)

O h my, looky there, that's Frank O'Berry. I surely would like to meet him, and now's my best chance." The red-haired Martha O'Donnell whispered under her breath.

April in Florida often brings sudden showers, but the Baptist Church in Alligator Town, known in later years as Lake City, was having their monthly church dinner on the grounds, anyway. The little, white Baptist church was in the middle of a small oak grove. Spanish moss waved lazily in the afternoon breeze.

Martha had known about Frank O'Berry for some time now and admired him from afar. She was only fourteen, but she was smart and mature for her age. She walked near him looking the other way and bumped into him, almost knocking him over.

"Well, I do declare, I . . . I'm just a clumsy girl today. I'm Martha O'Donnell. Please pardon me."

"Oh, that's okay, err, hi, um, my name's Frank O'Berry."

I wonder what that's all about, but nothing bad can come of it I'm sure, Frank thought to himself.

Frank James O'Berry was over six feet tall, broad shouldered with a squared chin and high cheekbones. He was both handsome and tough looking, but soft spoken most of the time.

"I never saw you at one of these dinners before Martha, but then again I haven't been to many, as I take Sunday afternoons off so I can work my other business."

"And just what business is it that you don't come to church on Sunday?"

"Oh, I do, most times. Just not to the dinners on the grounds I mean. I run a fish trap operation down behind my step-pa's place. You'd be surprised just how many fish I catch and the profit that's in it. Have you ever been to the Town Diner? Those fish dinners are my fish they fry up."

"Can't say that I have, as I'm a pretty good cook and know how to fry fish myself, as do my three sisters. But, maybe I will go there someday just to see if they do it differently. You work for your step-pa, don't you? I saw you pull down a horse to doctor him one day so easily that I almost thought the horse fell of its own accord. I also saw you last year fight a big fella and walk away with him knocked plumb out."

"Well Martha, I'm not partial to fighting anyone, but he deserved it. He was drunk and spoke poorly of the women of this town."

"Well, good for you. I suppose to have a job and a business keeps you very busy?"

A big black cloud moved over the church grounds.

"Well yes, but Martha, I smell rain."

Suddenly, a huge clap of thunder sent all the folks at the dinner scurrying as the rain began to come down in buckets.

"Come on, let's get to some shelter."

He took her hand and they ran over to the shelter of the wood shingled overhang at the back of the church.

"My, that was sudden, I surely got a chill from that shower, I wish I had a coat."

"How bout I put my arm around you, would that be okay?

"Why, why, I . . . well, okay, I guess."

That worked out pretty good, she thought to herself.

She giggled and looked up at him, as she was only five feet five inches and Frank was way over six feet tall.

"You're very tall, taller than either of my two brothers."

Frank looked down, tilted her chin up, smiled and kissed her.

"Careful what you do Mr. O'Berry,"

A strange sensation went through her.

"Oh, you didn't like it? But you kissed me back."

She giggled again and grabbed his hand. Inside the church they could hear the congregation singing "The Old Rugged Cross".

"We'd best get ourselves inside before the rain starts up again or somebody comes looking for us," Martha said, giggling again.

Frank O'Berry, Junior was born of strong Irish stock. His immigrant Irish father was killed in the Civil War. Frank's only memory of his father was that he had a long beard and laughed a lot. Frank, his older sister, Bonnie, and his mother lived in Cowford, Florida, later known as Jacksonville. A few years after the war with the north ended, Frank's mother, Ada, met a horse trader named Siegfried Shultz from Alligator Town, later known as Lake City, Florida. Ada and Siegfried soon married and they all moved back to Alligator Town. Not long after that, Bonnie, Frank's sister, married and moved back to Cowford.

Frank grew up in the horse-trading business with his stepfather. Frank was now a strapping six feet four inches, and at seventeen years old, could handle a man's job.

"Frank, we need to fix that gray mare's hoof and keep her off it for a while," Siegfried called.

"Yes sir, I'll get right on it."

Under the tutoring of Siegfried Shultz, Frank developed into a first-class, successful horse trader.

It was the summer of 1878, when Frank met Martha O'
Donnell. Martha was graced with a full head of Irish red hair
and freckles that Frank took a shine to. Both of her parents
were immigrants from Ireland. Although only five feet five
inches tall, and fourteen years old, Martha was somewhat
of a tomboy. Her brothers taught her to ride, shoot, and skin
a deer faster than most men.

Together, Frank and Martha were the tall and the short of
a couple. Their feelings ran deep, and they were nearly always
together at any social gathering. Martha had turned into a
mature fifteen and Frank, a hard working seventeen-year-old.
Their parents made sure they spent plenty of time together,
and their impending marriage was anticipated by both sides.
Today was not actually their first real date totally alone, but
it turned out to be very special.

Frank's fish traps were in the branch of the river that
ran through the swamp down behind the orange grove that
backed up to his stepfather's house.

"Frank, isn't it about time you collected the fish out of
your traps?" Siegfried asked.

"Yes, and Martha and her dad are due to be here soon.
I'll see if they want to go with me."

Half an hour later, a buggy drove up to the front gate, and
Martha jumped down with a basket on one arm.

"Hello Martha," Siegfried said and then called out. "Aren't
you going to step down and visit Mr. O' Donnell?"

"I have some errands to run, Mr. Schultz. I'll be back in
a couple hours and visit when I pick up Martha."

Frank turned to Martha and took her hand. After a short
huddle, Frank turned to Siegfried and his mother. "Martha
has agreed to go with me to pull the fish traps. We'll be back
in a couple hours."

"Frank, you two be careful and watch for snakes," Franks
mother, Ada, cautioned them.

"We will Ma." Frank said heading for the unpainted barn
and corral. They hitched up a buggy and made their way

down the rutted road, ducking a low hanging branch heavy with Spanish moss. It was a beautiful summer day, with huge, white billowing clouds and a slight breeze as they headed for a cypress creek called the West Branch.

Frank's stepfather, Siegfried, sitting on the porch in his rocking chair, puffed on his pipe and thought to himself as he watched the couple drive off in the buggy. Siegfried kept a full beard with a lean face and frame that stretched nearly six feet tall.

"Mother," he said to his wife. "Don't you worry about those two one bit. That boy is of good stock, is grown, and will do the right thing. He will take care of her and nature will take its course."

"Well I certainly hope so, it seems that the love shines brightly in their eyes." Ada replied.

Ada's lean, pretty face was complimented by her grey-hair and mild temperament.

"And we will miss them when they go," Siegfried whispered under his breath.

As Frank drove the rig down the little used road, Martha took his hand, leaving him to hold the reins with his other hand.

"What you got in that basket, Red?"

"Well, if it is any of your business, Frankie, my name is not 'Red' ." She jerked her hand away from his. "And I was planning on having a picnic with or without you. However, I do have fried pork meat, some collard greens and biscuits, plus guava cobbler, all packed in jars. I also brought two jars of milk."

"Boy howdy, that sure sounds nice, Red. We'll put the jars in the flowing well to keep them cool when we get there."

"You might go wanting for anything that looks like lunch if you keep calling me Red, Frankie O'Berry." A muffled chuckle and a grin was his reply.

After about a mile, they turned off the rutted road, made their way through a wire gap and headed across a pasture toward the swamp where the fish traps were located. As they came around a bend Frank suddenly halted the horse.

"Look over there, Martha," Frank said, pointing with his free hand. A big Florida panther was sitting behind a bush, looking at a calf being born. The newly born calf was no doubt on the panther's dinner list.

"Oh Frank, we can't let that ole cat get the calf,"

"No Martha we can't, I bet that animal weighs 200 pounds. However, I can't be sure I'll hit him from this distance," he whispered, "and it wouldn't be good to just wound him."

Frank slowly drew his saddle gun from under the seat of the buggy.

He raised the gun and fired into the air. The cat crouched, then turned and ran off into the swamp behind him. A bald eagle that had been perched on a bare limb in a tall pine tree jumped from the limb and took flight as the shot echoed through the swamp. The calf moved off on wobbly legs along with his mother and the herd as they moved away from the sudden noise of the shot.

"Well, I do declare, that was most disconcerting. I hope things go quietly from here on," Martha sighed.

"Don't count on that."

The fish traps were set out in the swimming hole that been widened and dug out by his step father about 100 yards from a flowing (artesian) well. The steady water pressure from below made the well flow all the time. It was in the middle of an open field, guarded by just one small, scraggly oak tree.

They stepped off the buggy and Frank tied the horse to the oak tree while Martha walked over to the well. *The well was a pipe sticking up about a foot above a small pool.* It bubbled into a small run off, like a tiny creek, toward the cypress swamp. She gently put the jars into the pool where the water was cool and clear as air.

Frank watched her and smiled as he turned and picked up his saddle pistol and tucked it into his belt. *When working cattle, it was easier and more comfortable to attach the*

holster to the saddle horn without the belt, hence, the name
saddle gun. In the old days, a saddle gun was usually a rifle.
But once in a while a saddle gun would be needed to keep a
wild steer from goring the rider's horse.

Frank smiled and took another long look at Martha and
asked, "Whose girl are you, Martha?"

"Why, like it or not, Frankie O'Berry, I am your girl, and
that's the way it is," she said bashfully as she turned away.

Frank smiled thoughtfully. "Well, don't I have anything
to say about that?"

"Not a thing, Mr. O'Berry," she replied as they turned
toward the swamp.

They walked toward the towering cypress trees along the
creek. A downed pine tree blocked their path, its branches
singed black from a long-ago woods fire. *A woods fire was*
often set by cattlemen to bring back fresh grass, which also
keeps the thick brush down.

A log lay crosswise over their path. Frank started to step
over it but then peered over it first as was his habit. Sure
enough, there on the sunny side of the log, lay a water moccasin warming himself, right where Frank would have put
his foot.

"You want to shoot him, Red, or do you want me to?"

"I certainly do. Hand me that pistol." Martha said with
a grin.

She shot the snake, and the blast echoed off the swamp.
A great blue heron and a tall white egret fled off through the
pale green and gray cypress trees. The sound of the shot also
startled a gator on the bank across the swimming hole. The
gator, who had been aware of their presence ever since they
arrived at the flowing well, quietly slid into the water and
disappeared. Frank stood on the bank and checked out the
area. He picked up a stick and threw it at a moccasin lying
in a low hanging branch over the water. The snake fell into
the water and wriggled off down-stream.

"I don't see any more snakes Frank," Martha offered, keeping a wary eye on the water.

Now everything seemed clear and they waded into the water to pull the traps. The swimming hole was like a small pond. Martha hiked up her dress and tied it in a knot so it wouldn't trail in the knee-deep water.

"This one's heavy. You should take the small end," Frank pointed.

Martha helped him pull in the first trap. The chicken wire trap was full of catfish, warmouth perch, and some small black bass. The second trap only had a few fish in it. Evidently a small gator had gotten in and ripped it open trying to get out.

"Gee, I'm going need a bath after doing all this work, Frank."

"Well your help is much appreciated, Red, and there is always the flowing well." Martha gave him a wide-eyed stare knowing what he meant, and a strange tingle ran through her. Taking in a breath, she grabbed the third trap, which was also full of fish.

Together, they loaded the fish into a box on the buggy. Pulling the traps had been a wet and smelly chore, leaving them both wet and uncomfortable.

"Let's clean up before lunch, Frank. I reckon this lunch shouldn't be a fishy one."

Martha laid out their lunch on the grass next to a blanket and started to wash in the flowing well. Frank took off his wet shirt and held a bucket of water for Martha. She washed her hands and looked up at Frank for a long moment. Frank set the bucket down and pulled her close.

"We'd best get you out of those wet things," he whispered.

"Now, Frank O'Berry, do you know what you're suggesting right here in front of God and everybody? Kissing is one thing, but . . ."

She stepped back with her hands on her hips, with a hard questioning look on her face.

"Yes, I do darlin, and I'm planning on marrying you if you'll have me."

"Really? You mean that? When?"

"Yes, I do mean it, with all my heart, and we'll get married just as soon as we can arrange it. I have enough money put up to get us started, so there is nothing stopping us."

"Oh Frank, that's all I have ever wanted, and I feel just like you do. But, we need to wait until we are married, you do understand, don't you?"

"Of course, I do darlin', you know I'll do most anything for you, Red."

"I'll forgive you just this one time for calling me Red," she smiled.

They hugged and kissed and then began to get ready to go back.

They were married the next month.

One year later, they were in their little Florida cracker house, the floor of which was about three feet off the ground, with a high-pitched roof and a porch all around it made to keep the house cool in the Florida heat. The house had a wood shingle roof, with a detached kitchen behind it. This was a safety precaution against the wood stove burning the house down. As Martha gazed out the window, she saw something across their potato field.

"Frank, you'd best look out there."

Frank followed her gaze past the porch to the other side of the potato field. A huge buck deer was standing along the edge of the woods. The sun was barely up showering shafts of light through the trees and the morning mist silhouetting a big buck deer.

"Martha, would you hand me my rifle, please?"

"That's a couple hundred yards Frank, you sure you don't want me to shoot it?"

"I suppose I'll manage."

Grinning, she handed him his new shiny blued 30/30 Remington lever action rifle with an octagonal barrel and the Marble full buckhorn rear sight. The butt of the stock was concaved and finished in brass so it would rest snuggly on his shoulder. Frank traded a good horse for that rifle. He raised the sight on the riser one step, as he knew the gun shot dead on at 100 yards and dropped a couple inches for the next 100 yards. He eased his straight chair to the porch, sitting backwards on it with the rifle resting on the top of the chair's back. The gun's report echoed against the wood-line on the other side of the field. Before the echo could be heard, the deer dropped in its tracks.

Well, Red, I kilt that deer, so my job is done. You want to go fetch it?" he asked, as she took the rifle back and hung it back on the wall.

"Whoever kills it brings it in and cleans it, Mister Joker Man!"

"I'll remember that," Frank said grinning at her, as he headed to the barn to saddle his horse.

The deer was skinned, quartered, and packed in salt so they could take it with them. Then he went back to the chore of getting their belongings ready for a move. The next day they were to migrate to central Florida to the Reedy Creek area near Kissimmee town. Their friend and nearest neighbor, Joshua "Wolf" Johnson, would accompany them on their trek south.

Joshua "Wolf" Johnson

MARCH 15, 1881

They were married a little over two years, when Martha looked out the front window of their little cracker house across the stubble of last spring's corn field. She saw a man at the edge of the woods coming their way. Martha called out to Frank.

"Look yonder, Frank. Here comes that tall, underfed friend of ours, Joshua, and his no-account hound, Matilda," she shouted to Frank in the back of the house.

"Matilda is a good ole hound dog, Marthie, and you know wolf man Johnson is the best friend we got. See, there, both right on time! Hand me those blankets there, please, Martha."

Frank and Martha lived just outside of Alligator Town, which was named after a former Indian cattleman in the area, nick-named Alligator.

Joshua Johnson, also known as Wolf, was a tall, gangly man, with a full bearded face and a casual attitude about most everything. He was good on a horse, good with a rifle or pistol, and honest as the day is long.

The three of them were preparing to migrate from Alligator Town (Lake City) Florida, down to the Kissimmee River Valley area, where wild cattle roamed the woods free for the rounding up. They were going to be ranchers instead of buying and selling horses. They expected to be on the trail for about a week.

"Frank O'Berry, have you spoken to that stubborn soul Wolf, about leaving those wild wolves alone? Besides, jumping off a perfectly good horse and bring down a wild cow is no way to behave. This is going be a long and hard trip and it needs to be a safe one," she said with her red hair flaring as she spun around to face Frank.

"Now, now, Martha. He knows we don't need no unnecessary shenanigans. Besides, there isn't many wolves left and I can't tell another man what to do for fun," Frank offered.

"Glory be, Frankie, he's got scars all over his arms and neck from jumping off a good horse to wrestle wild horned cows to the ground. Heaven knows for what reason. I also hear tell that he's kilt more than a hundred wolves too with that pistol of his. We surely won't need such nonsense on our trip."

"Now, Red, a man does need some little recreation, don't you think?" Frank said grinning.

"Recreation is it now?" her Irish temper flaring. "Seems more like jumping out of the top of a tall pine tree to see where the ground is if you ask me. I declare! I suppose you'll be trying it next, Frank O'Berry," she said pouting.

"Well, not likely. But, if I did, I'd want to jump on big healthy panthers or bears first. I wouldn't' want to steal Wolf's thunder," he smiled.

"Well so would I, but I'd shoot em first," she retorted.

"That you would darlin; that you would."

Frank couldn't help himself. Her response made him laugh at first. She looked so feisty and sexy at the same time. It reminded him of the first time they met.

"Don't worry about Mr. Johnson, Red. Besides, there ain't nobody better to ride a dangerous trail with than Wolf Johnson. What self-respecting desperado would dare try to hold up a party with the likes of him in it?" Frank grinned again and opened the gate.

"Do you suppose there is such a chance, I mean to run into thieves and robbers?"

"There is always a chance, darlin, just keep your rifle where you can get to it."

About that time Wolf rode his horse up to the gate.

"Good morning to you, Mr. Johnson," Martha said as Wolf Johnson approached the front porch.

"Morning to you too ma'am," Joshua Johnson tipped his hat.

"Come on in and set a spell," Frank said.

Wolf Johnson stepped down off his dappled grey horse, his grizzled be-whiskered face showing a toothy grin under an old felt hat. As he stepped down, he looked at the dog, Matilda, pointed to the ground and the big blue tick hound lay down immediately. Franks dog, Blue, a big Redbone hound jumped off the porch and approached Wolf's hound. Both bristled nose-to-nose but then their tails began to wag. They were content, as they knew each other, and had been on the hunt many times together.

"Blue," Frank spoke in a low tone.

Blue, turned and lifted his leg, marking his territory on the gate post and jumped back on the porch.

"I feel like I'm already halfway to Reedy Creek," Wolf said.

Wolf strode towards the house, pulling on the lapels of a dirty brown buckskin jacket. The jacket had no fringe or other fancy trimmings, as wolf was a plain man. He was wide at the top, at six feet five inches tall; about the same height as Frank.

"Come on in, Mr. Johnson, and help yourself to some biscuits and buttermilk," Martha said.

"Mrs. Martha, you shore know how to say good morning to a body. Biscuits and buttermilk is my favorite breakfast ma'am."

Wolf followed Martha into the small, weathered cypress house. Wolf came out of the house with a plate of biscuits and a pitcher of milk and a blue speckled cup. He poured milk

in the cup and sopped the biscuit in the milk swallowing
the biscuits whole. Matilda, Wolf's dog, cocked his head and
stared at Mr. Johnson.

"Here you go boy," Wolf said to the dog, as he threw a milk
sopped biscuit into the air. The huge blue tick hound leaped
into the air from a sitting position and caught the biscuit. He
threw another to Blue, Frank's hound.

"Is that all you brought with you, saddle bags and a bed
roll, Wolf?"

"Them are big saddlebags Frank."

"Yes, I reckon they are at that. Well, bring em in and we
will finish loading the wagon, we'll get a good night's sleep
and set out in the morning."

"I'm not interrupting your breakfast, Wolf?" Frank commented dryly.

"Oh no, you folks go on about your business; don't you
folks pay me and Matilda no never mind," Wolf jibbed back.
"However, if there's any little chore you might need tended
to, I'd be obliged to help."

"Well, now that you mention it, Mr. Johnson," Frank
grinned. "We do need a way to haul all these trappings south,
so would you mind hitching up the oxen to the wagon if you're
a mind to?"

"Come on, Matilda; let's go poke those quick footed oxen
into action." Wolf told his dog.

At the words "let's go", Frank's dog, Blue, jumped off the
porch to follow, growling and biting playfully at Matilda's ear
as they headed for the barn.

"Martha," Frank called out into the house, "would you
bring me my Johnny Reb blanket when you come this way?"

"You know, Frank, in the time we have been together, I
have learned to love your parents too and now we're to go
trapesing off to who knows where."

"Well girl, if we don't do something we'll never have nothing of our own. I want more for us Martha. Just remember what ole Elijah Morrison said about Osceola County.

Remember when he spoke of all those wild range cows down there just for branding? And if it's true, a man could get a good start in that country. So don't you worry your pretty little head about this trip, Marthie. You know there ain't nothing going to happen to us. Besides that, we got the dogs and they will eat anything or anybody!"

Wolf moved the oxen back to their pen, they all ate supper and turned in for the night.

It was the next morning and the sun had been up about an hour—the beginning of a new crisp Florida spring day. To the east, shafts of sunlight filtered through the thick pines. Wolf brought the ox cart around to the front gate, with a milk cow, and both Frank's and Martha's horses trailing behind.

"Now this is quite a rig you got here, Frank," Wolf quipped. "Good cypress slab construction with cowhide cover and a board seat that will hold two people. A good rig for sure. By the way, what are the oxen named, Frank? Greased Lightnin' and Speedy Boy?"

Well, Mr. Johnson, for your information, those boys had no names until now. But I think you just named 'em, if that meets your approval?" Frank said with a grin.

"Well I reckon so," Wolf declared smiling.

Frank started to load the cart. Even with all his height he could just barely reach the top.

"What do we need that we haven't loaded, Frank?" Martha asked.

"Well, let's see, we got chickens, the pigs, Fatty Boy and Side meat, Buttercup the milk cow, rifles, and plenty of cartridges. What else do we need other than feed for Greased Lightnin' and Speedy Boy, and our two horses," Frank reported.

"Oh, I need to get the seed box too," Frank exclaimed.

"Well if you forget my rocking chair, you will rue the day," Martha reminded them.

"What rocking chair would that be, missy?"

"Well Mr. Funny man, the one as I already saw you load, I was just testing you," She laughed.

"We could use a bigger wagon, husband; it's loaded as tight as a tick. I swear, it looks as if it might topple over sideways. I put your slicker in so you won't catch your death of cold when it rains, and I got mine too." Martha said.

"Why thank you kindly ma'am." Frank exclaimed.

"Don't 'ma'am' me Frank O'Berry; you just get us there in one piece."

Frank tied his horse next to hers and the cow behind the wagon and stepped up on the seat.

"Hand me your rifle and step up missy," Frank beckoned.

She handed up her 25/20 lever action rifle that looked a lot like Franks rifle, only smaller.

"I see you got your traveling clothes on, Red, your laundry dress and a felt hat."

Frank wore work pants with a long sleeve dark shirt and hat.

"I assume my dress meets your approval?"

Frank just smiled, but said nothing, popped his cow whip to get Greased Lightnin's and Speedy Boy's attention.

They moved off to the east, in order to cut the trail south with Wolf and the two dogs leading the procession. So with the oxcart loaded with everything they owned, they started off on the adventure of their lives. None of them could anticipate the trouble that lay ahead.

The Wagon

Back on the trail, after the attempted hold-up, and the wild alligator wrestle, they joined up again and resumed their journey, but much more alert. The dogs got down and ranged out in front of them, scouting the way. After about an hour, Wolf pulled his horse to a stop and waited for the wagon. Wolf whispered in a low tone.

"Folks, I smell smoke."

They all became very alert knowing that many of the unpopulated areas had bands of thieves operating in them, and they had already experienced one encounter. This could also be the two hold-up men they had recently encountered.

"The source of the smoke most likely wasn't the pair we already encountered, as they wouldn't build a fire because it would bring attention to them," Frank whispered.

"Now Martha, you just ease off this wagon and sit your horse again and leave mine. Take your rifle and trail after us, I'll move out first with the wagon. Wolf, you come along behind me a spell," Frank said in a low tone.

"Well, I guess I can keep your ornery hide a-covering your liver old friend," Wolf muttered.

"Likewise to you too, Mr. Johnson," Martha chimed in with a grin.

The cypress trees gave way to thick head high palmettos on either side of the trail. Frank could barely see oak trees

draped in Spanish moss in the half light. The palmettos
stretched for several hundred yards before breaking into a
large oak hammock. If there were anyone there, they would
be camped somewhere in the oak hammock.

Frank pulled his saddle gun and laid it in his lap under
his wet jacket as the wagon and oxen broke out of the palmettos and into the oak hammock. Up ahead he could see
smoke through the trees and began to rest a little easier. No
self-respecting band of renegades would build a fire with that
much smoke close to the trail.

"Hello the camp," Frank called out. Okay for me to come
in? No need to fret."

As he approached the fire he could see a large
closed-in wagon.

Hmm, Frank mused, *looks like a drummer selling things
or a medicine wagon with elixirs to cure everything known
to man, most likely it's a drummer but there are no markings
on the wagon."*

There was a coffee pot and a cook pot hanging over the
fire, although there was no one in sight.

I reckon I'll find the owner of that coffee pot soon enough.

He stopped the oxen next to the fire and waited. All at
once, a voice boomed out from what appeared to be coming
from up in the big oak tree that covered the campsite.

"If'in you're friendly, and would like to share a little camp
coffee, kindly show your hands and step down," the voice said.

Blue jumped up from the seat and growled.

"It's okay Blue, down," Frank told his dog.

"Sounds fair friend, I will just put my hog leg in its holster
here on the wagon and step down."

"Mighty fine, stranger." I reckon no scoundrel of a thief
would be a driving a wagon pulled by oxen," the voice replied.

"Well, if I was a robber man, my two oxen, Speedy Boy
and Greased Lightnin' might be my disguise, and they are
pretty fast for a getaway," Frank quipped.

Frank looked up and saw the man with his rifle pointed at him.

"Well good evening, mister, I ain't had any coffee since before sun up this morning at breakfast."

A hoot owl called out nearby, easing the tension.

"Okay go ahead and step down stranger and I'll do the same. Oh, you are alone ain't you stranger?" The voice asked.

"No sir, I am not. If you look to your back, you might see my partner looking at you." But don't fret we are peaceable folks relocating to the south and headed for the Reedy Creek area. All we want is a little conversation and a taste of coffee." Frank answered.

With that, Wolf moved out from a clump of palmettos about forty yards away, tipped his hat and said, "Howdy do friend," as he put his rifle back in its scabbard and ambled his horse into the clearing.

"Well, if that don't beat all. You fellers are careful like ain't cha?" The man scrambled down the big oak tree, rifle over his shoulder and holding it by the barrel showing he meant no harm.

"Bring your outrider in and we'll have a cup of coffee. My name is Jefferson Hopkins and you both are welcome to a cup of coffee and a plate of beans and back strap."

Hopkins was clean shaven with bushy pork chop side-burns. He wore a bowler hat, a vest, and a jacket, with a gold watch chain showing. He was about five feet ten inches tall and 160 pounds.

"That would be nice, Mr. Hopkins; a feller can't be too careful these days. I'm Frank O'Berry and this here is Blue, my dog. The outrider over there is the almost famous Wolf Johnson," Frank explained.

"Frank O'Berry, it's nice to meet you, and I may have heard of Mr. Johnson."

"What did you say brought you fellers to these parts, Mr. O'Berry?"

Hopkins walked over and leaned his rifle against the wagon wheel.

"We're on the way to Kissimmee and the Reedy Creek area," Frank replied.

"I do need to warn you though, Mr. Hopkins, there are two hold-up men in the area, we ran into them just before dark and ran them off. We didn't get a good look, but one was tall and the other short."

Wolf led his horse into the campsite and tied it to Frank's wagon.

"Well thanks for the warning, I guess you folks look peaceable enough, but after you soak up a plate of my beans, you might not think I'm so harmless." Hopkins said.

"Haw, I kin eat anybody's beans, Mr. Hopkins, cooked or dried!" Wolf replied.

"Well, see'n as how we are all so cozy like, you fellers sit a spell and we'll talk."

"Wolf Johnson here will eat you out of vittles if you let him Mr. Hopkins," Frank said laughingly.

"Oh, Mr. Hopkins there is just one more, little thing," Frank said nicely.

"Come on in, Martha," Frank called out.

"What in tarnation? Mr. Hopkins stood up, eyeing his rifle.

"It's okay Mr. Hopkins, that's Martha, my wife, and she don't eat much," Frank explained.

Martha came out from the dark surrounding the camp with her rifle lowered, leading her horse, looking as pretty as a picture.

"Meet my wife Mr. Hopkins, Martha O'Berry, the best rifle shot in Florida."

"Well, howdy-do missy, pleased to meet you, I hope," Mr. Hopkins' voice trailed off.

Martha tied off her horse, put her rifle in the wagon, and moved up to the fire.

"Wolf Johnson huh?" Mused Mr. Hopkins.

"I think I've heard of you. Ain't you the feller that traps wolves and jumps on wild cattle and brings them down bare handed?" asked Mr. Hopkins.

"Well I've been known to skin a few wolves and taking down a wild cow or two has come in handy when I was out of vittles." Wolf replied.

"But, that ain't nothin' Mr. Hopkins. Frank here bit the tail off a live gator this morning and we have it with us for supper to go along with those beans, Wolf cajoled.

"Shucks, I shore feel better about camping in these parts with you folks in camp, let's get that gator cooking and have some beans," Mr. Hopkins said laughingly.

Wolf cleaned the gator tail and then Martha pulled out an iron skillet, a little fat back to grease the pan. Along with the meal, Wolf told yarns by the bucket full. As the fire died down and it was time to get some sleep, Wolf grew curious about Mr. Hopkins wagon.

"I guess you'll be resting in your wagon Mr. Hopkins?"

"No, I generally sleep by the fire. You see, it's my catch wagon that I keep my animals in until I can ship them north to my partner. He sells them to the zoos, it sorta smells to high heaven in there," Hopkins explained.

Wolf wondered just why then, it wasn't open so it could air out, or why he didn't sleep under it in case it rained. It seemed as if there was something in that wagon that Mr. Hopkins didn't want them to know about.

"That's interesting. You got a wagon full?" Wolf asked.

Hopkins shifted his weight and stammered a little.

"Oh, well, not really, I'm looking mostly," Hopkins explained nervously.

Wolf walked over to the wagon which was closed tightly.

"Smells like you had a herd of goats in there Mr. Hopkins?" Wolf commented.

"Well, I've had all sorts of varmints in there, including a bear and a panther, a big black male panther at that!"

Frank could tell where this was headed and decided to change the subject.

"More coffee anyone? How about you, Mr. Johnson?" Frank asked.

Frank figured that Mr. Hopkins might have more in that wagon then he was letting on, but it was his business and decided not to worry about it.

"I'll feed and tie off the livestock, Frank." Wolf remarked.

Frank and Martha unrolled their bed rolls under the wagon, to keep the dew off. Wolf lay by the fire across from Mr. Hopkins, who lay by the fire away from the wagon. This increased Wolf's curiosity even more. *"Why would anyone not sleep under their own wagon?"*

The fire died down, and the last of the smoke wisped up through the trees and the only sounds were a gator grunting down by the swamp and a whippoorwill in a nearby tree.

As Mr. Hopkins snored soundly, Wolf stirred from under his blanket. He eased the blanket off and put another pine knot on the fire.

"I've been lying on the ground stewing about what might or might not be in that wagon long enough, I have to find out. I just got to know why Mr. Hopkins was so nervous about what's in that wagon. Besides, Hopkins didn't seem like a violent sort, so even if I was discovered prowling around the wagon, not much would come of it, Wolf thought."

He waited another few minutes, squatting near the fire, then rose and eased over near the wagon.

Wolf studied the hinges and decided to make his move. The wagon had a tailgate, then a latched door. The tailgate swung down quietly, as the hinges were made of thick cowhide.

Over by the fire, Mr. Hopkins rose up on one elbow, watched Wolf for a second or two and mumbled to himself.

"Oh no, he's a going to do it. I knew he would. He was just too damned curious. Well, serves him right." He lay back down with a long sigh.

Wolf swung one side of the door out and peered into the blackness of the wagon. He peeked around the corner and looked where Mr. Hopkins lay and all looked well. He struck a match but couldn't see much.

"Nothin in there purring at me or clawing to get out, but it did stink in there." Wolf muttered to himself.

He put his foot on the step rail and pulled himself up into the wagon. He struck another match, and still couldn't see much. He took another step and bumped a burlap bag on the floor of the wagon. As Wolf's eyes adjusted to the match light, the burlap bag moved and began to rattle, then the other bags on the floor came alive and started to rattle. Wolf froze in his tracks as the hot flash of terror filled his body. He realized that he was in a wagon full of live rattlesnakes! Now, few things worried Wolf, but snakes were one of them. "Snakes," he whispered, "Snakes he shouted, snakes!" and leaped backward out of the wagon, sprawling flat on his back with such a ruckus his horse tied nearby reared, broke the halter rope, and galloped out into the night.

Both dogs came howling over to him and began to bark at the wagon that was still buzzing with several dozen disturbed rattlesnakes.

"What the Sam Hill is going on over there?" Frank yelled.

Mr. Hopkins had leaped up and was standing over Wolf, who was still trying to catch his breath.

Hopkins bellowed, "Now you done it, dad burn your hide, your trespassing's done caused your horse to run off and disturbed my sleep."

"What in thunder were you doing in that wagon, Wolf?" Frank asked.

"Well, I just couldn't stand Hopkins here being so secret-like about that blessed wagon, Frank. I had to know what was in there."

"Mr. Hopkins, why didn't you tell us about your rattle-snakes?" Frank asked.

"I didn't tell you cause most folks wouldn't have stayed in this here camp with me if they knew the wagon was full of rattlers. Besides, it was nobody's business but mine," Hopkins replied.

"Well you are right about your business. However, having a wagon load of rattlesnakes in camp and not telling us wasn't exactly a neighborly thing to do." He turned to Wolf.

"Breaking in to a body's wagon to satisfy your curiosity is not a just thing to do either is it, Mr. Johnson?"

"Well Frank, he was so dad burned secret like about that wagon. But I guess you're right, except what if he had a bunch of stolen goods or kidnapped somebody or something?"

"Whatever I was a hauling was my look out, not yours," Hopkins countered.

"Now gentlemen, I suggest we have here a case of too much curiosity and too much secretiveness. I suggest you both shake hands so's we can get some sleep!"

"Well, Mr. Johnson shouldn't have done it," mumbled Hopkins.

Wolf began to grin, "Tell you what Mr. Snake Man, maybe we can work something out after all."

The gleam in Wolf's eye was obvious and made Hopkins curious. Just what do you have in mind, Mr. Johnson?"

"First of all, please call me Wolf; all my friends do. Now I don't rightly like rattlesnakes, but I been told those critters are very good to eat."

"You mean you want one of my snakes to eat?" howled Hopkins.

"I'll pay you a fair price if you show me how to handle it," Wolf replied.

"I get ten dollars in New York."

"Well this ain't New York! So, I'll give you two dollars."

"Sir, you insult my profession, five dollars is a little more fair."

"Three dollars," Wolf said with finality.

"You're robbing me, but okay, I'll do that just to end this nonsense. Now you know you need to eat that snake fresh, so I'll throw in a bag for you to carry it in." Hopkins conceded.

Frank asked, "You ain't planning to eat that critter raw are you Wolf?"

"Well no, I guess not," Wolf replied.

"Don't look over here, Wolf Johnson, for I ain't putting a rattlesnake in my wagon and I ain't cooking no rattlesnake neither," Martha announced.

"Well wait just a little minute, if your snakes are worth ten dollars apiece, you must have a hundred snakes in that wagon, yonder? That's a lot of money to be hauling around these parts.

Ain't you afraid of being robbed of by some yahoo?" Wolf asked.

"Well, Mr. Johnson, I just was, at three dollars a snake."

"Let's figure all that out in the morning so we can get some sleep," Frank said.

"Okay, let me see if I can whistle up my horse first. Good night folks, it's about time you folks got some sleep," Wolf said sheepishly.

The next morning, Mr. Hopkins was up first.

"Good morning folks, I trust everyone is ready to get up and get on the road?" Mr. Hopkins said as he greeted the crew. He had poked up the fire and put some coffee on.

"It ain't light yet," growled Wolf.

"No, it ain't Mr. Johnson, but I've got to get on the road. I have to get these snakes on a boat in Miami, bound for New York City," Hopkins replied. I wonder what boat captain would take rattlesnakes on a boat," Wolf mumbled under his breath.

"Okay, Mr. Hopkins, I'll jump up and maybe you can show me how I aim to carry that rattlesnake on my horse."

"I'll show you how to carry it alright, but the horse might not agree with either one of us."

Frank was already up, fed the horses and oxen and then had his horse saddled and tied to the back of the wagon.

"You want me to saddle that ole broken down mare of yours, Wolf?" Frank asked.

"Thank you, kindly Frank, but I'll take care of her. You get you some breakfast."

"I have some boiled eggs and beef jerky for both of you men," Martha announced.

"Mr. Hopkins, I got enough, if you would like some too."

"You got boiled eggs?" Hopkins grinned.

"Well, I wouldn't mind a couple hen's eggs if you kin spare them," he answered with a big smile.

"It's been quite a spell since I tasted eggs."

Breakfast didn't take long, and Mr. Hopkins brought over a croaker sack and handed it to Wolf.

"Dad burn, you mean that snake is in this flimsy little sack? What if he decides he don't like it in that sack and starts to bite out of this thing?"

"Don't fret Mr. Johnson, as long as he can't see, he is docile as a worm in dirt."

"It's your horse you got to fear, when he smells that snake," Hopkins grinned.

"All you need to do is to tie that snake to the saddle horn and the snake will be as good as a lamb."

Wolf, with snake in hand headed for his horse that was tied to a tree limb.

"Easy boy," Wolf said in a low calm tone. The horse smelled the snake, snorted and looked wild eyed.

"Watch out Wolf!" Frank called.

Wolf's horse shied away. After a couple of times, Wolf got an idea. He put the snake on the ground and led the skittish horse up near the snake sack.

About that time, the snake found a small opening where the sack was tied up and began to wriggle out of the sack.

"Look out Wolf, the snake is loose," Martha shouted.

Wolf started to back up as fast as he could until he backed into his horse which bolted out of the camp again. While Wolf retrieved his horse, Martha walked over to the snake, with most of his body still in the bag, put the butt of her rifle on the snake and picked him up by the neck, calmly placing him back into the bag. She set the bag back on the ground and stepped back. No one said a word.

Wolf eased the sack up and tied it to the saddle. The snake lay quiet in the croaker bag.

"Ok, that was easy, thank you kindly, Martha," Wolf commented as he put one foot in the stirrup. About that time the dogs started barking at the smell of the snake. The horse shied with Wolf hanging on with one foot. He finally got in the saddle as the horse started bucking.

"Hang on Wolf," Frank called out.

Frank, Martha, and Mr. Hopkins all started laughing as the horse banged into the wagon, started the snakes inside to begin rattling again. Both dogs were barking and Wolf's horse almost threw him off. Finally, after a couple of minutes the horse calmed down, with Wolf talking low and stroking his shoulder.

"Mr. Johnson, we all thank you kindly for the rodeo show and I'm glad you survived it without getting throwed," Hopkins announced.

"Well you folks are quite welcome, anytime you need entertainment, you just call on me and my horse," Wolf replied.

Hopkins mounted his wagon and pulled it out onto the trail heading for Miami with his rattling cargo.

"Don't let the gators get you, Mr. Hopkins," Wolf chided.

"You keep that varmint tied up tight," Hopkins warned.

Arthur Wesley Blakie

Arthur Blakie, part time wrangler, part time gambler, and sometime family man, headed his horse drawn buckboard wagon east, trailing his saddle horse behind the wagon on the trail toward Osceola County. He was looking for a new place to begin their life all over again. His wife, Ruth, sat quietly with their two children, Ezekiel (called Zeke) and Caroline, sitting between the two adults.

Blakie was drunk when the fire started in their kitchen. It burned from the kitchen which was attached to the house by a common roof. It wasn't supposed to, but it burned down both the kitchen and the house and everything in it. They had been at Fort Brooke, later known as Tampa, on Florida's West coast. The landlord and the sheriff were still looking for them. Arthur sat with his lips pursed tightly.

"I don't have much to cook with tonight, Arthur," Ruth said with a sigh.

"The fire took pretty much everything we had."

"Don't bother me with your gibberish woman, you burned down the house, not me."

"I know, I know," Ruth replied.

"I did it, I did it, Lord help me, I did it."

"Quit your sniveling woman, I can't stand it."

"Well, if you hadn't been so drunk you might have stopped it," Ruth snapped back.

Without looking, Art swung his arm in a backhand motion, across the children, striking Ruth across the mouth, almost knocking her out of the wagon. The wagon fell silent, with the daughter clinging to her mother in fear as the wagon continued to bump its way along a primitive, narrow road through a dismal cypress swamp.

"I'm gonna pull over to those oak trees yonder." He pointed to an oak hammock about a hundred yards to the south.

"You get the camp settled, whist I see if I kin shoot us some meat for supper. I might find a deer, or with a little luck I don't seem to have of late, maybe I can roost a turkey."

"Zeke, you and your sister collect the wood and get everything out of the wagon for your ma," Arthur instructed.

"But Pa," Zeke chimed in.

"I'm fifteen and you promised to take me hunting with you. I sorely would like to go pa!"

"Don't talk back to me boy. Your sister is only four, which is too young to be gathering the wood alone."

"But Arthur," Ruth reminded her husband cautiously, "You promised the boy."

"Don't worry me none woman, you just see to it if you can get the camp ready without burning it down." he said menacingly.

They entered the oak hammock and stopped. It would be dark in an hour or so. Art saddled his horse and swung into the saddle. He rode off through the gall berry bushes that surround a nearby swamp, his shotgun across his lap. Ruth sighed.

"Children, please unload the wagon, and then go look for some lightered pine knots for the fire. As the sun began to set with pinks and yellows sifting through the trees, Ruth busied herself, getting the biscuits ready. She opened a jar of dried beans she'd been soaking. The children had brought back two loads of pine knots, charred and aged but full of sap to burn easily.

Caroline was only about three feet tall and would drag Zeke's old sharps rifle by the barrel along behind Zeke, just in case he saw something to shoot on the wood gathering trips. Caroline was too small to carry much firewood but could drag the rifle just fine.

Ruth called out, "One more trip children, but this time, see if you can find some oak for the fire. You'd best hurry as it will be dark soon."

A whippoorwill called—a calming sound in the coming darkness. Ruth had built a nice fire and started the supper of biscuits and beans. It would soon be dark and the children were down by the swamp gathering the wood. Caroline was loading the last piece on Zeke's outstretched arms, when a terrible high-pitched screech rang out through the woods, stopping the children in their tracks.

It was the cry of a panther, which was thought to sound like a woman's scream to some. It put a chill of fear through both Caroline and Zeke and they froze in their tracks.

"What was that?" Caroline whispered to her brother.

"Don't worry baby sister; it's just an old bird or something." Zeke shrugged it off, but he knew the sound of a panther, and it was close.

"It was just an ole bird saying goodnight, Caroline," Zeke mumbled, not wanting to alarm his sister.

"I'm a-skeered, Zeke," Caroline whispered.

"Hey, don't be skeered, Caroline. You got that gun, don't you? And you got me here too, don't you?" Caroline nodded her head in agreement.

"Come on, Caroline, Ma needs this here wood."

Zeke hurried down the game trail through the palmettos and gall berry bushes, with Caroline trailing along behind.

Zeke could barely see the path as darkness fell quickly and thinking Caroline trailed directly behind, turned from the trail that skirted the swamp and moved up through the gall berry bushes toward the camp. Caroline, in the half-light and dragging the rifle was lagging behind and didn't see Zeke make the turn. She continued on down the trail, pushed past some palmettos and into a clearing. Not seeing Zeke in front of her, she stopped abruptly.

"Zeke?" she called out.

Zeke, making his way through the head-high dog fennels, called back to Caroline,

"Sister, you'd best get up here with me, it's near dark; Sister? Caroline!" Zeke shouted, "Where are you?"

Back in camp, Ruth heard Zeke call out and stood up in the fire light to listen. Caroline, looking for her brother, peered across the clearing in the near darkness, only to see the huge panther rise up out of the grass.

She screamed and shouted out, "Mama, mama!" At first the big cat was startled, but quickly sensed that the child was helpless. In three bounds, the cat was on Caroline, knocking the gun to the ground as Caroline screamed one last time.

"Sister, sister," Zeke called out as he heard his sister's cry and chilled him to the bone as he dropped the load of wood.

"Zeke?" Ruth screamed, Where's your sister?"

Ruth threw the biscuits on the ground and grabbed a burning lightered knot by the cool end and ran toward the sounds.

"Zeke, where are you, where is your sister?" as she approached the boy's location.

"Oh Ma, she was behind me and then she wasn't, I guess she's back a-ways."

"Caroline," Ruth shouted.

The sounds of her voice echoed across the swamp, but the swamp was silent and dark.

"Lead the way Zeke, where you last saw her,"

Ruth's imagination was running wild and she moved with difficulty. They retraced Zeke's steps and found the trail. At first, they went the wrong way shouting Caroline's name. Soon they turned back and found the clearing.

"This is too far Ma," Zeke exclaimed.

"I didn't come this far."

By the light of the flaming pine torch they saw a glint of metal in the grass.

"Oh no, look Ma, my rifle is. . ." His voice broke off in mid-sentence.

"Caroline," Ruth's voice cracked.

They both saw the blood-soaked wire grass near the rifle. Bloodied drag marks lead off into the swamp. As Ruth sank to the ground in disbelief, Zeke took the flaming torch from his mother and stared at the bloodied spot. He moved toward the swamp and began to follow the blood trail. Ruth sat on the ground sobbing, as Zeke followed the trail out of sight, softly calling her name.

"Caroline, Caroline, can you hear me?"

"My baby, my baby," Ruth cried as she clutched the rifle, which was the last link between her and her daughter. She stared at the ground for a few moments: then she stared at the rifle in her hands. It was the last thing her daughter had touched.

"The Lord has truly abandoned me," she whispered.

Calmly, Ruth placed the butt of the old sharps rifle on the ground. She cocked the hammer back, put the barrel to her chest and pulled the trigger. The roar of the rifle was the final interruption in the pain of the black night.

Arthur Blakie rode into the dark camp, slumped in the saddle, with a deer tied I front of him and uttered a curse.

"Ruth," he bellowed, "where the devil are you woman? Are you asleep? Well, at least you didn't burn up the camp." He slid the deer off the horse onto the ground. As he stepped down off his horse, he saw the biscuits on the ground and heard sobbing from beneath the wagon.

"Zeke, is that you under there?"

"Papa?" Zeke whispered.

"Get yourself out of there boy. Where's your ma?"

"Ma's out there," he pointed toward the swamp and started to cry again.

"Ma's with sister and they'd both be dead," he sobbed.

Sister was eaten by a panther and Ma killed herself with my rifle," he said with bluntness that even disturbed Arthur Blakie.

The next morning they dug a grave for Ruth, with a little mound next to her. Then they butchered the deer, wrapping the meat in cloth until they could process it. The twin mounds under the huge oak tree at the campsite gave the once picturesque place a somber atmosphere. Arthur and Zeke buried Ruth next to the mound for her daughter even though there were no remains of her. They cut down pine saplings and piled them over the mounds to keep the wolves from finding them. The smell of pine sap and the pile of saplings hopefully would deter the wolves.

Arthur turned towards his son. "Boy, I been leaned on all my life. I never had nothin and I got less now. But that's all gonna change now Zeke, my boy. From now on, we are gonna take whatever we need," he said with finality. His face grew dark with pain and hostility.

"No by God, we'll not just take what we need. We'll take anything we want! You understand me boy?"

For the next two months or so, the pair robbed travelers around Fort Brooke. They were hell bent on taking whatever crossed their paths. Then they drifted east toward Osceola County and the Kissimmee River valley. They heard rumors of a trail being cut from Orlando down the lower east coast so the telegraph people could string a wire all the way down to Fort Lauderdale and planned to work their way down that way, but first they would see what they could find in the Kissimmee, Reedy Creek area.

Reedy Creek

The trio of Frank, Martha, and Wolf, continued south towards Reedy Creek, near Kissimmee town. Wolf scouted ahead, while Frank and Martha came along behind the oxen. Their two horses trailed behind the wagon. It was late April, and the Florida weather was breezy and not too hot.

"Well Marthie, we've been out two more days on the trail. That means we only have a day or two more to go."

"I do hope so, Frankie and you keep calling me Marthie and you might find yourself riding in the dust behind this wagon mister. If I had my druthers, I'd like to be called Martha or even Red, instead of Marthie, Mr. Funny man."

"Now darlin', don't go getting your apron in a knot over a little thing like that. I was just seeing if you were awake over there."

Wolf, who had been riding point through the tall pines, noticed something out of the ordinary. He pulled his horse up abruptly and sat there, thinking. Then he rode back toward the wagon.

"Well looky here, there comes Mr. Johnson," Martha exclaimed.

"What is it Wolf?" Frank asked.

"Remember the two trails a while back that cut our trail going east? Well, they done it again, only this time going west! Come on up and I'll show you."

At the trail, Frank got down to look at the tracks.

"How old?" Martha asked.

Wolf answered, "Not very, seems about an hour, maybe two."

Frank touched the tracks and nodded in agreement.

"It looks to me like those two we ran into a couple days ago doesn't it?"

"It sure does," replied Wolf.

"I reckon we'd best watch our step from here on boys," Martha commented.

They all looked at each other in agreement.

"Yep, looks that-a-way," Wolf replied.

"It looks as if the only time they cut the trail, is when the going gets rough on either side," Martha said thoughtfully.

"You mean they are riding alongside the trail, trying not to be seen, maybe looking for someone to rob?" Martha asked.

"It's hard to tell, but sure seems that-a-way. Looks like they are up to no good," Frank answered.

"Okay, Martha, we had best split up again. Did I say it right, Martha?" Frank grinned at her.

"You'd best watch it mister."

"Wolf, you ride about thirty or forty yards out, I'll follow on the wagon. Martha, you trail shouting distance behind on your horse."

"Well, if I get the chance, I might like to turn my pet rattler loose in their camp tonight. Then we'd see what they are made of," Wolf chuckled.

They rode behind the two mysterious horsemen for two more nights. They kept a cold camp both nights to prevent detection as smoke can be smelled a long way off.

On the fourth day of their journey, they approached the settlement of Reedy Creek. Reedy Creek was just north of Kissimmee. They began to notice more trails indicating civilization. This area was mostly tall pines and palmettos with a few cypress stands in the distance. The trail was deeply rutted and sandy.

Wolf rounded a thick stand of palmettos and saw what appeared to be a general store with two horses hitched out front. Wolf looked at the tracks leading to the store, and sure enough, they were the same horses they had been trailing. He pulled his horse up and whistled a bob white whistle. Frank turned in the saddle and motioned for Martha to stop.

Frank pulled the wagon slowly up beside Wolf.

"Looks like a store with two customers," Wolf said, nodding to the store.

"Yep, could be our guys," Frank answered.

Martha moved up just behind the two men.

"Martha, you take your rifle and ease off through the woods that-a-way, whilst me and Wolf will approach the store head on. You cover what happens, which I trust will be nothing," Frank explained.

"But you be really careful, you hear? You with child and all," Frank warned.

"Looks as if we got at least three people in that store, Frank," Wolf surmised.

"Yep, it figurers. There is another horse in the coral out back. That is no doubt the two we had the run in with and we saw crossing our trail," Martha said.

"Well, let's go find out," Wolf said with a grin.

"Okay Frank, you boys take care now," Martha said as she stepped off the horse. She picked up her rifle and began to make her way toward the store through the woods.

Frank pulled the ox cart right up to the left of the two horses, while Wolf went to the right. This would help flank anyone coming out of the store, or at least give them two ways to have to look. Frank stepped down from the wagon, seeing Martha about 40 yards out behind a huge pine tree.

"Blue, get in the wagon," Frank barked loudly to get attention from inside the store.

Blue jumped up on the seat. Wolf remained silent as he figured Frank would get noticed first, giving him time to act.

"You on the horse don't move. Don't neither of you move, we got you both covered from inside." a heavy voice snarled out from inside the store.

"Throw down them pistols, now! The voice commanded. Wolf spoke first.

"Whoa now! What we got here, Frank?"

"Oh, I'd say we got ourselves some mean desperadoes picking on a poor store keeper, Wolf."

"Don't seem fair, Frank. Those fellers outnumber that poor store keeper.

"Hey in there," Wolf called out.

"If you make us put our pistols in the dirt, we will be forced to side with that store keeper feller, then the three of us will outnumber you," Wolf continued to bait the men inside.

"Mister," the voice called out, "I ain't got time for you two. You're most likely the feller that shot at me I figure a couple days ago. You got two seconds to throw down them guns or you'll be lying beside them."

"I saved your life mister. I didn't shoot to kill."

"Well I guess now you wish you had."

"They got no sense of humor, Frank, they just cain't take a joke. Here is my pistol mister thief." Wolf antagonized.

"And mine," Frank dropped his pistol on the small boardwalk in front of the store.

Meanwhile, Martha moved a little closer, but kept out of sight behind some palmettos.

A skinny, angry, scared young boy stepped out of the store, pointing a very large .45 caliber pistol at Frank and appeared to be no more than fourteen or fifteen years old.

The second man pushed the store keeper out in front of him like a shield and approached Wolf. He pushed the shopkeeper out of the way and said, "Set down."

The store keeper sat down on the boardwalk.

"You, the smart mouth." Let's see what you got that I want.

"You the boy's Pa?" Wolf asked.

The boy shouted out excitedly, "Pa, he knows!"

"Shut up Zeke, he knows nothin."

"You ain't much of a pa are you pilgrim?" Frank spoke for the other side.

The gunman whirled toward Frank. "Shut up," Arthur Blakie said through clenched teeth, but Wolf brought him back.

"Shore mister, we'll give you whatever you want. However, we're just settlers moving to a new place, we ain't got much. We got a little deer meat and maybe two or three dollars. We are just travelers trying to find work."

The boy took a couple of steps toward Frank and poked his pistol in Frank's stomach.

"Gimmie that watch, your money, and anything else you got," the boy demanded.

Ole Blue, realizing the unfriendly manner of the boy growled and bared his teeth at the boy.

"You know son, that dog is part wolf and if he gets a holt of you, he won't let go until you're dead," Frank warned flatly.

"You better hope he don't move; as the second shot, would be yours mister."

The dog snarled.

"You really think it would work out that way, son?"

Wolf had thrown a twenty-dollar gold piece on the board floor in front of Arthur Blakie.

"What else you got smart mouth?"

"Well, just a half bottle of my Packin-Ham whisky and some smoked deer meat," Wolf lied.

Frank became very alert, for he knew there were no whisky and no smoked meat in the wagon or on Wolf's horse.

"Throw it down now!" Arthur Blakie bellowed and motioned with his pistol.

"Now, mister," Wolf whined meekly as he patted the burlap bag holding the snake.

"You wouldn't take a feller's poke and leave him with no whisky or meat, would you?"

Wolf had started to untie the top of the snake bag as he spoke.

"Throw it down now!" the man commanded again.

The bandit assumed Wolf was taking it off the saddle.

"Mister," Frank spoke sternly.

"You know you can take our money and valuables, and we'll be alright, but it ain't right to take a man's food."

"You got three seconds to throw it down smart mouth, and you over there shut up."

Wolf had the snake bag open now, so he detached the leather loop that held it to the saddle horn and carefully, but discretely, held on the bottom corner of the bag.

Frank, watching carefully, figured Wolf was going to present the bandit with a fresh rattlesnake, was coiled like a spring, ready to move. As he reached for his watch with his left hand, he looked the bandit boy in the eyes and said calmly:

"Blue. Don't move,"

But the dog was ready.

Wolf, raising his voice said, "Okay mister here you go, now don't drop it, you hear?"

He swung the bag back as if to pitch it to the man, then swung it forward, holding on to the bottom corner. This flung the twisting venomous snake out of the bag and through the air, right at the man.

Blakie, seeing the snake just before it hit him in the chest, yelled and fell backward trying to ward off the snake. His gun went off. At the same time, Martha, who had moved up to the building just around the corner from the porch, fired over the boy's head, at the taller thief. With the snake scene and a loud hot muzzle blast distracting the boy for just a fraction of a second, Frank saw his opportunity.

"Blue!" Frank yelled, as he grabbed the gun in a downward motion from the top, just as the boy pulled the trigger.

The hammer fell, not on the firing pin, but on Frank's hand between his thumb and forefinger, keeping it from discharging.

The dog leaped as Frank jerked the pistol out of the boy's hand. Blue grabbed the boy by his shoulder near his neck. Martha was standing over him with her rifle pointed at his chest.

Blue had the boy good, and he yelled so loud you could have heard him as far as Orlando.

"Ow, ow, owie. Get him off me," the boy shouted.

But the dog had caught many a hog and was in no mood to let go.

Wolf had jerked his rifle out of its scabbard and held the man at gun point. Meanwhile, the shopkeeper, being careful of the rattlesnake, picked up the thief's pistol and pointed it at the bandit.

But the snake had done its job and taken its toll. Arthur Blakie was bitten on the face arms and hands. The snake slithered off a few feet and coiled. The store keeper who had not said a word as yet finally broke silence.

"I never seen anything like you two. They were talking about killin' me so I couldn't identify 'em."

"Glad we could be a little help then mister," Wolf replied.

Frank had pulled out a rope from the wagon and called the dog off the boy. He tied the boy bandit to the tree next to the store and left Blue to guard him.

"Let's see if we can salvage this snake-bit varmint for the law," Frank said.

He walked over to the man who was breathing hard and beginning to turn purple on his face and neck where the snake had struck him.

"I'm afraid yore a goner," Wolf surmised to the bandit.

The man looked up and cursed them.

"Well mister, you made your own bed and now you're gonna die in it," Frank told him.

"Die in it? Frank, you're a poet," Wolf remarked.

The man died in about fifteen minutes.

From the tree, the boy who was recuperating from the dog incident, shouted.

"You killed my pa, I ain't gonna forget that!" he spat out.

Frank walked over to the boy close up to his face.

"Son, what you did, and what you were gonna do, murder the store keeper and us has put you in a very bad light with law abiding citizens. Because you're so young, you may get off with only a couple years in prison. But, let this be a lesson to you. You cannot take what is not yours without expecting retribution. Your pa died because he threatened to shoot someone. You got off lucky, I let you live. I hope you won't ever forget that. If you do, you'll end up dead, like your pa," Frank told the boy.

The shot had attracted a couple of local men from down the trail.

"Pardon me gents, I'm Silas Abernathy and that there is Horace McCelvey," Silas said.

"This here man you saved is Nat Brown, a good friend to us folks around here. If you'd like we would be willing to take that live young varmint into Allendale, err, uh, I mean Kissimmee to the town marshal for you, as a thank you and by your leave." Kissimmee used to be Allendale a few years back, but they changed it to the Indian name of Kissimmee."

"That's mighty nice, I'm Frank O'Berry, this is Martha O'Berry my wife and this is Wolf Johnson and we accept your offer, don't we Wolf, Martha?

They both nodded and the men began to put the boy into their wagon.

Unnoticed in the fray, the shopkeeper had killed the snake with a garden hoe. When Wolf realized that his snake was dead, he confronted the shopkeeper, Nathanial Brown.

"Nathaniel, what in tarnation did you kill my snake for? That was my pet snake Rattle Boy. Rattle Boy was the only snake alive that could capture outlaws and live to tell about it. Well, for a little while anyway," As Wolf's voice trailed off.

Frank began to laugh, and then Wolf began to laugh along with the shopkeeper and the two neighbors. This eased the tension and put things back to normal.

"If you folks are looking for a place to settle, I might be able to help you find a place to rent or buy. In the meantime, you three are welcomed to come and stay with me and my Jenny till you can get settled," Nathanial Brown offered.

"Frank," Wolf exclaimed, "I knew Reedy Creek was a nice place, despite the kind of customers Nat here allows in his store,"

They all laughed again.

"Mr. Brown, we do sincerely appreciate your offer and if you could just spare a spot for us to set up camp that would be wonderful," Frank said.

"Well then, that settles the matter Mr. O'Berry, glad to help. I'll take you folks on home in a few minutes, as soon as I can close up the store. You can park by the barn and use the barn as your camp. You'll eat with us of course and welcome."

For many years after the rattlesnake incident the story would be told in bar rooms, around campfires, at round ups and even barn dances. These stories made Wolf Johnson even more of a celebrity.

Since the boy had not killed anyone, the judge sentenced the boy bandit to six months in the local jail, and one year in servitude to a willing rancher, unless a relative could be found. Tom and Rebecca Simpson took the boy in after the six months in the lock up and then the fun began.

The Simpsons lived near Kissimmee, east of Lake Tohopekaliga.

"Ezekiel Blakie, where are you son? Git yourself out here boy, I got something to tell you," Tom shouted as he stepped out onto the porch and into the yard. In the barn, which was situated off to the left of the house about fifty yards away.

Ezekiel (Zeke) heard Tom call to him. Zeke had just finished shearing off one of the horse's tail with the sheep sheers. Admiring his work, he laid down the sheers, stuck his head out of the barn and called.

"Yes sir Mr. Simpson, I'm coming, Yes sir."

Tom looked over and saw the boy as he came running and reached into his pocket and pulled out a letter. As Jake approached he sat down on the steps and said, "Well boy, you won't be throwing the fresh churned butter in the dirt or painting the hoofs of my horses with tar and riding on the backs of my hogs much longer, because you'll be moving out soon, back to Fort Brooke to live with your Aunt."

"Yes sir, that'll suit me fine," Zeke said with belligerence in his eye, for he remembered how his father died and he hated the whole town for it.

Zeke also knew that if it was found out that he cut off the horse's tail, he wouldn't be getting any supper, so he said.

"Mr. Simpson, I know I ain't truly been to your likin' and this place ain't where I'd wish most to be, but if you like I'll feed and water the horses tonight before supper."

"That-a-way I will get supper and be able to clip the other two horse's tails before I leave," he thought.

Tom, was the trusting soul that God created, and he agreed and went to wash before supper.

The next morning, instead of pancakes and eggs, side meat and cornbread, Rebecca Simpson fried a couple of chickens and made a batch of huge biscuits she called catheads, as they were so large. Those, along with a pan of sawmill gravy made out of flour, milk and bacon drippings would round out both breakfast and lunch for the boy. She wanted to pack him good lunch in spite of his disrespectable shenanigans.

The townsfolk arranged for Ezekiel to ride to Fort Brooke with the mail rider. The mail rider rode the circuit between Fort Brooke and Kissimmee. That morning the boy went to the barn to saddle a horse for the ride and feed the other horses. He left the horse in the barn as it had no tail.

"Well boy, here comes your escort," He could see the rider coming through the pines.

"I'll get my things," Zeke said with a twinge in his voice, for the boy knew that these people had been good to him, even though he hated it here. He was almost sorry he had to leave, almost!

"Howdy folks, I'm Robert Ferguson, the mail rider. I understand I'm to escort a boy back to Fort Brook?"

"That's a fact," Tom said dryly.

Zeke was on the horse and kept the horse pointed towards the two men so they could not see that the horse's tail was missing.

"This here's the boy," Tom gestured towards Zeke.

"That's Ezekiel Blakie, Mr. Ferguson."

"Ezekiel, say hello to Mr. Ferguson,"

Zeke nodded.

"Well son, if you are ready, we need to be moving on. I'm a good half hour behind already. Now Mr. Simpson, as I understand it, I'm supposed to sell the horse the boy is on and bring you back the money on my trip next week? Is that what you want?"

"I'd be much obliged. Would a five-dollar gold piece make it worth your while?"

"No need for that," The mail rider said.

"The townsfolk are paying me to do this job and I figure that this small chore is part of my job."

"I appreciate that very much Mr. Ferguson, but here is the gold piece anyway." Tom flipped the gold piece in the air at the mail rider, who caught it with one hand.

Thank you, very kindly Mr. Simpson, you are very kind,"

"*You've no idea how much I would pay to get rid of this boy,*" Tom said under his breath.

"What's that, I didn't quite catch what you said," the mail rider asked.

"Oh nothing, you have a good trip."

Mr. Ferguson, the mail rider, turned and started down the road. Zeke realizing his prank was soon to be found out, skedaddle on down the road and started to gallop the horse past Tom to catch up with the mail rider.

Tom and Rebecca, now standing on the porch couldn't believe their eyes.

"My God, would you look at that, would you look at what he did to my horse?"

"Now Tom, don't get excited. Just because he bobbed off the tail of one of our horses is a small price to pay for getting him off the place,"

"Oh no! The horses, the other horses," He leaped off the porch and ran towards the barn.

After a week or so at Nathanial Brown's, the store keeper's home, Frank, Martha, and Wolf, went to a boarding house in Kissimmee where they stayed until they could acquire some land. Early one afternoon, after looking over a parcel of land up on Shingle Creek, Frank and Martha stepped out of the local store that doubled as a land office, into the bright sunshiny day where their horses were tied.

"Well Red, we've done it," Frank hugged Martha twirling her around before putting her down.

"We got us ten acres of land with a house!" We're about four miles from town, the place has one acre planted in orange trees, and a small California box style house."

This style house was made with vertical planks and strips of cypress over the cracks to keep the warmth in and the cold out.

"Now all we have to do is put the house in order Martha, but that won't take long. With Wolf and a few of the other folks helping us, I'm sure we'll be in that house in less than a week."

After the house was renovated and while they figured out the next move, Frank and Wolf took odd jobs to keep a little money coming in. They fenced the house, and the odd jobs turned into a service business. At this point, the first of ten children were born to Frank and Martha. James Adolphus O'Berry, was born to Martha and Frank, into the world of raising and working cattle on June 20, 1885.

Then they began to contract cattle services to other ranchers. Since more often than not, the cattle ranchers didn't have enough help to do everything.

"Wolf, we have to gather up Robert Braswell's cattle, mark and brand them. Then we'll drive them to Tampa to the meat packing house."

"How many and what are they paying, Frank?"

"They offered 25¢ a head or might even pay us in cattle." Frank answered.

Over time, this arrangement allowed them to build a sizeable herd. In fact, in a span of six years, Frank and Wolf were selling their own cattle.

Jim O'Berry at six years old had a lot of chores to do, but on occasion, he and a couple of the neighbor boys would get together and play a rodeo game called "Buck the Rider". They would tie an old McClellan saddle between two ropes in the barn. One rider would get on and the other two would jerk the ropes in an effort to throw the rider off. These games usually ended in a horse manure fight, since horse manure was mostly in baseball sized clods.

Frank had an old horse called Peanut. Old Peanut was as calm as a blue-tick hound. Often two or even three boys would mount Peanut and ride him bareback. On occasion one or more would fall off. That's how Jim's nose got broken the first time.

Sometimes the boys would play hide and seek on horseback. That usually took a couple hours, as the rules were that no one could dismount, and must stay within five hundred yards of the base tree. When the hidden horseman was found, he could race back to the base tree. If he beat the person who found him, he was home free.

Unfortunately, on a ranch, childhood was a fleeting moment in time. By the time the boys reach ten years, they were riding as good as the men, and could shoot almost as well. The girls could cook and sew at that age too.

Jim Lee with cousins enjoying a ride.

1895

Ten years later, Frank and Martha sold their place and bought a much larger tract of land below Campbell Station. Here, there was a Florida Cracker style house for them to live in. The family now grew, prospered and all was well. However, one night the silence of sleep was broken by the high-pitched squeal of a hog.

"Frank, wake up, Frank," Martha shook him.

"What is it, oh, I hear it. Something's got one of the hogs."

Frank jumped up, grabbed a rifle and met Jim at the door. Jim O'Berry, now ten years old, already had his rifle in hand. They rushed out the door and in the blackness of the night they could barely see an animal being carrying off, it was a young sow pig. Before they could shoot, the thief and its prey disappeared in the dark.

"Dad burn it," Frank growled.

"That was a good sow, well, let's get some sleep. We'll deal with that bear tomorrow. That's one for the bear zero for us, but we'll fix that very soon," Frank declared.

"Pa, that weren't no bear," Jim said. "It was not big enough for a bear, a wolf maybe."

"Well son, if that was a wolf we could be in for trouble. Where there is one wolf there are usually more.

The next morning, Frank sent Wolf and Jim off to find the remains of the sow that was taken and set there until he comes back. Then, they could even the score. Wolf and Jim set out horseback with two dogs slow trailing the hog scent.

"Look yonder Jim, where the palmettos get real thick, about two hundred yards out," Wolf pointed.

"Well I'll be, that is a very big wolf," Wolf whispered.

"Let's get down, tie up the horses and the dogs, then we'll go on foot," Wolf said.

Moving very slowly, it took about a half hour to creep up on the wolf who appeared to be guarding the dead pig's carcass. The wind was in their favor, blowing from the Wolf to them, so the wolf didn't smell them. As they closed in, the wolf could not be seen, due to the palmettos and dog fennel weeds. Wolf held up his hand for Jim to stop and pointed.

"Shoot him in the heart if you get a clear shot, Jim."

"Yes sir," Jim whispered.

Two wolves came out together from behind a clump of palmettos and Jim fired, and the first wolf dropped where he was spotted. This was followed by Wolf's shot at the second wolf, a mere second behind Jim's shot. The wolf leaped in the air, biting at the place he was hit, and was running blindly towards the two men. Jim took deliberate aim and shot the wolf nearly between his eyes. He tumbled down within five feet of their boots and stayed down.

"Whew, that was a little bit scary," Wolf exclaimed as he poked the wolf with his rifle barrel.

"No, it was a lot scary," Jim answered, lowering the hammer on his Winchester to half cock.

Frank, with Wolf's help, continued to contract cattle services to other ranchers. They would mark, brand, gather up, and drive cattle to the pens for ranchers who didn't have enough hands to do so. After a time, Frank joined the Kissimmee City Council which gave him even more contacts.

Cattle Drive

As the years passed, Martha had three more boys, Charles, Martin, and Roy, and a few years later she bore five more girls. James was Martha and Franks first born and was added to the daily routine. James (Jim) O'Berry, ten years old now, carried out his chores like any man. Frank had contracted with several ranchers around Kissimmee to drive their herds to Fort Brook and Tampa on the west coast of Florida.

"Wolf, why don't you gather up a few hands, about ten will do, along with you, me, and Jim. We have a herd to drive over to Fort Brooke and Tampa."

"What about those cattle thieves we been a warned about?"

"Make sure all the boys bring their rifles and no one brings any liquor."

Also, tell them we take care of our own, and should anyone get hurt, he gets a twenty-dollar bonus.

"Are we picking up the cows a few at a time?"

"No, the Brown brothers have already done that for us. All we have to do is go to their place and pick up a herd of about 800 head. It should take ten to fifteen days to drive them to Tampa from the Kissimmee area, if all goes well."

Frank's son, Jim rode point with Wolf, who knew the way. Jim, was to look for the unusual, which could mean trouble from cattle thieves, but that usually happened at night.

Jim was sturdily built, blonde, five feet ten inches, with a good sense of humor and a twinkle in his eye. He could ride, work cattle, and shoot with the best. Although Jim was his father's right hand, Frank rarely confided or consulted with him.

Even so, Frank had a plan. He knew the story of how the Spanish had brought cattle to America and how they lost some of them as strays or stolen by Indians. This was how cattle had first come to Florida. Joshua Marshall was the cook and drove the cook wagon. He was baffled, by the half-mile of rope Frank made him carry in the cook wagon, in addition to three weeks of food stores.

"Pa, I've found a good place to camp tonight," Jim said excitedly.

"How's that boy? Frank replied.

"Well, there is a thick swamp with an oak thicket to one side. Like you said, we can rope off the whole area. The cows will stomp down the gall berry bushes next to the swamp.

With the swamp at our backs we have half the area blocked off. We can spread out in front of the herd and nobody could stampede the heard from behind and with fires all around they won't be able to surprise us.

"That sounds like it should work," Frank answered.

"In the morning, we'll send out scouts to check the trail ahead. It pays to be careful, but the way I figure it, they won't hit us until we are about half way or more. Then they'll try to tie us up so they can get the herd to Tampa or Fort Brooke before we can catch them. The critical times are after dark and just as we start out in the mornings."

By the time the herd was brought in, Jim had the rope coral almost finished.

"Push 'em in tight boys, Frank ordered his crew, as cow whips popped around the edge of the herd.

They were bedded down for the night and the herd was quiet.

"Okay boys," Joshua Marshall called out. "Possum and dandelion roots, or would you gentlemen like something else for supper?" The cook said with a grin.

Joshua Marshal, or Josh as he was called, was a short round man, who always wore an apron and a white western hat. At supper time, his word was law.

He was standing by a beef hind quarter hanging on the cook wagon which he had just taken out of the salt barrel.

"Josh, quit your joshing; you know your gonna hack us up some steaks off that critter hanging there," one of the hired hands told him.

"Well now, maybe I will and maybe I won't, but if'n I do, you'll eat it the way I cook it or its mush tomorrow, with no possum," he responded.

Joshua hauled out the biggest frying pan ever, as it must have been three feet across and on three legs. With steak sizzling, potatoes boiling, coffee and biscuits, he fed the group well. In another pot, a huckleberry cobbler was baking in the coals, with coals on top for even baking.

"Hot steak, warm center he called out, come and get it," The cook yelled as he banged a pot with a spoon to get their attention.

Each man got coffee, a biscuit, a steak, a boiled potato and more coffee with huckleberry cobbler later.

"I'll say one thing Joshua." One of the men eased up to Joshua.

"Serving a potato with our steak was a step up from beans. Thank you kindly."

"Well I'm partial to beans myself," came a voice in the dark.

Everyone laughed, as they all knew better.

"Mr. O'Berry wants healthy drovers," Joshua commented.

"By the way boys, tomorrow night instead of steak and potatoes, we'll have steak, collard greens, and biscuits."

The next morning, with the sun shafting between the cypress trees, grits, a little side meat, and biscuits with butter and coffee was the breakfast fare. Frank sent two riders out early to scout the trail. One on point and one a couple hundred yards back just in case.

"Well, Frank," Wolf drawled.

"I suppose we should be a little more careful here about. I saw signs yesterday of what looked like a rider that could have been scouting the herd. Nothin' real positive, but it could have been someone up to no good,"

"Well, ain't that just dandy," Frank replied, "I'll send out scouts of our own. Who would be your pick, Wolf?"

"Bob Canfield. He knows how to slip around in the woods better than any of the rest of 'em."

"How's that?"

"Well, young Bob is sweet on Daniel Webster's daughter, over in Kissimmee town and I hear tell they been slippin' around in the woods for about six months, dodging Webster who was looking for them."

"Fine, tell him what we are expecting and get him on his way."

They got the herd moving, as Jim O'Berry took down the rope fence. The next two days were like the first. However, on the third day things began to change.

"Who's that rider coming in so fast, Wolf?" Frank asked.

The rider came galloping up to the two and stopped up short.

"It's our scout, Bob Canfield, Frank,"

"Mr. O'Berry, I saw' em. There were about ten men, but they didn't see me."

"Saw who, Bob?"

Bob's horse was all lathered up and was wheezing.

"Riders, just planning to ambush us. They are about a mile up where the two cypress swamps come together making a pinch point," Bob explained as he caught his breath.

"I'd say they might be intending to let us get the cattle through the pinch point, then try to stop the most of our crew from going through, while they take our herd to Punta Rasa or hide them somewhere."

"Now Bob, think hard, do you believe you saw all of them?"

"Well sir, I don't rightly know, but it seems to me it would take eight or ten riders to move the herd, and at least that many to keep us pinned down. Maybe less if they shot a couple of us right off," Bob explained.

"So, they could have about twenty men. Sounds like that bunch that shot some of the cattle drovers down south last year, doesn't it?"

"Obviously, they have scouts out too. They could be watching us now. We need to find them now," Frank muttered.

"Where would you be, Wolf, if you were watching us?"

"I'd be sidling along the flank with the lead cattle, Frank."

"Okay, Wolf, take one man, and the two of you take the left flank. Bob, you take another man and take the right flank. Bring back whoever you find, alive if possible."

"Jim, you follow Wolf and then find us a different way to push the cattle west if need be."

Wolf, Jim, and a rider named Dennis rode out further than anyone watching the herd would be and circled well ahead of the herd. Jim kept riding, looking for an alternate route. Soon, Wolf and Dennis were hidden behind a palmetto patch when they saw a rider coming. They pulled their rifles from their scabbards. When the man got within 30 yards they challenged him.

"Stop that horse, put your hands in the air or we'll shoot you off your saddle," shouted Wolf.

The man, startled, abruptly stopped his horse and debated whether to pull his own gun, but could not see who had challenged him.

"There are two of us mister, don't do nothin' your liver will regret," Wolf warned.

"What are you two got in mind, you gonna rob me?"

"Put that rifle, down on the ground along with your saddle gun, and do it very carefully," Wolf commanded.

"Okay, mister, as you say," the rider responded as he dropped his weapons.

The three of them rode into camp and found Bob and his man were already back and had found nothing.

"Step down stranger and have a cup of coffee," Frank invited.

The man stepped down off his horse and immediately had his hands tied behind his back.

"I don't' know what you people think you are planning, but I ain't done nothing to warrant this kind of treatment," the rider said.

"I'm Frank O'Berry, mister, what's your name?"

"I don't think that's any of your business."

"Ah well, it doesn't really matter much, does it? We know what you were up to. We also know what your gang is planning and we intend to deal harshly with the likes of them. Now you have two choices, mister. You can talk to us, or if you keep quiet, you'll be tied to a tree for a while and then go to jail after this fracas is over . . . if you survive. However, if you tell us what we need to know, you might just get out of this alive and a free man. That's your choice. You have thirty seconds," Frank said.

"If you know so much you don't need nothin' from me," the outrider said.

Looking the man in the face, with a grim look Frank said.

"Okay Wolf, you boys take him out and find a good tree, tie him to it and put a little of that honey you like so much, all over his clothes."

Wolf exclaimed, "Damn Frank, won't that draw ants and most likely a bear to the man or ants at the very least?"

"His choice, just do it."

"Okay, okay," The rider said, "What do you need to know?"

"Ah yes, the power of the bee," Wolf whispered to himself.

"How many riders?" Frank asked.

"Twenty, but without me that leaves nineteen."

"What is their plan and formation?"

"Well, about half of them are to stop your men as the cattle go through the narrow pinch point between the two swamps. The rest were to drive the cattle to a hidden coral near Fort Brooke, outside Tampa. They were to hide behind the gall berry bushes on this side of the swamp, five on each side of the pass through."

"How long will they wait for us to show and what was your part to be?"

"Oh, they will most likely wait until you get there. I was to tell them when you got close. But they will expect to at least hear from me by three or four o'clock at the latest."

Okay men, as soon as Jim gets back, me, Jim, and three others will take the left side. We'll ride out of sight and hearing, then walk up on them afoot and take them prisoner or shoot them down if they resist.

"Wolf you take another three on the right side and do the same. But before we do, lets round up the herd over by that oak thicket and rope fence them until we get back," Frank explained.

"Won't that be a bit risky leaving the cows unattended?" Wolf asked.

"Yes, but we'll leave the one man with them, hidden. A gunshot by him will tell us we have a problem."

"What if there is a gunshot while we're trying to corral these fellers and the other eight riders come running through?" Wolf queried.

"Some risks must be taken, Wolf. My party will leave ten minutes before yours. With any luck, we'll have ours under control so we can help you, or if it doesn't go right, you can be the ones to help us. Then we'll deal with the other eight any way we can. Besides, we have three extra men to back us up."

"There comes Jim now, but he doesn't look happy," Wolf exclaimed.

Jim jumped off his horse.

"Pa, unless we go through a swamp, it's a good three miles to a clear spot. They will catch us before we can get around I'm afraid," Jim reported.

"That's okay son, we have another plan. Jim, you take these three men and make a quick rope corral over there by those oaks. The rest of you put the cows in the corral as quick as you can. Is everybody ready?"

With the cattle in the corral, the plan was about to begin.

"Mister," Frank addressed the outrider. "You apparently have cooperated so far. Care to tell us your name now?"

"I'm Curtis Batson from Alabama. This is the first time I rode with these men, I really don't know much about them."

Well, riding with those fellers could have been the last of you, and it ain't over yet. However, if your information is good, we'll be back here in a couple hours, but in the meantime, we are going to have to tie you up for that time. Understand?"

"Yes, sir I do, just don't forget me," Batson said."

"Don't worry," Wolf said,

"No honey required, yet!"

Both teams moved out, and about an hour and a half later, the first team was in place and started to make their way through the gall-berry bushes. The bushes were so thick and tall the outlaws couldn't see them coming. Ten minutes later the second team dismounted and began to make their way up behind the other group of outlaws.

Back with the cattle, the lone guard sat in a small oak tree, behind a patch of palmettos, where he could see the cattle. However, he could not see the rider tied to the tree. After about an hour, another rider came from the east, out of sight from the guard. He dismounted and slipped up on the man tied to the tree. It was the second outrider Frank's crew could not find.

"Curtis, where is everybody?"

"Get me untied and I'll tell you about it. Hurray we don't have any time to dawdle."

"I thought you was dead, but here you are."

The second outrider untied Curtis.

"I dodged that bunch trying to catch me, but I see your luck sorta ran out; temporarily."

"Yes, until now. But watch out, there still is a rider guarding the herd. You need to skedaddle outa here now and warn the others. Where's your horse? You got another gun?"

"Yes, I have a rifle back at my horse I can loan you, but what you gonna do without a horse?"

"Oh, I'll get me a horse, don't you worry none," Curtis said with a grin.

"You got a chaw you can spare partner?" Curtis asked.

"Sure do friend, here you go," the second rider tossed a plug of tobacco to Curtis.

"Thanks, pard; it's been a while."

They worked their way back to the second rider's horse where the man pulled his rifle out of the scabbard and handed it to Curtis. It was a well-worn 30/30.

"Thanks for the use of the rifle," Curtis said with a smile. He checked the rifle and levered a shell into the chamber, then shot the second rider in the chest where he stood.

"What . . ." Was the last sound the man uttered.

Then Curtis took the man's pistol belt and climbed up on the horse.

"Thanks again pard, I told you I'd get a horse," Curtis said, looking down at the dead man and headed north. He intended to put a lot of distance between himself and this outfit of cowmen.

The gunshot startled the cowboy guarding the herd, but he stood his ground as he heard a horse ride off to the north. He eased down off his perch in the oak tree and made his way very carefully about 200 yards, to where the shot had come from. He had no idea what he might find. What he found was puzzling, but apparently, Curtis shot this man, whoever this man was, and then left.

Meanwhile, Frank's crew disarmed five of the rustlers without a shot being fired.

They quickly tied them up and moved toward Wolf's group. Wolf was not so lucky. His group of rustlers was a little more strung out.

"Hold it right there," the rustler drew his pistol on Wolf. "How'd you get over here?" He asked Wolf, thinking he was one of them.

"Oh, I had to answer the call of nature," Wolf replied as he stepped up to the man and hit him in the jaw, with the butt of his rifle. The man's reflexes pulled the trigger, shooting wolf in his left foot.

"Who fired that shot?" a deep voice called out.

Wolf, jumping up and on his good foot, with one of his men stifling a snicker, called back.

"He did the bastard; he shot my toe, the stupid idiot. Who gave him a gun anyway?"

"Who was it shot you in the foot? How are we gonna ambush anybody with shots being fired here?" the agitated voice replied.

"I don't rightly know who he is; I hit him with my rifle butt and knocked him out. He'll be okay in a minute or so, I'll let you know then."

Wolf could hear the men coming their way, He signaled his men to get down. All but Wolf crouched down in the gall-berry bushes.

Four men came up within ten yards of Wolf.

"Who the hell are you, I don't remember you?" the leader called out.

At the same time wolf's men stood up rifles leveled at the rustlers.

"Don't move; don't say a word either. Drop those rifles and unbuckle those gun belts." Wolf demanded.

"Well now, I don't know, we got our rifles too, and we can shoot the likes of you down like a rabid wolf," the leader challenged.

The voice of Frank from behind the rustlers bellowed out, "I thought he told you not to speak. Which one of you wants to die first, I got five men here to help him out."

The leader half turned around. "Okay boys, we don't really want to fight those odds. Drop your rifles men," the leader said.

"And those pistols too," Wolf said, and then he heard a rifle shot coming from back toward where the cattle were corralled.

"Frank, did you hear that shot?" Wolf asked.

"Yes," Frank answered as he approached the leader.

"Okay mister, who fired that shot? Are you missing any men?"

"Why should I tell you anything?"

Frank half turned, swung his rifle barrel into the man's face, and he went down hard.

"You may not hang for attempting to steal our cattle, but the way you're going, you might want to. Now answer my question, please," Frank said nicely.

The man made a valiant effort to answer.

"Two men scouting you," he said, holding his jaw.

"Ah," Frank said. "We have one of them, Curtis is his name."

"Well, either one of 'em shot our man, which I doubt, or he got shot. We'll know soon enough," Frank said.

"Curtis is a bad one," the leader said.

"That's interesting, isn't it, Wolf," Frank said.

"Shore is, I thought we had him coming our way," Wolf said.

"You'd best think again mister," the would-be rustler said through his bleeding mouth.

"Okay another question. How many more men you got?"

"None, this is it."

"Wrong answer, mister," Frank raised his rifle, like he was to hit the man again.

"Okay, okay, we got eight more riders waiting to run the herd."

"I guess that no good bastard Curtis gave you that information?"

"Amazing ain't it, Wolf, Curtis actually told the truth," Frank mused.

"If it's any consolation, he had no choice, if you know what I mean," Frank said.

"I suspect the rest of this group will send someone to investigate that shot, Wolf. We best get some men out there with a reception party."

"Ruined my nearly new dad gummed boot, not to mention my toe, I loved these boots," Wolf lamented.

Wolf, limping on his gunshot little toe, moved his crew over to the trail, but out of sight. The sound of pounding hove's alerted the group, as all eight riders came thundering through the narrow pass. When they got close to Wolf's men, the reception party stepped out of the gall-berry bushes, rifles at the shoulder with a bead on the men. The first two realized they were at a big disadvantage, pulled up with the intention to stop, while the last three or four men thought they had a better chance. They already had their rifles out of the scabbards intending to fire.

"First man to raise a gun dies," shouted Wolf. Two of them didn't care and got off three or four shots before they were dead in the saddle. Seeing the distraction, the first three men kicked their horses into a flat gallop, riding low in the saddle. One of the shooters shot one of Wolf's men in the shoulder and he went down. The other three that were left reigned in with their hands in the air.

"Wolf, are you and your boys okay?" asked Frank as he approached the group with the five men tied up and in tow.

"They shot Johnny, but I think it's only a flesh wound and he should mend okay.

"Dad gum it Johnny, did you get yourself shot just so you could collect that bonus I promised anyone that got hurt?" Frank chided.

"Well, no sir, Mr. O'Berry, I don't rightly think so."

"Well, I'm sure sorry you got shot son, you did a fine job and you deserve a good bonus with no reservations," Frank said with a grin. "You will also get your share of the profits as well," Frank indicated.

"Thank you kindly Mr. O'Berry and I hope you will use me again down the road."

"You can bet your boots on that son, no doubt about it."

"Mr. Johnson, you think you can take a couple of the boys and round up that other bunch on the other side, while I figure out what we're gonna do next?"

"Why Mr. O'Berry, I would be most happy to oblige," Wolf chided back.

"But whilst yore pondering a thought, I got me a whopper of an idea about what to do."

"Well spit it out Wolf man."

"Well sir, most likely we won't encounter any more cattle thieving banditos, but wouldn't it be nice if'n we did, that we had a party of body guards riding along-side us?"

"What in thunder are you talking about Wolf?"

"Well, we got to do something with these fellers, so if we tied them together in a string along either side of the herd, it would not only help keep the herd together, but look like they were guarding our operation. Then we can take 'em on to town to the marshal there in Fort Brooke."

"Well, if that don't beat all, Wolf. You done solved us a major problem and did it with style," Frank said.

"But, hold on just a minute," Frank added.

"Jim, take Mr. Johnson's toe here, and four others back to the cattle, find out what that shot was about, and if all's well, start the cattle moving to catch up to us."

"Yes sir Pa, I'll get it done," Jim O'Berry replied.

"Wolf, you get the cook to fix up that toe of yours and then come up here to fix up Johnny too."

Wolf hobbled over to Frank, so most couldn't hear.

"One more thing Frank, those two men that got away, I doubt we'll get any trouble with them, but the second one behind the leader look awful familiar like," Wolf whispered.

"You recognized him Wolf?"

"It happened fast, but that rider was the spittin image of Zeke Blakie, whose daddy I kilt with that rattlesnake," Wolf explained.

"Lordy, if that don't beat all, but unfortunately it does sorta add up doesn't it Wolf?"

"Well, we'd best be keeping a sharp lookout," Wolf replied.

Wolf led the rustlers into Tampa Town (formerly Fort Brooke) with all of them tied from one horse to the other in a long string.

"Well I'll be," said the Sheriff, sitting in a chair leaned back against the front of the jail house.

"Harley, get out here and look at this," The Sheriff called out to his deputy inside the jail.

"Well, bless my soul. We ain't got a jail house big enough for this bunch, sheriff and it looks like that's where these other fellers are planning for them to go."

Frank approached the sheriff.

"Howdy Sheriff Bradley."

"Howdy Frank, what you got there, all tied up in a bow?"

"Well, these fellers tried to steal our herd, shot two of my men, but two of 'em got away."

"I recognize a couple of them. I suspect the rest are from down south, but Frank, I ain't got room for all of what? Eighteen men?" he complained.

"Perhaps you can farm some of 'em out to the sheriff down at the cattle docks, until the judge passes sentences on them."

"I suppose that might work, Frank, but if you got any spare vittles to help me feed this bunch, I would much appreciate it, as my budget just ain't that big."

"We most likely got a half a haunch of beef we could leave with you. I'll also throw in some potatoes and biscuit makin's if that would help."

"Mighty nice of you Frank, seein's how you filled my jail with varmints."

They sold the cattle for a good price and had a good night on the town. The return trip back to Kissimmee town went without incident.

For the next three years, the ranch ran smoothly until the Cuban cattle buyers came onto the scene. James (Jim) had turned 14 years old and could handle most anything that came up. The Spanish American War ended in 1898 with part of the countryside devastated and food scarce in Cuba as all the cattle had been killed or eaten, leaving no beef in Cuba. This opened up a whole new market for cattle.

Cuban Gold

Over the next year, many cattle from central and west Florida were sold to Cuban buyers. Jim was now 14 and looked much older. He was five feet ten inches and one hundred sixty pounds of muscle. Cattle sales to Cuba put the central Florida cattlemen front and center in the effort to repopulate the cattle herds in Cuba with new livestock. Times were tough in Cuba. The Cuban cattle buyers would travel to Florida with saddle bags full of gold coins and purchase up to fifteen hundred head of cattle each time. Of course, this spawned more robberies and killings of the Cuban emissaries. The next three years brought Frank's ranch and business to a point he needed to sell cattle to the Cuban buyers. Jim was now 17 years old, but advanced mentally and emotionally beyond his age.

Frank had received a request for 1500 head of cattle to be cut out of the herd by the buyer's representative. The herd was to be driven to Punta Rasa and put on cattle barges. Frank and his men rounded up 2500 head of cattle from various ranches including his own. Since robberies were a real threat, Frank sent four riders to Punta Rasa to meet the representative at the docks to safeguard the rider and his gold.

Jim O'Berry, Wolf Johnson, Bill Brown, and John Wilson rode to meet the Cuban cattlemen.

They made camp a mile or so out of town that evening and the next morning, went to find the Cuban representative. Jim saw him first.

"Okay Wolf, I think I see him over there," Jim said.

Senior Riaz was over six feet tall, dressed in a blue shirt and typical Cuban work pants.

They rode over to the corral.

"Senior Riaz?" Wolf asked.

"Si Senior, I am Raoul Riaz at your service. I assume you represent Mr. Frank O'Berry."

"Yes sir, we do, this is his son, Jim O'Berry, and I am Wolf Johnson, foreman. These men are Mr. Brown and Mr. Wilson, all trusted men employed by the O'Berry's for quite some time."

"Here is the letter you sent, so you will know we are who we say we are," Wolf said.

Riaz took the letter, read it and said:

Seniors,
    I am very glad to meet all of you. If you should you turn around, you will meet my companions who will also escort us and help drive the cattle back here to the docks.

They turned and saw three riders approaching them.
"Sir, I suspect your saddlebags are holding the payment? We are here to make sure you and your companions get the cattle you need and enjoy your stay in Florida. However, we have something we'd like to try.

"Sir, because some disrespectful thieves often gather in large numbers we have a plan for a little more insurance. We have a saddlebag loaded with rocks we would like to tie over the real money, just in case something happens beyond our control. Then we can throw the rock filled bag down to give us time to get out of gunshot range," Wolf told the Cuban cattle buyer.

"Si, my friends, that seems like a good precaution. If you would give it to me, I will attach it."

"Now we are eight men moving in a group, which makes the trip much safer, as the trail is a long one," Jim said.

They started out the ninety odd miles to Shingle Creek, keeping a fair pace two by two. The Cuban riders didn't look much different than the boys from the O'Berry Brand, so unless someone was spying on them at the cow pens, things should go well.

"Senior Riaz, it will take most of five days to get to the ranch, and we'll arrive around noon of the fifth day. This means four camps along the way," Jim told the Cuban leader.

"Si, and have you decided if we should have cold camps or not?" Riaz asked.

"I would prefer cold camps as that might keep us free of unwanted visitors."

About five miles out of town Jim reigned in his horse.

"Wolf, shouldn't we put a couple outriders on our flanks."

"Makes sense to me Jim. Mr. Brown and Mr. Wilson, would you mind scouting ahead a little and on our flanks?"

"Makes good sense to us too," Brown answered.

"Senior Johnson, I was thinking our risk would not be so as great as you seem to make it," Riaz said.

"Well, it was a just a few years back we got jumped. We were driving about 800 head of cattle to the docks and we captured one of their scouts who told us we had about nineteen men left waiting for us at a tight place in the trail between two cypress stands. We dealt with them with only a few minor gunshot wounds."

"I suppose that would make you cautious," replied Riaz.

"But back then, there were no riders carrying twenty-dollar gold pieces, so we thought we'd best be safe. You can imagine as soon as the word gets out there will be robbery attempts, but we decided you fellers wouldn't be the first ones," Wolf explained.

"Interesting story amigos, I see we were correct in bringing more men from Cuba." Ruiz commented.

On the third night, they made camp in the middle of a huge field of palmettos and posted a guard at the place where they left the trail. Sure enough, along came a lone rider following the trail of the eight horses. He turned and went back the way he came before the guard could get close enough to challenge him and then he reported back to Wolf.

"A lone rider, watching our trail and turned around when he saw we had turned off the trail. Well, that sure ain't a good sign," Wolf remarked.

"I'm thinking we might move on a little further, Wolf," Jim said, thinking out loud.

"You got a right smart idea Jim, we can move out of here, avoiding the trail and in the morning they will think we are still here. I need a volunteer to stay and see how many hombres we are dealing with."

"I'll do it," Jim volunteered.

"Now Jim I know you could do that, but your daddy would shoot me if anything happened to you, and you're not full grown at seventeen, so let's let one of the hands do that," Wolf responded.

"I would really like to do it," Jim said.

The Cuban drovers laughed.

Jim O'Berry, at seventeen, was nearly grown. He only measured about 5'10" tall but was filled out and muscled. He could outshoot most of the other men, pick the heads off quail running in front of his horse on the ground with a cow whip, and to hear him tell it, could throw a baseball straight up out of sight. Nobody thought much of that baseball yarn, but Jim was respected by the men, and he didn't drink or chew either. Two of the men had witnessed Jim kill a steer trying to gore his horse on the last trip; something you have to be quick to accomplish.

"A volunteer?" Wolf asked Brown and Wilson.

"I'll stick around a while, I've seen enough of you three anyway," said Jim O'Berry with a grin. First let's build a small fire so they will be able to smell the camp when they come in. Bobby Brown built a fire and put a big piece of downed oak on it so it would burn all night.

Robert, "Bobby" Brown's build had a shorter stature than the rest of the troop. A lot like Jim, but heavier and tough as nails. His skill with a gun was as good as anyone's too. He wore typical cow puncher clothes, a bit dirty after the six days on the trail.

"Okay then, let's ease on out of here and make like a possum a-leavin' his garden at first light," Wolf remarked.

They all quietly set out through the swamp a hundred yards from the camp. Jim O'Berry cut off to the left and circled around behind the camp behind a big area of palmettos and gall berry bushes where he saw a stump he could stand on. He put part of a palmetto fan on his hat and smeared his face with soot from the burned stump he would stand on, so he would be camouflaged.

Just before dawn, four men leading their horses approached the camp. Jim was sitting on the stump, dozing. Their approach alerted him. However, the four riders only found the camp empty.

"What do you make of this?" one man said to the others.

Jim could hear them talking and could barely understand what they were saying. He could see them as dark shadows pretty well in the moonlight.

"Well, they either lit out a little while ago, or never stayed. If they never stayed they had to have seen you John and figured to put some distance between us and them," the second man said.

"If that's the way it went down, then they must have something worth running for," a third man figured.

"Well, what do we do now?" the third man asked.

"There were eight of them. The only reason they would move like that is if they didn't know how many of us there were," the first man said. The first man was John Zuckerman and the leader of the bunch. John was not real tall, stout with a half-grown beard and a fat face.

"So, boys, we could use a couple more men," John said.

Zuckerman shouted to the last man, "Zeke, you hightail it back to the coral and pick up those two boys from Alabama, Mike Gray and Curtis Batson."

Jim heard that much plain as day.

"With surprise on our side, we can even the odds a little and maybe catch 'em unawares altogether. You see, since they are gone, they still don't know if we came back or not and how many of us there are. I would bet that they were just being cautious."

"We'll slow trail behind 'em Zeke and you hurry and catch up. You can catch up with us by nightfall tonight, or sooner," the first man said.

"Okay, John," Zeke said, "but think on one thing. If these riders are from the O.B. brand, they are pretty smart. They ambushed the last bunch of twenty riders I was with and only four of us got away while under a crossfire." Zeke mounted his horse and galloped back to the west.

"Let's go boys, they could be at least a couple hours ahead, maybe four, but we had better go with caution," John said, as they all mounted and began to walk down the trail the eight men had taken. John, the leader, was cautious and calculating. He figured he and his boys could pull this off with little trouble, eight men or not.

"Two of you move out front and to the sides just in case they are watching for us." John said, as two riders moved out.

Jim waited thirty minutes, then walked his horse back around to the other side of the main trail. He mounted and worked his horse at a fast walk. When he figured he was way ahead of the thieves, started to run his horse at a slow loping pace for about twenty minutes, then slowed to a walk for another thirty minutes to give the horse a rest. Then he loped the horse another period, and so on until he found his group after about three hours of riding. The sun was beginning to slice through the pine trees to the east.

"Here comes Jim," Bobby hollered up to the rest, as he was riding about forty yards behind the group. Jim rode up to the group.

"They came in alright, four men, afoot and up to no good with rifles ready. When they saw we were gone, they sent a rider hightailing it back the way they came, then they started slow-trailing you boys.

"Okay, Jim, how would you figure this one?" Wolf asked with a smile.

"Well, I see two possibilities, Wolf. We can out-ride 'em and never look back. Or we can catch them in the act and put 'em away for good," Jim replied.

"What about the rider sent back?"

"Oh, he was sent for two more men," Jim chimed in.

"Senior Ruiz what would you do?" Wolf asked.

"Well Senior Wolf, this will not be the last time I wish to make this journey, I am certain. There are many cattle buyers in Cuba. If this trip is successful, I will be asked to come again. The fewer banditos to watch out for the better, so I think we should catch them and put them in the jail house, or whatever occurs when we try," Senior Ruiz replied.

"You're a right smart hombre, Senior Ruiz. We'll do just that," Wolf declared.

"Okay boys, here's how she blows. We'll make camp with a fire, set out our bedrolls, filled with grass & leaves. I figure they will be here tonight as that rider will only take a couple or three hours to get back to the others," Wolf said.

Then Jim spoke up, "If we do that, we'll have all of them to fight, won't we?"

"Well shore-enough Jim, what are you thinkin'?" Wolf asked.

"Well sir, right now there are only three riders coming our way. Tonight, there will be how many?" Jim asked.

"Hmmm, boy you got a point, yes you do. There will be six by then. Go ahead finish it out," Wolf said.

Well, I figure they know how many we are, so they will try to get at least that many to go up against us. But, if we take them in small groups, it might not be so risky. In other words, we ambush the three that are coming along and then wait for the rest, reducing the odds by three gunmen. If we leave the men on horseback, horses hobbled and them with no guns, the new bunch would ride right up to them. With enough persuasion, they'll keep quiet and we can get them without a fight, maybe," Jim finished.

"Dad gum Jim, that is a purty darn good plan, let's do 'er. We'll need to know how far back to go. One rider will go out front for an hour. The rest of us will follow and if we haven't found them in an hour, well set up an ambush."

"I'll head out first," Mr. Wilson told Wolf.

"Okay boys, Willy is first up, we'll be along in a little while, Willy," Wolf informed everyone.

William "Willy" Wilson was a long, tall cow puncher. He wore a brown shirt and denim pants and sat a brown horse. Unless he was moving, he would be hard to spot amongst the bushes and trees. He was quiet and thoughtful, so he was a good man to locate the group without being discovered.

"Let's go boys, let's head out and catch up with Willy. I don't want him out there too far ahead of us," Wolf said as he mounted his horse.

Willy had been out about two hours, he had passed through some heavy palmettos about seven feet high and was now entering an area with dog fennels and tall pines and just low growing palmettos. He thought he saw something off to his left and pulled his horse up and stopped. He could see a rider about fifty yards off, riding parallel to the trail. "That must be the outlaws' out-rider," he said to himself.

Willy was too exposed to move, so he held still until the rider got out of sight, then whirled his horse and made it to the palmettos. With a little luck, he could get far enough ahead of him to make it back to the group.

But luck was not with Willy, for there was another rider on the other side of the trail that saw him. The next thing Willy knew, a bullet cut one of his reins, as the report of a rifle was heard, spooking the horse who took off at a gallop. Willy, riding low and trying to grab the cut rein, was about fifty yards past both riders. Another shot rang out from the right and missed. Willy knew they were trying to stop him from getting back to his group, which meant the main body of outlaws was not far behind.

About a quarter mile back, the group heard the shots.

Wolf ordered, "Spread out, get off your horses, and take cover. Tie them off and use your long guns."

The seven men spread out about a hundred yards wide and got in place. It wasn't but a few minutes when Willy came galloping through their line. He saw Jim, with his rifle on the ground, so he reigned in, jumping off behind a big pine tree with rifle in hand.

"Two riders, the rest must be close behind them or they wouldn't have shot at me." Willy relayed loud enough so others could hear.

The outlaw bunch, now numbering six riders were riding hard toward the gunshots.

Thirty seconds later in rode five men, rifles out, looking for their target.

"Stop or die," Wolf yelled at the top of his voice.

Three rifle shots went towards Wolf's voice.

"Fire," Wolf commanded.

The first fusillade of shots downed three of the five riders, but the other two split off to the left and right, trying to turn around.

Zeke, thinking it was the O.B. brand riders, had held back about fifty yards, and when the shots were fired. He jerked his horse to a stop, peeled out of the saddle and began walking his horse back further out of range.

One of the other riders that was not hit almost ran over Bobby Brown. That rider was Curtis Batson, and in the mêlée, Bobby was knocked over, dropping his rifle. Curtis leaped off his horse with his saddle gun out and was standing over Bobby.

"Don't even move your mustache. You're Bobby, aren't you?" Curtis said.

"I got Bobby under my gun over here," Curtis called out.

"Stop where you are or I'll kill him," he shouted.

"Where did you come from and what's your name mister?

"Mr. Batson to you," Curtis said with a smile.

"Tell them your situation," Curtis told Bobby Brown.

He's got me under a gun, Wolf," Bobby yelled back.

"What do you want, Batson?" Wolf called back.

"I figure you got a saddle bag full of gold coins from those cattle buyers that came in yesterday," Curtis said.

"Okay, boys, he's got the drop on me and wants the saddlebag," Bobby called out.

Then Curtis shouted, "Everybody gets back a hundred yards on your horses. One unarmed rider will bring the saddlebag, and nobody follows. I'll let him go about a mile down the road."

Wolf Johnson got the saddlebag full of rocks from Senior Ruiz and rode over to the gunman.

"Well look here what we got," Wolf said.

"Our murdering outrider got a new job." he shouted.

"I thought you'd still be high-tailing it out of the state," Wolf said looking down at the man, his saddle gun out of sight in his lap.

"I ought to kill you where you sit mister," Curtis replied.

"Let's get a few things straight Mr. Batson. First off, I'll give you the saddle bag. Me and Bobby will back off with the others and give you an hour start," Wolf said.

"Now why in the world would I do a thing like that?" Curtis replied.

"Cause that's the best deal you're gonna get. Now, I am a man of my word, so you will get an hour, which is all you would get if you took Bobby with you, only I figure you'd kill him at first opportunity," Wolf said.

"Well, if that's how you feel, what if I just put a bullet in you where you sit right now?" Curtis replied.

Well, two reasons, "Mister" Batson. First, what you don't know is two of our boys are already flanking you with rifles. Since you been on the ground for a spell you couldn't see. But, most of all, and finally, (Wolf had his gun still hidden, but in hand and cocked) if you move that gun an inch, I will kill you," Wolf said.

The look on Curtis' face was telltale. Now he knew for sure Wolf had a gun in his hand. He doubted he could beat him to the draw.

"Hmmm, only one hour? How about two hours?"

"You heard the terms, Mr. Batson."

Alright, you take Bobby here and back off to where you said you would, I'm holding you to your word," Curtis said shakily.

"Fair enough mister. Okay, here it is; take your ill-gotten gain and go fast, as one-hour ain't much and we will be behind you."

Bobby moved back to Wolf's side and Wolf threw the saddle bag on the ground between them.

"If you make it, you'd best spend that gold wisely in another country mister," Wolf finished.

"Back up out of range," Curtis ordered.

"Walk behind me, Bobby," Wolf ordered as he backed his horse out of pistol range, while slipping his rifle out of the scabbard.

Curtis, knowing Wolf couldn't see him well, picked up Bobby's rifle. He knew he could hit Wolf easily at 30 yards. Without thinking twice, he spun around to shoot Wolf, just as a shot rang out from Wolf's right. Curtis, hit by a bullet at close range dropped like a sack of potatoes.

"You okay, Wolf?" Jim shouted.

"Is that you, Jim? It sure looks like you shot just in time, as I was a-gonna kill that no good murderer myself," Wolf hollered.

"Well Bobby, what are you waiting for, go git your rifle and that 'valuable' rock filled saddlebag that Jim done got back for you," Wolf said.

"Then I expect we'd better bury him," Bobby answered.

"No, I don't think so. We ain't got far to go, and the way I figure, they will have a re-ward out on this fella."

"Hey Wolf, I like your plan, that would be extra pay for all these shenanigans wouldn't it, Bobby?" Jim replied.

"Okay, then it's settled," Wolf said with finality.

The rest of the trip was without incident, and 1,500 head of prime beef were cut out of the different herds gathered up in a field outside of Kissimmee. Payment was tendered, and the cattle were driven back to Punta Rasa. There they loaded the cattle onto barges bound for Cuba.

This was one of many such cattle buys, and most of them were of little difficulty. The next few years were without any real problems, with Frank and Martha's family growing.

Campbell Station, 1903

As Frank's assets grew he bought more land bordering Lake Tohoptaliga on the east side south of Kissimmee. It was a very large plot with excellent grazing and farming land. This piece of real estate ran all the way below Campbell Station where the house was located. Jim was 18 years old and the eldest of nine children. He and his four brothers, Charles, Martin, Frank and Roy were a great asset to Frank senior as well. Frank and Martha also had five daughters. Frank had truck crops, cattle, horses, hogs, sheep, and goats. Everything he touched seemed to prosper.

"Jim, I want you and Wolf to oversee the butchering of three steers, six sheep, and two dozen hogs and then get them ready to put on the train. It's cool now and getting colder. Start today and take them to Campbell Station to the train early tomorrow," Frank ordered.

"Yes, Pa," Jim quickly replied, knowing his father was not feeling well and was very strict about carrying out his orders. No one knew just how sick Frank and another member of the family would get.

Jim and Wolf, along with a couple of the other hands, butchered the animals in their small slaughter house and prepared them for transport.

"Wolf, if you and the boys are ready, I'll go hitch up the horses to the wagon and bring it around."

Jim brought the two huge Percheron mares around to pull the big load.

Jim said, "We have about 2,500 to 3,000 pounds of meat, so let's pull out early so we can get to the railroad way before the train gets there."

Jim and Wolf Johnson pulled out just before 2 a.m. wearing heavy coats, as the weather had turned bitterly cold.

They built a fire immediately after arriving at the Campbell Station train stop. The pine knots blazed yellow and released black smoke from the pinesap in the black thirty-something Florida night. The two shadows of Jim and Wolf bundled in big jackets and droopy hats, crouched close to the fire, danced against the pine slats of the tiny building in contrast to the cold black night.

"Well, Wolf, its nigh on four in the morning. What time is that train supposed to show?"

Now, Jim, you ain't got no place else to go, so we'll just keep warm until she shows."

"Jim did you bring something we can set on fire to flag the train with?"

"I sure did. I got a whole newspaper in case one burning flag doesn't work. Say, is that Lykes Brother Meat Packing Plant very big Wolf?"

"I guess it's the biggest around, since most of the beef, sheep, and hogs are no longer bound for Cuba, Lykes Brothers puts it on a train or a boat, bound for wherever they want it to go."

In January, the bitter cold brought on higher humidity in Florida, so a thirty plus degree temperature made it feel colder than it really was. Jim turned to Wolf, his straw blond hair poked out of the old rumpled hat he wore.

"You think it's freezing, Wolf?" Jim asked.

"Not quite Jim, about thirty-four to thirty-eight degrees I reckon," Wolf replied.

In the stillness of the night, they heard the train a way off.

"There she blows, Wolf. I'll get that torch ready," Jim said as he rose and stepped over to the paper.

"I can see the train about a quarter mile away," Jim said as he waved the burning paper.

From the cab of the train, the engineer saw the burning signal, and started slowing down. Jim lit another torch just to make sure, and the train stopped and out jumped John, the conductor from the caboose.

"What you boys got for us tonight?" John asked.

"Mutton, hog, and beeves, the best you ever saw. Here's the manifest," Jim said as he handed the paperwork to John.

"Okay, start loading and I'll count 'em up."

Jim backed the rig up to the open car door and they loaded it with the carcasses and shut the door on the freight car.

"See you next week, John," Jim called out.

"Oh, no you won't boys, this is my last run. John took a sip from a flat brown bottle.

"I'm going to work down over to the East coast railroad. A feller named Flagler tried to build a track clean across the ocean to Key West, but it was blown away by a hurricane and they need workers again to rebuild it, so's I hear tell."

"What in blazes do they need with that?" asked Wolf.

"I don't rightly know. But, working there would shore beat this run. I know every bend and switch tail of this old piece of track, and I'm due for new places and prettier faces."

The engineer blew three quick impatient blasts on the horn, so John waved his lantern at the engineer and climbed back aboard the caboose.

"Take good care now," John called out.

Jim waived. They would miss their old railroad friend.

It was a good seven miles back to the homestead and the sun was turning the cold southern morning pink and grey. As the old rut road turned to the east, the sun reflecting off the frost was almost blinding. Jim gazed into the snow-like frost and turned to Wolf. "Wouldn't you like to go somewhere like old John?"

"They will never build a railroad that will stay put over that much ocean. It's too deep and they have too many storms down there. Besides, your pa would never approve of you scurrying off to somewhere like that."

"Wolf Johnson, you ole cow hunter, you'll stay around this place until you drop. They'll bury your bones under a lone flat woods pine tree where they'll find you.

But not me, you'll see, I ain't afraid of pa. He may be tough, but he is fair."

"Well, Jim boy, even if you did get down south, there's still Indians down Miami way."

"Ha, shows all you know," scoffed Jim, "Miami is a big city."

"Have it your way boy," Wolf replied, with a knowing glance. "But you're still your pa's first born," Wolf said quietly.

"You'll see," Jim's voice trailed off.

A flock of curlews flew low over the wagon and the whistling noise their wings made caused Jim to look up. As they disappeared over the trees, Jim thought about his pa and what he would think about him venturing off. Well, he did it, didn't he?"

Jim was strong, sturdily built, but got his height from his mother, which was a bit shorter than usual. Like his mother, soft spoken, but opinionated and strong willed like his pa. He was born four miles west of the town of Kissimmee, Florida. At six years old, his pa had put him on a horse and taught him to ride whether he wanted to or not. At sixteen, he could break the meanest mustang horse brought in from Texas or Oklahoma. He could shoot a saddle pistol quick enough to down the meanest bull that happened to turn on him and make his twelve-foot cow whip crack like a Winchester. He, as well as the other cowhands, moved cattle with the whips. They were continuing the practice as the original "Crackers" did. He was also very proficient with a rifle.

Jim O'Berry was raised in a devout Christian family but was not totally guided by his faith until later in life. At eighteen, Jim had a twinkle in his eye, loved the outdoors and a good laugh. But he never drank, gambled, nor swore. He tried tobacco once, but it hurt his nose so bad, he stuck the chaw in the dirt to make the smell go away.

He did have some interest in the ladies, however. He met Elizabeth Lanier at a town party one September evening, and a good friendship blossomed. As the weeks and months progressed, he saw her quite often when he had time. He courted her at her home and her parents liked him, mostly because they respected his father.

But right now, they had to get out of the cold and put the horses up.

The Fever

Wolf Johnson, driving the horse and wagon, turned back to a southerly direction and down the rut road towards the aging Cracker house. The grasses on the side of the road and between the ruts were frozen and glistened. The morning sun continued to sparkle and glint off the frost covered grass as they came within sight of the back of the house.

"Who's that out back, Jim?" Wolf asked.

"Oh, that's Pa, looks like he's gonna put a bridle on my horse Cola."

"Well, ole Cola done shied away from him twice," Wolf replied.

"Oh no, he just did it again. This doesn't look good; you know Pa's temper, he used to cut a guava sprout and tan my hide over nothing."

Frank went inside the house through the back door.

"He's coming out again, Wolf, and he's got a shotgun.

The horse fell before the sound of the shot could be heard at the wagon.

"He killed my horse. He killed my horse," Jim shouted, standing up in the wagon.

Frank turned at the sound to see his son standing in the wagon glaring at him.

Frank staggered and then collapsed onto the hard ground.

"What's going on, why did he fall?" Jim asked.

"Let's get there quick, Jim," Wolf said excitedly.

Wolf slapped the horses with the reins and the startled horses took off at a trot, knocking Jim back to the seat. Wolf guided the wagon toward the fence, stopped, and threw the reins over the fence to hold the horses and both men vaulted over the fence.

"Ma, come quick, Pa's down on the ground," Jim yelled.

They got him in the house, he was conscious but weak and it was hard for him to breathe.

"Jim, saddle a horse and go find the doctor," Martha ordered.

"Wolf, bring me some cool water please," Martha asked.

Doc Suddath got to the house about four o'clock that afternoon. The whole family gathered around the bed where the doctor was examining Frank.

"Well, Martha," The doctor turned toward her.

"Looks like he got the fever."

"Oh no, what fever? Why? From where? Martha cried out.

Martha had a sinking feeling in the pit of her stomach, one of her daughters had been sick for three days and she couldn't figure out why.

"Well, I believe its typhoid fever, at least it ain't the yellow fever. Where he got it might be hard to tell, but I do know one thing. We all here have been in contact with Frank, which means we are all quarantined for the duration. So Martha, let's get started to get this place cleaned up. Evidentially Frank ate something contaminated. Try to find out what he ate in the last 48 hours. Clean out your kitchen with anything old or that doesn't smell right. If you have any vinegar, wash everything down in the kitchen with it. Be sure to wash the eggs you cook and cook them done. Boil the underwear and pants he wore, including bed linens and table cloths. Send a message to the crew not to come to the house. Oh yes, lime the privy, really good."

"Is the well close to the privy?" The doctor asked.

"No, they are 100 yards apart, but Doc," Martha said grabbing the doctor by the arm. "We may have a worse problem. One of my daughters has been sick for three days," Martha explained.

The doctor quickly went to look at the baby and sure enough, she had the fever.

"Martha, I can't give you much hope, her condition is not good, so be strong during these times," the doctor said.

"Have any of your crew eaten inside, or shared the water bucket dipper with him?"

The water bucket with a communal dipper was on the back porch for all to use.

So, the siege began. In spite of the cold compresses and attention, two days later, the baby died.

Some of the crew was also under quarantine. It lasted seven days until Frank pulled through, and no one else got sick.

"I've got to get out of here," Frank complained. I started the purchase of the new Edgewater place on the lake a couple weeks ago," Frank said weakly.

"Now, funny man," she said with a smile. "You're too weak to go riding off to town. I'll send Jim to let them know you will be in a week or so," Martha replied.

The next two weeks went fairly well, as Frank regained his strength. However, as it often happens on a ranch in the wilderness, nature takes its course. One night, about three weeks later, there was a big commotion outside with a hog squealing and dogs barking.

"What in tarnation is going on? Frank leaped out of bed and grabbed a rifle. Jim was on the porch with his rifle, but the squealing of the hog indicated whatever had the hog squealing was well out of range.

"It was a bear this time, Pa. He grabbed a big black sow and ran off before I could get out here to shoot," Jim relayed, as all four boys stood around on the porch.

"Well, that bear succeeded once, much like the last one. That means he will be back, and we can't let that happen again. In the morning, Jim, you go over to see Eliza Jones and get him and his dogs and see if we can't find that critter and make bear meat out of him," Frank said.

The next day, late in the morning, Martha walked out on the porch.

"Good grief, its pandemonium out here" Martha said, as the Jones's dogs, along with Sears, Roebuck, and ole Blue were howling and barking.

"Morning Mize O'Berry," Eliza said, seeing Martha.

Eliza Jones was a tall black man with nearly white hair and beard and a gentle face.

He was neatly dressed in a khaki brown shirt and khaki pants of the day.

"Why good morning Eliza. Can I get you a cup of coffee or a biscuit and milk before you go bear catching?"

"Thank you kindly, Mize O'Berry, but I'm just fine. Bear meat for supper would be what I'm a thinking about now."

"Bear meat sure sounds good, Mr. Brown; good luck and I hope your dogs fair well," Martha replied.

Satisfied the hunt was under way, she went out back where the wash pot was boiling. It was a big black iron pot about three feet across that she boiled the work clothes in.

"Okay Eliza, let's us go get that bear," Frank said as the dogs were loosed on the bear's trail.

The bear hunt party was made up of Frank, Wolf, Jim, and the next eldest of Jim's younger brothers, Charles, in addition to Eliza and one of his boys, Jerimiah.

Charles was taller than Jim, blonde and neat. But Charles was not cut out to be a cowboy. However, he did often drive the chuck wagon and cooked for the cattle drovers.

They trailed the bear down to the swamp west of the house, where they found the remains of the pig. The dogs kept running on the bears trail after milling around a few minutes.

"Not much left of the sow, is there Pa?" Jim mused.

"Nope, which means that bear is full and that will slow him down a bit," Frank replied.

The trail wound off to the north toward a place called Buckles Bend.

"Listen to the dogs, sounds like he's treed," Eliza turned in his saddle to alert the others. They picked up to a gallop to get the bear before he hurt the dogs.

The bear was a big, black male about 300 pounds and was about half way up a big oak tree. He met his end with one rifle shot by Eliza.

They all jumped in to skin and break down the meat, so they could carry it back. Eliza had an extra horse to pack about a 150 pounds of meat back to the O'Berry place. Martha was on the porch to greet the returning group, having finished the wash. Eliza was first to ride up to the porch.

"Howdy Mize O'Berry, I know you folks allow me the meat for using my dogs, but I'd like you to have a hind quarter, as I know how much you folks love bear meat," Eliza said.

"Why thank you kindly, Mr. Jones. I do like bear meat myself," Martha replied.

"Eliza, this Sunday after church, I plan to cook up some bear meat, roasting ears of corn, sweet potatoes, and collard greens. Why don't you, your wife, and family come to supper with us about 4:30? There will be my four boys, my daughters, Wolf Johnson, our crew, and Frank and me," Martha elaborated.

"Why Mize O'Berry, we'd be most happy to set supper with you folks," Eliza replied.

"Then it's settled, we'll see you Sunday around 4:30."

Eliza had four boys that worked part time for Frank working the cattle. They were good at their jobs and nice boys. There were four tables out under a big oak tree. All the Jones family occupied one as was the custom. The O'Berry family and crew sat at the others.

Jim always liked working with one of the Jones's boys during marking and branding time. One of the Jones boys would grab the hind leg, then Jim would reach over, grabbing the front leg on smaller cattle or horns of the larger ones and pull them down so they could be held down, marked with a cut in their ear and branded. Jim knew any one of those boys would not let go of the leg, or he would suffer the consequences of a half-grown beef cow with two feet flailing around.

Soon after the bear incident, the O'Berry's moved to their new Edgewater place, south of Kissimmee by a sand road.

"Jim, our sweet potato crop has seasoned long enough, take a couple of the men and go rake them out into the bushel baskets and take them to town to the grocery wholesaler," Frank instructed.

"Sure, Pa."

Jim and two of his brothers, long lanky Charles and stocky built Martin raked the sweet potatoes out of the layered pine needles where they had been aging under a shed out back. Early the next day, Jim brought a large wagon, pulled by one of the big Percheron horses up by the house with two of his brothers to help sitting beside him.

"Pa," Jim yelled at his father on the porch. "Got forty bushels of sweet potatoes to deliver, we should be back later this afternoon, or at least by dark."

"Be sure to say hello to the Lanier's for us, as I know you will no doubt visit Elizabeth," Frank shouted back.

Jim grinned, as he had tied his horse behind the wagon for the side trip he had planned to visit Elizabeth.

Frank had bought his truck farm at the Edgewater location from an Englishman, grew corn, sweet potatoes, and egg plant in abundance.

Frank waved at the three boys on the wagon as it rattled down the sandy, rut road, with the sun just peeking over the trees making shafts of light through the pines. As usual, a flock of curlews whistled overhead. The wholesale grocer would give them 40¢ a bushel credit at the store. After they off loaded and had lunch, they began to gather up stores to take back to their commissary.

Elizabeth Lanier

Alright boys, lets load the wagon for the commissary and the house. I need two barrels of crackers, two barrels of flour, a barrel of sugar, a barrel of corn meal, three 100 pound bags of salt, and 50 pounds of lard." Jim gave his two brothers the list.

"Where are you going?" Charles asked.

"I got a little errand I got to run, so I'll be back by the time you get loaded, or at least before dark I figure," Jim told his brothers as he loaded a sack of potatoes on his horse.

"Oh, I know where you're off to, with your hat on straight. Hey, you got on a clean shirt too. You're headed over to see Elizabeth Lanier ain't you?

"Is that a problem you need to be fretting about gentlemen?" Jim remarked.

"Well, don't be too long, okay?"

Jim rode the mile over to the Lanier house, where he figured he'd find Elizabeth at home. He stepped down off his horse and went up on the porch.

"Is anybody home?" Jim shouted at the front door of the Lanier house.

The house was a rambling old unpainted house with a big front porch and a swing on it. There was a barn and horse stable out back.

Elizabeth came crashing out the door, almost slamming the door into Jim. She was a handsome big boned woman a little taller than Jim, with long blonde hair. She was wearing a gingham gown with a white apron.

"Why Jim O'Berry, what in the world are you doing here at this time of day?"

"Why I came to see you Elizabeth, if you got the time."

"Ah shaw, well come on in Jim, mama wants to know who's here," Elizabeth said with a big grin. Elizabeth was tall and sturdy with a little meat on her bones, but not too much.

"Mama, look who's come a callin'," she said with a big smile on her face.

"Well Mr. O'Berry it's nice to see you again, it's only been a week or two," Mother Lanier said sarcastically sweet. She was making fun of Jim, since he came over to the house every chance he got.

"Howdy ma'am, I came to town with a load of sweet potatoes and thought I'd stop by and see you folks and spend a little time with Elizabeth if you can spare her," Jim cajoled.

"I also brought you a bag of sweet potatoes for you folks too," he said as he dropped them on the floor.

"Well thank you kindly for the sweet potatoes, Mr. O'Berry, and you and Elizabeth can run along to the porch and visit," Mrs. Lanier said.

"You know, Jim, you keep a callin' like this and I will begin to think you are getting sweet on me," Elizabeth said.

"Oh, I wouldn't want you to think too much about that, I just like to see your funny nose and listen to you laugh," He said smiling.

They talked until about 3:30 in the afternoon when Jim told her he must get back to town so he and his brothers could get home by dark.

Elizabeth leaned over and they kissed.

"Now I expect to see you again soon Jim O'Berry, or I might just find me a boy that will spend more time here," she teased.

"And just who would that be?" Jim asked indignantly.

"Well, you never know," she said teasingly.

I don't know, if you go flitting around like that, you might not be the kind of woman I might want to marry," Jim came back.

"Who-haw," Elizabeth let out a big laugh.

"Since when are you a marrying kind yourself?" she came back.

"Seriously, Elizabeth, I got some things I got to do, but if you can wait about a year, I'll come and get you."

"Well, I don't know. "

"Here, take this," He handed her his best pocket knife.

"I know it ain't much, but I don't have a ring yet," he said sheepishly.

"Oh, Jim, yes I'll wait for you," she threw her arms around him and kissed him passionately.

His horse felt like a flying carpet all the way back to town. He was going to marry Elizabeth Lanier, the prettiest girl in Kissimmee-town.

"Ma, Ma," Elizabeth said running back into the house.

"He asked me to marry him and I said yes."

"Well daughter, don't get too excited just yet, he hasn't asked your pa yet."

Back in town Jim and his brothers climbed on the wagon and started towards home, their mission was accomplished. Eventually they would send the produce north on consignment to New York, Philadelphia, or Baltimore.

The Cowhide

Most everything Frank did made money. They ran about 3,000 head of sheep and goats, both common and Angora. There were roughly 800 head of range hogs in addition to 3,000 head of range cattle, spread out over Osceola County.

However, all was not always easy. It was a hard life and disaster always loomed ahead in some form or another.

"Who is that riding in so hard, Wolf?" Frank asked as a rider was galloping hard toward the barn.

"That idiot, he'll run that horse right into the barn and kill himself and the horse," Frank said.

The rider was Willy Wilson. He pulled his horse up short in front of the two men and jumped off, throwing the reins over the fence.

"Mr. O'Berry, we got trouble, I'm sure of it," Willy said, breathing hard.

"Spit it out, Willy," Frank growled.

"Well you remember that feller whose daddy Wolf killed?

"What about him," Wolf chimed in?

Well I seen him and two other fellers had dug a hole and were filling it in as I rounded a patch of palmettos. They didn't see me though.

"What did they bury?"

"I ain't sure, but they most likely killed a cow, or somebody and they were burying it, whatever it was," Willy said.

"Gather up a couple more men, Wolf. Willy, get yourself a drink of water and a shovel and then you lead us back there," Frank ordered.

A couple of hours later, they carefully approached the area. Willy pointed to the burial site, "There it is".

"Well they didn't try to hide it did they, Frank," Wolf said.

"Okay boys, lets us see what's in that hole," Frank directed.

It didn't take long before Willie pulled up a cowhide.

"Well look at that Mr. O'Berry, It's one of our neighbor's fresh cowhide. Now why did you suppose they would bury that here?"

"It's plain whose property that hide is on, as well as whose cow that was. I smell a dead possum," Frank said.

"Willy, take that hide and move about a mile off of our property and carefully re-bury it, and careful not to be seen," Frank directed.

"That's good as done, Mr. O'Berry."

Jim, you hightail it home, get that small lock box from under my bed. It's got a few gold coins in it. Bring it back here and bury it. We'll see what happens.

"You want me to stake this place out to see who comes and goes Mr. O'Berry?"

"Thank you for volunteering, Bobby, but I think that won't be necessary. I think they will come looking for us," Frank predicted. The rest of the group went back to the home place. Nothing happened until the next morning.

"Look out front, Frank, we got company," Martha called.

"Why, it's Sheriff Bob Walker, and what looks like a posse of six other men. What a coincidence," he said sarcastically.

Good morning, Sheriff," Frank greeted as he walked out on the porch.

"Good morning, Frank, I'm sorry to tell you that some very serious charges have been levied against you and we need to settle it." The sheriff said.

"Well Sheriff, I ain't shot nobody lately, so what seems to be the ruckus?" Frank asked.

You have been accused of killing one of Mr. Mc Cafferty's beeves and hiding the evidence on your property."

"Really, and you believe that, Bob?" Frank replied.

"Doesn't matter what I believe. I just have to do my job," the sheriff replied.

Well, just who is making such a nasty accusation, Bob, Mr. McCafferty?

"Well no, a feller from over Tampa way the name of Tom Baker came into the office and said he heard of a cow killing and later saw someone burying a cow hide on your property," he replied.

Well, I believe I am due the consideration of facing my accuser, is he with you, Sheriff?" Frank asked.

"I'm Tom Baker," A voice said as he moved his horse closer to the sheriff.

Tom Baker was tall and thin, had the look of a card player. His eyes were dark and unfriendly.

"Well, Mr. Baker, I guess that makes you a liar, but let's give you the benefit of the doubt before the sheriff arrests you for false accusation, or I shoot you, or worse," Frank said.

"Jim, go get my horse and whoever is around to accompany this group to where ever they want to lead us," Frank ordered.

"Hold on there, O'Berry, you . . ."

Frank wheeled so fast it startled Tom Baker.

"You what, Baker?" Jim snarled as he stared Baker down.

"In the meantime, Sheriff, why don't you fellers step down and have a cup of coffee and a biscuit while we get ready to ride?" Frank offered.

"Even you, Mr. Baker, you too are welcome; for now," Frank added.

The posse stepped down off their mounts and Martha brought cups and a big pot of coffee out to the porch, along with enough biscuits to go around.

"Tell me, Mr. Baker; didn't I see you a few months ago, in the company of a young man by the name of Zeke Blakie?" Frank asked.

Mr. Baker nearly dropped his coffee cup.

"Well, uh, no-er, I may have run into someone of that name I can't remember."

"I see," Frank said starring at the man, knowing a lie when he heard one.

"What has this got to do with anything, Frank?" the sheriff asked.

"Well, Sheriff, if you remember, Wolf Johnson and I were involved in stopping a robbery attempt a few years back, surely you remember?"

"Oh yes, the rattlesnake incident, everyone remembers that one, why?"

"Zeke Blakie, son of the man killed and some of his cohorts have tried several times to steal our cattle and kill us in revenge, so I don't put much past him," Frank replied.

"One more thing, Sheriff, do you know how many cattle I have within fifty miles of Kissimmee? I'll tell you. I have somewhere between three and four thousand head, so why would I steal someone else's beef?" Frank said as he stood up, his face red with anger.

There was no answer.

"But enough talk, Sheriff, let's get to it," Frank said sternly.

A bewildered sheriff followed Frank off the porch. About an hour later the group arrived at the spot Baker led them to. "See there is fresh dirt," Baker pointed.

"You boys get down and let's see what's what," the sheriff said.

"Hand me that shovel," Baker ordered.

In a few minutes, the shovel hit something.

"Why, it's a box, Sheriff," Wolf exclaimed.

"No, not a box," Baker's voice diminished as he dug deeper.

"Where is the cowhide, Baker," The sheriff asked sternly.

"I, I know it was here, Sheriff, I saw them," Baker whined and stopped short, knowing he was outclassed.

"Wait a minute, Sheriff, that looks a lot like one of my strong boxes from the house," Frank exclaimed.

"Are you sure Frank?"

"It should have about a hundred dollars in gold pieces in it," Frank said.

"Now I don't know what's going on here boys, but something smells mighty rank," the sheriff said.

"Look here, there are five, twenty-dollar gold pieces in there, just like you said, Frank," The sheriff said as he showed the open box around.

Wolf Johnson chimed in, "It looks to me like someone stole the box and stored it here, planning to get it later."

They all turned to Baker.

"Now look here, don't go looking at me," Baker said, backing up.

"Baker seems to me like you started something you can't finish. For tying up a duly elected official of Kissimmee Florida, I hereby fine you twenty dollars or twenty days, take your pick. If it goes to the judge, you won't get off so easy," the sheriff said glaring at Baker.

Frank pulled the sheriff away from the crowd.

"Now, Sheriff, you know that me or any of my people would never rustle a cow from another rancher, especially one I do business with. I suspect this was an effort by Zeke Blakie to try to do me or my reputation some harm."

"Besides, if I did need a beef to eat on the trail, I'd pay the rancher top price for it. Further, you might like to contact the sheriff over at Tampa town to be on the look-out for Zeke. He tried to rustle a whole herd from me but got away. I'm certain you heard about that incident," Frank confided.

"Yes, I have heard, and I'll do just that Frank."

"Okay boys, it will soon be noon and time to eat, so if you like, please come and sit for the noon meal. I told Martha to expect you and she makes a mean pot of chicken and dumplings.

"By the by, Mr. Baker, that invite does not include you," Frank said with a glare.

Head Count

Things went well for the next few months, except for some of the riders noticing an occasional stranger riding through the area. There was no word on Zeke Blakie.

One morning, Frank gathered up a few hands, including William "Willy" Wilson, Bobby Brown, Wolf, Jim, and four more hands on the front porch.

"Boys we need to know how many cattle we have west of Campbell station. I figure it will take eight of us about three days to get a decent count. We'll be moving them to Ballast Point next month. This month we're going south to Lake Okeechobee and move those cattle to Punta Rasa. So, pack up your saddle bags and bed rolls and we will move out in an hour," Frank announced.

"Oh, and by the way, the grub will be good, as Charles will be driving the chuck wagon," Frank said as an afterthought. At that point, Martha appeared on the porch.

Martha chimed in. "I wish I could accompany you boys, but I did bake a sack of four dozen cookies you can snack on tonight after supper and I will see you all a few days from now when you get back."

Martha was pregnant again.

The drovers from the O.B. brand had been on the trail for two and a half days, when they saw six riders coming toward them from their right flank about a couple hundred yards away through the pines. Frank pulled out a pair of new field glasses from his saddlebag.

"Let's see if I can tell who's coming to greet us," Frank told the group.

"Hmmm, I don't recognize, wait. Yep, It's Zeke Blakie and his bunch, with rifles in their hands."

"Okay, dismount and get behind a pine tree," Frank ordered.

About that time the first shot echoed across the flat pinewoods.

"Evidentially, that bunch was hunting us," Frank yelled.

Charles pulled the chuck wagon up and scampered behind it.

Willy, riding beside the wagon jumped off and rested his rifle on the seat of the wagon. His rifle barked once, and one of the men was knocked off his horse. "Good shot, Willy," Frank said, that will make 'em think twice.

Willy stood up and was hit by a bullet.

"Dad burn it, I been nicked in the arm," Willy cried out.

"I got another one, Pa," Jim yelled.

By this time the six riders were down to four, they wheeled around to run.

"Let's go over easy like and see if those two fellers are dead or alive," Frank said.

They walked over the hundred yards or so to where the men lay.

"I never seen this one, Pa," Jim said.

"Well looky here," Bobby Brown exclaimed.

"If it ain't, Mr. Baker, the cowhide burying skunk and he's dead as a doornail." Bobby exclaimed.

"Well this is a fine bucket o' slop," Frank said.

Now we got to do something with them. We don't want the sheriff thinking we killed these men just because. Charles, you bandage Willy's arm, and Jim, you go over yonder and pick up his horse. We'll put them both across that horse, since the other one ran off and have Willy take them to the sheriff and get his arm fixed up properly.

"Yes sir, Mr. O'Berry, I'll get her done, I'll tell the sheriff just how this went down, you boys take care now."

Will rode off toward Kissimmee leading the horse with the two bodies.

Frank gathered the remaining six riders around him.

"Okay men, divide up into three groups of two men per group, and keep your eyes peeled. Wolf you take Jim and work south, me and Charles will work west. The rest of you work north and north west and see how many cattle you can count. I doubt we'll have any more incidents, as they will be licking their wounds for a day or two. We'll meet back here tonight for supper.

Jim and Wolf rode south counting cattle. During a lull Jim rode up close to Wolf.

"Wolf, can I ask you for some advice?"

"Well, I reckon, but can't guarantee what kind of answer you might get."

"That's fair enough. I have made some decisions and I want to run 'em by you. You know Pa is talking about retiring and settling down in the city?"

"Yes, Jim, I have discussed that with him."

"Well, there won't be any land left to work cattle on and I never wanted to be a cow man anyway, so I'm thinking about farming tomatoes. You know Pa's truck farm brought in good money, and the tomato crop was the most profitable."

"Well, with no land, just where would you do your tomato farming?" Wolf asked.

"I've been doing some thinking on that too. There is plenty of land for the asking over in the Bahamas on Andros Island, where you can farm year-round. There is also land down in south Florida, below Miami. I got a little money saved and will sell off some of my cows to boot."

"You talked to your pa about this Jim?'

"Not yet, I wanted to run it by you first, besides that, my friend over Orlando way might want to go in with me too," Jim replied.

"Well, Jim, it sounds like you have a plan working, just remember to get your father's blessing and plan it carefully."

"Yes, I figure it will take Pa about a year to get to the point where he doesn't need me. Besides, Charles and Martin already have jobs waiting for them at the Lykes Brothers Meat Packing plant. Frank and Roy are slated to join the army."

"One question, Jim, I know you worked the Okeechobee farms, but are you sure you know how to farm tomatoes?"

"Yes sir, I do. I been doing some experimenting at the farm and I think I got it down pretty good," Jim responded.

"I'm in the middle of planning how much money and supplies it would take for two of us to move to Andros Island and start a farm.

In addition, you may have noticed my garden patch out back of the house. That's my tomato patch and is sort of an experiment. I'm using cow manure for fertilizer."

The cattle count went well and the next week Jim, Wolf, and the other drovers started the round up, driving the cattle from Kissimmee to Tampa.

Martha wanted to go but had too many children to watch out for and she was still pregnant with her next child.

Martha

The first few days the men were gone went well and Martha tended the children and organized the chores for the older children to take care of.

Frank Jr. was outside chopping wood, when he noticed three riders approaching the house. He ran inside.

"Ma, three riders are coming in about 100 yards out and they don't look like anyone we know," Frank Jr. said.

"Find your brothers and call them inside," Martha said.

Martha picked up a six-shot pistol and put it in her apron pocket.

"Martin and Frank Junior, get your rifles and Frank Jr. you stay with the girls and keep them out of harm's way and watch what happens through the window. Martin, you head to the barn and protect it. If you see me shoot, you back me up, okay?"

"Sure ma, we will cover you. Do you think they are trouble?" Martin asked.

"We don't know yet do we boys? Remember our riders have been attacked several times; and now they are all on the headcount. We are on our own, so let's be very careful and don't be afraid," Martha explained.

Martha stepped out on the porch as the men approached the gate on the fence in front of the house.

"Good morning gentlemen, what can I do for you?"

"Is this the O'Berry Place?"

Yes, I am Martha O'Berry.

"Nice place you have here," the leader said.

Meanwhile, two of the riders rode slowly over toward the barn.

"Just you two hold-up there," Martha ordered.

"Now we were just going to look over the barn, no harm ma'am."

"My barn is of no concern of yours, what is your purpose here please?"

At that, the two men kicked their mounts into a dead run toward the barn.

Martin saw and heard the whole thing, as Martha shouted out her orders.

"Boys, get ready, you know what to do."

The two men pulled up in front of the barn, pulled out torches and started to light them.

"Mister," Martha said, as she drew the six-gun, "If they light those torches you are a dead man. Boys, shoot the first one that lights a torch," Martha shouted.

"You're bluffing, lady."

"Never bluffed in my life, mister, call your men back and leave while you can still do so sitting upright in your saddles. They may be boys, but they are crack shots," Martha warned.

Realizing he was at a crossroads, the man turned his horse, as if he were leaving.

He spun his horse around pistol in hand, but never got the chance to shoot, as Martha had already understood what he was attempting to do. She was already aiming with both hands and with a loud explosion, the bullet slammed into the man and knocked him off his horse.

One of the other two riders spun around and headed at a gallop toward Martha.

A shot rang out as the second rider who was lighting a torch was shot off his horse, falling on the torch.

The third rider heading toward Martha realized he was outclassed and made a quick turn to the left, running his horse toward the grove of small oak trees a little way from the house.

Martha fired her pistol straight up in the air, not wanting to kill him, figuring the message he would take was be even better. However, he seemed to ride faster hearing the blast from the .44.

Frank Jr. came out of the house.

"Good shot ma," Frank Jr. said.

"Martin, watch that man until we get there."

Frank Jr., keep that skunk covered, let's go see how bad off he is.

They walked out through the gate and approached the man. His gun was on the ground about six feet away and his hands were in plain sight.

"I thought you were bluffing, he wheezed, what did you shoot me with; a cannon?" The man whispered."

"My .44 if it makes any difference. How bad are you?"

"I think I'm done,"

"What's your name and who hired you?"

"Names Jessie Browner, please put that on my grave,"

"Okay, but only if you tell me who hired you," Martha replied.

"A young blond-haired feller over in Tampa gave us a hundred dollars to burn your barn. Don't know his name though."

"Zeke Blakie is his name," Martha said.

"Frank Jr., keep him covered, if he moves shoot him in his head, I'm a-gonna roll him over," Martha instructed.

"Let's see how bad you're shot," she said.

"That doesn't look too bad, Mr. Browner; you might just make it, if you survive the wagon trip to town.

With that, Browner reached inside his boot and came out with a two-shot derringer.

At such close range, the shot was deafening as Frank Jr. shot him in the head.

"Stupid fool," Martha said as she stood up.

"Come on, Frankie, let's go see what the other one has to say."

Frank Jr. stared at the dead man he had just killed.

"I really didn't want to kill him, Ma. But he shouldn't have pulled that gun. I think he would have shot both of us," Frank Jr. said sadly as he looked up at his mother.

"I know son, you did well. Always remember it was you or him. You did the right thing."

Martha and Frank Jr. approached the other man.

Martin came down from the barn and also approached the man.

"He's dead," Martha declared.

"And badly burned."

"I'll get the buggy ma, so we can take them to town," Martin said.

"No son, you saddle your horse and go get the sheriff," Martha instructed.

"We want the sheriff to see what happened here."

The sheriff and the undertaker arrived later that afternoon.

"Well, Martha, it looks just like your boy, Martin, described it. This one pulled another gun, and the other one tried to set your barn on fire," the sheriff noted.

"Do you have any idea why they would want to burn your barn Mrs. O'Berry?

"Now Sheriff, I believe you already know the answer to that. Zeke Blakie hired them to most likely murder me and my children and burn the place down," Martha said with fire in her eyes.

"Did he say that?"

"No, but he described him down to the blonde hair. He did say he was paid $100 from a young blonde haired man in Tampa to burn the barn down though, and there is only one man that would do that, fitting that description. Frank is not going to be happy the way this keeps happening, especially now, here at home," Martha answered.

The next day, the crew rode into the yard. The tally had gone as expected. Hearing the news, Frank decided to mount a posse to find Zeke Blakie. He went to see Sheriff Bob Walker to get his cooperation.

"Yes, Frank, I found a $120 on the body, and yes, Martha said he implicated an unknown man, but did not name Zeke Blakie. I admit, the evidence is convincing, but I don't have enough to legally arrest him," Sheriff Walker explained.

"Bob, you know I am a law-abiding man. However, that man tried to burn my barn and murder my wife and boys. I am going after him with a vengeance he will not be able to avoid."

"I know how you feel Frank, bring me proof and I'll lock him up. So far all we have is hearsay," Bob explained.

"You most likely know that I am in the process of divesting myself of all the land and cattle I own. I have bought a two-story house on the court house square here in Kissimmee and intend to retire. But, I want this thing resolved before I do. It will take about another year to complete the sales I expect. In the meantime, I have to keep looking over my shoulder to see what's coming at me and my family, and that is no way to live."

"Frank, I'll do what I can here. I will also contact the sheriff over in Tampa to keep an eye on that feller."

"You can tell the sheriff we are coming for Blakie, dead or alive," Frank swore.

"Now Frank, I don't think you want to turn into a vigilante, you're too smart for that."

"Sheriff, I will take him to the sheriff where ever we catch him, unless he shoots first. I'll even ask the sheriff if he wants to join us."

Hunting for Zeke Blakie

It took two days to divide up their men and get up a posse of six men including himself, with another eight to take care of the ranch and watch their cattle. Frank left Wolf Johnson in charge of the home guard. Bobby Brown, Willie Williams, Martin O'Berry, George Stockman, and Jim O'Berry made up the posse. The day they were to leave, Martha who was two months pregnant, walked out with her rifle.

"Now Frank, I'm going with you. I have already loaded the buckboard with food and supplies to keep you men fed. I want that skunk as much as you do," Martha exclaimed.

The silence was deafening, as all six men stood stock still.

"Now, Martha," Frank started.

The look he got from her spoke volumes.

Frank looked away, thought for a second, shuffled his feet and said.

"Boys, would one of you go and get Martha's buckboard and bring it around?"

"I'll go Pa," Martin said, running towards the barn.

"I'd say she earned her place in this posse when they tried to burn the barn down and kill her," Frank continued.

"Now boys, I appreciate you all throwing in with us on this hunt for Zeke Blakie, but there may be gunplay and if any one of you has a bad feeling about this, I'll put you on the home guard." No one moved.

"Okay then, we'll move out in a few minutes."

About a half hour later, they all left the ranch, headed for Tampa. Martha was in the wagon, trailing the group. They made good time that day, eating up about twenty-five miles before stopping for the night. It would be a four day trip, so they traveled until just before dark. Their camp was easy to set up, as Martha's beans were already cooked, and they had a huge three-legged fry pan called a spider, so all she needed was a fire to cook the steaks on. When she did, the smell permeated the camp site as they gathered around.

"How are we going to go about finding Zeke, Pa?" Martin asked.

"We'll camp outside of Tampa. Too many of us going into town might spook him if he is there. Our job will be to locate him without spooking him.

"So far, he has had someone else to do his dirty work. It's time he paid for it. But there is one thing for certain, I don't think he will come quietly," Frank explained.

"Bobby, how do you feel about nosing around Tampa for a couple of days?"

"Gee, I don't know, Mr. O'Berry, but with all those bars, I'm gonna have to drink a lot of beer," he said with a grin.

"I'm sure you can handle it."

"George, would you like to be his shadow, just in case?"

"Sounds good, Mr. O'Berry. Bobby and I can handle that, can't we Bobby?"

"You bet, and we realize that Zeke knows what you and Jim look like, so we'll gladly see what we can find out."

"One more thing, we'll have Willie and Martin hang out around town inconspicuously. Willie to follow anyone that gets spooked by Bobby, and Martin to come and get us," Frank explained.

"Okay," Bobby said.

"I'll mosey around, but, George, give me a few minutes in each bar so we don't look like we are together."

Three days later, around noon, they arrived at the west side of Tampa, along the beach area, near the water where the bars were.

Bobby was dressed like any cowboy, but wore his saddle gun, giving him the appearance of someone that meant business—any kind of business.

The crew worked the bars, and drank a good bit of beer, with little luck. There was only one more bar at the end of a long dock on the water. There was only one bartender and a lady of the evening in the bar.

"Howdy ma'am, can I buy you a drink?"

"Why sure cowboy, my names Julie and I could use a beer."

"Barkeep, could we have a couple beers for me and the lady?"

The barkeep put down two beers.

Behind the huge ornately carved bar, was an equally elegant back drop of mahogany woodwork and mirrors, as was the custom in those days.

About that time, George strolled into the bar, ordered, and received a beer. There was a table with cold food consisting of roast beef and a big loaf of bread ready to be sliced. The table also held gravy for dipping, hard boiled eggs and pickles. George cut a couple thick slices of bread and piled the roast beef high. He topped it with a slice of pickle and another slice of bread. He dipped one end into the gravy and began to eat. No one really noticed him.

"What brings you to this ole bar, Bobby?" Julie asked.

"Oh, I just got a little business to tend to . . . say, you wouldn't happen to know a feller by the name of Zeke Blakie would you now?

For a split-second Julie tensed and her eyes flashed, giving her away. Then she said, "And I was hoping you was just looking for little ole me. Uh, what's your name again?"

"Bobby, I was hoping I would find Zeke around these parts, but so far no luck. I hoped to hook up with him on a little job I got cooking."

"Then, you know Zeke?"

"Not really, but it sounds like you might. I just know of him. He came recommended by some of the boys down south. Does he come in here often?"

"Once in a while," Julie answered.

"Tell you what, here is a five-dollar gold piece and an envelope. You get that letter to Zeke and the five dollars is yours. By the way, is there a hotel in this town close by?"

Julie put the five-dollar gold piece in her bra, tucked the envelope in her garter.

"Yes, back in town, about a quarter mile east of here. You can't miss it."

"You are very generous, Bobby, is there anything else I can do for you, say for about an hour or so, while you're here?"

"Why thank you for asking, Julie. I'm gonna get settled in at the hotel, but I'll most likely be back later tonight for a little company if that suits you."

"You suit me just fine. See you then."

Bobby finished his beer and left.

"Excuse me missy, but could I buy you another beer?" George asked moving towards Julie.

"Sorry cowboy, I have to take a break now, but come back later and we'll talk," she said over her shoulder as she hurried out the back door.

Outside, Bobby mounted his horse, wheeled around and headed east, nodding to Willie. Willie saw Julie flash between the buildings, headed towards a boat at the end of the dock. George left the bar in time to see Martin mount up and head east, so he figured he was going to get the rest of the crew. George mounted and eased on down the street towards where Bobby had disappeared behind some buildings. They met up and decided to wait on the others to show up before approaching the boat. Zeke might even leave, so they could follow him.

Inside the boat, Julie was preparing to leave.

"Did you notice anything strange about the man that gave you this note?" Zeke asked.

"No, Zeke, he just looked like a cowboy with a little money to spend, and a loose gun," Julie answered.

"Is he coming back to the bar later?"

"He said he would come back to see me later."

"No doubt, Julie. Say, I'm planning a little voyage for a couple of days and would like a little company? Would you like to come with me?"

"Why sure, Zeke, you just say the word," Julie said as she stepped outside the cabin.

Julie left the boat and headed back to the bar. Zeke watched her as she walked toward the bar. He also noticed a couple of cowhands, hanging around outside the bar and across the street. That seemed strange, very strange, since the bar was the only attraction around.

"Come on girl," Zeke called to his dog, a big black hound.

He kept her around to guard the boat. He let her out on the deck to play around. We'll see if anyone notices."

Zeke pulled up a spy glass and could easily see the two men staring at his boat.

Martin and Willie both noticed the dog and stared at the boat, which made it obvious to Zeke that they were watching him.

"*I wonder why they don't come on to the boat,*" Zeke thought to himself.

"*Oh, I get it now, they are waiting for the rest of their crew. This looks like a posse looking for me because I hired those men to burn the O'Berry's out. One of them must have told them it was me who hired them.*"

The boat had a solid rail about a foot high, so he used that as cover as he slithered on his belly to the dock lines that held the boat to the dock. He loosened both the bow and stern lines. The wind was blowing from the east, so he could drift away fairly quickly.

"*Now if I can just raise that the main sail before they get too close.*"

The boat was already drifting westward, if only a few feet. From a distance Willie and Martin didn't notice.

Frank and the others appeared and they all began to move towards the boat with Bobby, George, and Frank on horseback. They headed towards the bar to throw him off if he was watching.

"Frank, the boat is moving, and there goes the sail," George called out.

Seeing the group coming at him, Zeke had raised the main sail and the boat was picking up speed. It was now about 50 feet from shore and receding into the bay.

"Come on boys, he's getting away," Frank yelled as he spurred his horse to a gallop.

The horsemen pulled up to the edge of the dock, realizing they were too late. The boat was underway. The riders had their rifles out, but Zeke was nowhere to be seen.

"Damn, he saw us coming and sailed away with us watching. Time to go home people and you'd best get them slickers out, I smell rain." Frank said.

The Wet Ride Home

It turned dark and remained overcast for the rest of the day. The wind came in gusts and the rain came down in sheets. The riders pulled their slickers off the back of their saddles. The other two got on the wagon with Martha and pulled a tarpaulin over them for temporary shelter.

In the early days in Florida, there were no warning signs of bad weather. It just happened.

As the seven of them rode out of town, the winds and rain got worse. They made about ten miles before it got too dark to continue. There was too much wind for cooking, so they ate a cold supper of beans, and tried to sleep under the tarpaulin, and under the wagon until morning.

"One of the worst nights I ever tried to sleep through," Frank bellowed.

Everything was wet, but Bobby and George picked up some lightered Knots. They split them to reveal the concentrated pinesap which would burn and built a fire. They made the fire beside the wagon, so they could cover it with the tarp, and cooked a breakfast of side-meat and eggs. The smell of bacon frying seemed to help everyone's spirits. The winds began to pick up even more, and the rains came and went.

"Martha, remember that storm we had when we went to south Florida one year?"

"Yes Frank, but that was a hurricane. Oh-my, you mean we might have a hurricane here?"

"Well, the rain seem to be coming in bands, just like it did then. This could get worse before it gets better.

The wind shifted from the north to the east and was blowing directly in their faces.

"Frank," Martha said, "If this gets any worse, we may have to find a place to hunker down."

"Yes, Martha, I agree, but first I want to get across Turkey Creek, before it swells too large to cross safely. From the looks of it, the storm went south of us. Unless it stops, we should be alright in a day or two."

About three hours later, they came up to Turkey Creek, the bridge had been swept away and the water was raging.

"What now, Frank?" Bobby asked.

"Well, we have to get across."

"Pa, wouldn't it be better to have a horse and rider on the other side?" Martin asked.

"You are right son, its only about fifty feet to the other side, I'll swim my horse over with a rope, that way I can help the rest of you. Here, Martin, you and Bobby tie your rope to mine, then we'll have just under 90 feet of rope to use."

Frank's horse hesitated, but he spurred the horse and he jumped in. Frank held on to the saddle, lying with his feet trailing in the water as the horse struggled to swim across. The current was swift and pushed the horse and rider downstream about thirty yards. A clump of hyacinth's smacked Frank's face, but he made it across safely. He stood up and led his horse back to the crossing.

"Okay, that worked pretty good. Bobby, George, bring the wagon horse over, then Bobby will come over and we'll hook up to the wagon and pull it across. George, give Martha your horse and take her rifle out of the wagon and secure it on the saddle so we don't lose it. George put the rope around one shoulder, in case you lose your horse, and come across. I'll hold fast here just in case."

Finally, everyone made it across and then it was Jim's turn. He was the last one left besides the wagon.

Jim started across, when he heard George shout.

"Lookout Jim, there's a whole cabbage palm coming at you."

A full-grown cabbage palm was sweeping downstream carrying some other debris with it.

"Don't let go of the rope," Frank yelled.

The root clump of the tree hit Jim and his horse hard. With no control Jim went under. The horse whinnied and thrashed as she got her front legs over the log and was swept downstream. Frank and George jumped on their horses.

"Martin, get the wagon across," Frank yelled as they rode downstream along the edge of the stream, looking for Jim.

Jim still couldn't be seen, and the rain was coming down in sheets again.

"I can't see Jim or his horse," George shouted.

The water kept getting deeper as the stream flooded into the swamp.

"We're headed into the swamp, Frank."

"George, the water's getting deeper, my horse is about to flounder. Turn around and we'll get to some solid ground and go around the swamp to the other side," he shouted.

Back at the crossing they could see Frank and George making their way back through the sheets of rain. As they approached the group, Frank shouted,

"Bobby, you and Martin go around the swamp to the east. George and I will go around to the west and look for Jim.

The swamp ran north and south, and it wasn't very wide at this point, but it was still deep. It took about thirty minutes to get to the other side, as the water was up to the horse's bellies.

"Look over there," Bobby shouted to Martin.

"Lord almighty that's not Jim, that's a bear," Martin said.

The bear was hanging on to a cypress tree, his legs wrapped around the tree trunk.

"Look Frank, what's that?

Up ahead, a form was taking shape.

"Huh, George, that's the horse Jim was on."

The horse clung to the cabbage palm log with his fore legs, keeping his head above water. The cabbage palm was lodged between two other trees.

Frank got off his horse and waded up to the other horse, calming him and taking the bridle in his hands, he coaxed the horse to stand by standing on the log and backing the horse.

"Fire a shot in the air George to let them know we found the horse. They must have found Jim by now."

It took about a half hour to make their way back to the crossing area. Frank saw Bobby who was not smiling.

"No sign of him, Frank," Bobby said.

Okay, it's starting to get dark, let's all get mounted make a big sweep around the other side of the swamp, about a quarter mile out," Frank ordered.

Two hours later they were all back at the crossing where the wagon and Martha were located, all wearing long faces.

"Martha, we have yet to see any sign of Jim, we'll resume the hunt at first light."

"As I recall," Frank said. "There is a grove of oaks a little way down the trail. We'll hunker down there until tomorrow morning and see how it goes."

They got everything together and moved to the oak grove where they used the grove of small oak trees and the wagon as a wind break, with a tarpaulin tied to the wagon as a roof, it covered them fairly well. The tarpaulin gave enough of a wind break for a small fire of lightered knots to burn.

The all sat in a semi-circle saying little.

"I hope this is not a wake, for I ain't dead yet," Jim said, his voice raised over the wind.

Jim was standing just outside of the circle of light from the fire.

"Lordy be it's, Jim!" Martha shouted.

The whole camp erupted, as they were all glad to see that Jim was safe again.

"Okay, Jim said, here's what happened. I was knocked off my horse and had to swim, crawl, and claw my way across the current. I was swept into a bear, holding on to a tree, but he paid me no mind. By going across the current, I managed to get to dry ground, but I was a good mile away by that time, so here I am."

They all gathered around the fire, with smiles on their faces in spite of the weather, Jim was safe.

The winds died down during the night, so when daylight came, with light rain and dying winds, they set out for home. Around noon of the fourth day, they arrived at the ranch. Evidently the hurricane had missed the home place, so all was well.

1903

Two weeks after the hurricane was over, Frank sent a rider out to their truck farming operation in southwest Florida to find Jim. Jim was easy to find and arrived back at the home place the next morning.

"James, I have something I want to discuss with you, as things are changing around here and I want you to be prepared," Frank said.

"Sure, Pa."

"First off, I think you should sell off the cattle with your brand on them, as pretty soon there will be no land for them to graze on, unless you have made other arrangements."

"No, Pa, no other arrangements."

"That should give you a good starter nest egg on whatever you decide to do. If you want to start a small ranch, I will keep eighty acres for you, but first I want you to finish your schooling. If you agree, I have made inquiries and will make arrangements for you to go to the Florida Agriculture college in Lake City, you know, formerly Alligator Town. They are planning to move the college to Gainesville in 1905 and will rename it the University of Florida. Since this is 1903, you may have to move to the new location next year. An old friend of mine is president and thinks a couple years would help you in the future. Does that sound like something you would like to do?"

"Yes, Pa. Gee, I never thought . . ." Jim's voice trailed off.

"I really do appreciate the opportunity to go to college and I accept your offer. That is very generous, Pa. I will go ahead and sell my cattle as soon as possible, but I don't believe I want to start a ranch, so don't concern yourself about any pasture land. As you know I like working the truck farm part of the business more than the cattle and intend to farm at some later date."

"Well, son, that sounds like you have given this a lot of thought. School starts in September of this year, which means you will get out in the summer of 05 or 06. By the time your schooling is finished, I will be out of the cattle business."

It didn't take Jim long to sell his personal cattle and put several thousand dollars in the bank. He took a little of the money with him to school for spending money and stayed in school for two years studying in the all-male college of agriculture and the University of Florida. Jim started school that year and finished in 1906. He worked part time at the College of Agriculture until they moved it from Lake City to Gainesville in 1905.

While at agricultural school, Jim had met another student, Thomas Atlee. Thomas Atlee was a string bean of a man, clean shaven, slow talking, slow to anger fellow but could hold his own in a fight when necessary.

They decided to throw in together and go to work on Flagler's overseas railroad down in the Florida Keys and then farm tomatoes after Jim's schooling was over. Thomas was graduating as Jim finished his first year. Jim had arranged a job for Thomas at his father's truck farm.

Later that year, Jim sat down again to talk to his father.

"One thing, Pa, you know Thomas Atlee, my friend from school?"

"Sure Jim, I hired him on your recommendations when he came home from school. He seems like a hard worker and is honest as they come,"

"Thanks Pa. I needed your take on him. Thomas and I may go in together after I finish my schooling,"

"Sounds like you've been thinking again Jim."

Meanwhile, Frank's other sons also began to leave home and seek their fortunes. Frank and Martha retired in style to a two-story house on the courthouse square in Kissimmee and enjoyed their retirement until mid-1914. At that point, the First World War broke out.

Frank, while winding down his retirement plans, started to go to town one day to close on the house on the town square where they planned to live. He'd bought a new open two-seater touring Cadillac automobile back in 1902. As he drove down a dirt road towards Kissimmee City, a man on horseback rode out from the cover of palmettos, directly in front of the car. Frank was barely able to stop just short of the horse.

"What in the devil do you think you're doing?"

"The rider pulled a pistol, pointed it at Frank and rode up on the driver's side.

"O'Berry, I'm Zeke Blakie," the rider said.

Frank, unarmed at the time and fully surprised just stared at Blakie.

"It would seem fitting to put a bullet through you O'Berry. If it were that Wolf Johnson feller, sitting here I definitely would. But I want you to suffer just like I have suffered all these years. You let me live once, so the way I figure it, if I let you live now, we're even. However, I'm here to tell you that I fully intend to have your son, Jim O'Berry, killed in the worst possible way. Not today, not tomorrow, but within the next two years or so. He will just disappear. That should give you something to occupy your mind for a while."

Zeke holstered his gun and dug his spurs into his horse's flanks and galloped off in the opposite direction toward a line of trees, thirty yards away.

Frank shouted, "I'll find you, Zeke Blakie, you are nothing but a worthless excuse for a man."

Frank did have a .44/40 rifle on the floorboard of the car in case he came upon a deer or turkey. He leaped out of the car and grabbed the rifle. But by that time, Zeke had reached the timberline moving fast, as three-shots rang out from Frank's rifle, bullets hitting the trees. Mumbling to himself, Frank continued on to Kissimmee to swear out a complaint with the sheriff, for whatever good that would do. Then he had best warn his son, Jim.

The Old Wire Trail

James Adolphus O'Berry, son of Frank James O'Berry, took the threats from Zeke Blakie that his father had told him about to heart. Back in the late 1800s, the O'Berry family had beaten back threats of death and disaster by the hand of Zeke Blakie more than once. The latest threat from Zeke to kill Frank's eldest son in order to make Frank pay in anticipation and agony for the death of Zeke's bandit father was perceived as real. Since Zeke had tried to harm the O'Berry's more than once, this was no idle threat.

"Thomas, you recall me telling you about Zeke Blakie? Well, he has made a threat to kill me in the next two years; I'm thinking if we are together that could include you as well."

"Well Jim, in that case you need someone to watch your back. That would be me, so don't you think any more about it. We will continue on our way, just a little more aware of our surroundings."

"Okay then, lets plan to work on Flagler's Railroad for a while and build up our money then how do you feel about farming tomatoes in the Bahama's? Unless Zeke Blakie got hold of this idea, he would not be able to find us, and the threat would die of old age.

"Wow, that sounds like a really adventurous plan. Let's see how it goes."

"Okay, I guess we got the wagon loaded with enough for a month or more."

"Yep, it's enough I'm sure."

"Ma packed us some good vittles and we have fishing poles, our rifles, and saddle guns along with plenty of tomato seed and farm tools," Jim enumerated.

No one noticed a rider, about a quarter mile away through the pines, who had been watching the O'Berry ranch with a spyglass for several days. Satisfied, the rider left the area and loped his horse as fast as he dared. When he got to Kissimmee, he went straight to the telegraph office and sent a telegram to Tampa. It read: "Two to travel east." A half hour later came a reply: "Two doubles the offer." The man left the telegraph office and immediately headed east toward the Old Wire Trail.

The best way to south Florida from Kissimmee was the Old Wire Trail, which was a rough wagon trail cut during the Indian wars to keep in contact via telegraph with the army in the south. The telegraph wire hung on brackets strung from pine tree to pine tree for the most part. The trail ambled through the palmetto and flat pine woods, across the Alapattah flats and around the cypress swamps for the most part. Then it ran across the mighty St. Johns River down to Jupiter. The Alapattah flats area was before the St. Johns River, forming a low stretch about twenty-five miles across and often covered with water from a few inches to two feet deep.

They set out early in the morning and did not stop for lunch or anything. The first day was easy. It wasn't until they neared the end of the second day when things changed a bit. When they reached the Alapattah flats, they noticed the water.

"It's getting mighty dark Jim, and the water is knee deep, Thomas commented.

"Yes, we're two days out, in the middle of a flooded Alapattah flats area. The horses aren't going to like standing in water all night," Jim replied.

I'm not partial to spending the night aboard this wagon with no fire either, and no place to stretch out," Thomas asserted.

"I think we should back track to where the ground is dry for the night."

After about ten minutes, they found a patch of dry land.

"I'm going to build us a small fire Jim, which will give us a little light." Soon they both grew tired and with the fire down to just a few red coals, they lay their bedrolls on the ground and went to sleep. Jim had roused a couple hours later for a nature call, and just as he started back to sleep, he heard a strange noise.

"Thomas," Jim whispered and poked him. "Wake up and listen."

Thomas sat up and they both heard what appeared to be a horse splashing through the flooded area to the east.

"It must be a rider coming this way, but riding in the dark?"

"Now, just why would someone be riding out here in the dark?"

"I don't know but he is headed straight for us."

"You think that's a coincidence?"

About that time the splashing stopped.

"Now he's afoot. Pull your bed up and put this extra blanket under it to look like you're sleeping. Be quick and let's step back behind that stand of palmettos."

It was a bright night with a half moon. The trees and bushes cast black shadows, which made keeping out of sight easy, unless you were walking from dark to moonlight, as the other person was doing. He stopped about twenty yards away. He raised his rifle and shot both blankets, twice each.

"Stand where you are! Move and you are dead," Jim shouted.

The man was an easy target, but Jim wanted to question him. He was staring in the dark, trying to determine where the voice came from.

"That was not very neighborly mister and you ruined several new blankets too. Who put you up to this?" Thomas said from behind a large pine tree.

"He's got me dead to rights, I'm gonna have to move quick. I might be able to shoot O'Berry or make him flinch so I could run." The man thought.

He wheeled and raised his rifle. Thomas was off to one side and could see the man clearly.

He was cut down by Thomas before the man could pull the trigger.

"Well, Thomas, I figure I owe you a can of peaches, thank you kindly, it's getting light, so I reckon we'd better bury this feller and be on our way.

"What a terrible night."

"The good part is we are alive to see the sun peeking through the pines. Now all we have to do is get across the St. Johns River without getting gator or snake bit."

As they approached the river, Jim noticed the great abundance of birds.

"Lordy be, I have never seen as many birds, ever," Jim exclaimed.

"Me either and look how many ducks there are? Grab a rifle. We ought to shoot us a few ducks for supper."

They both fired at once, killing two ducks, but before the echoes of the rifle shots ended, the sky was filled with thousands of birds that covered the sky. Ducks, Curlew's, pond birds, cranes, and some they had never seen before filled the sky.

They watched the spectacle for a half hour and then found that the best crossing was near the wire trail. Thomas went ahead of the wagon on his horse, while Jim drove the wagon.

"What's that? It looks like a mean ole gator?" Jim asked.

"Wow, that boy is ten feet long. He is coming right at the wagon. Careful, Jim," Thomas warned.

"Well, he can't eat the wagon."

At the last minute, the gator turned and disappeared under the water.

The river crossing was made without further incident and after another day of travel, they came to a split in the trail.

The Hurricane of 1926

They finally reached Miami, a town of about thirty-five hundred, which had just started running a street-car route through town.

"Here we are Thomas, in the big city, camped out on Brickell Hammock. Let's go over to the Devils Punch Bowl for some fresh water."

"Why is it called The Devils Punch Bowl?" Thomas asked.

"I really don't know, but it is a fresh water well dug out of hard rock by the Spanish.

They filled their canteens and remounted.

"I told my friend, Wolf Johnson, that I would see Miami Beach, so let's go see it."

After about an hour's travel, they tied their horses at the ferry boat ticket booth hitching post and boarded a ferry boat that would cross over to the barrier island which was Miami Beach. The ferry eased up to the bank, and one of the crew members put a plank from the boat over the mud bank, and the boys scampered over it to high ground along with a few others from the ferry.

After a few hundred yards, they could see the great expanse of the Atlantic Ocean.

"Wow, what a sight, Jim. It seems to go forever."

"I'm taking off my boots and getting in the water," Jim exclaimed.

"Me too!" Thomas agreed.

They spent most of the day walking the beach until the ferry was scheduled to return to the mainland of Miami.

"They went from Miami to Silver Palm settlement, the jumping off place where they boarded a small rail car and were ferried down to Marathon. Flagler's railroad was moving down through the Florida Keys and was being repaired from the hurricane of 1922.

"Boy howdy, there sure are a lot of fellers working down here in Marathon Jim," Thomas exclaimed.

"I figure about 150 men," Jim replied.

It wasn't long before they signed on and were assigned a place to stay.

"Gee, this is a better mattress than I had at home, no corn shucks in it," Jim exclaimed.

"I could get used to this," Thomas said. "It sure was hot last month, but it seemed to cool off a little now."

"Yes," Jim replied. "And the wind seems to have increased a lot."

The next morning, the winds were blowing pretty hard with a constant "blow-your-hat-off" breeze. The sky took on an eerie yellow-gray color and the winds became even stronger.

"This wind makes it harder to move these supplies, and it doesn't seem to be letting up at all," Thomas observed.

They were staying in a log house with several other railroad workers. That morning the crew foreman came over to address Thomas and Jim's group.

"Men, I'm sorry, but we're going to have to work in the rain until this storm is over. If the winds get up a little higher, we may have to cease operations for a spell. But in the meantime, go ahead and keep working," the foreman said.

That night, the rains came and went, but the winds kept increasing. By the next morning, the winds were up so hard you could hardly walk from one place to another. One of the windows in the log house crashed in, hit by a flying board.

All the men, awakened by the screaming winds, scrambled to cover the windows with miscellaneous boards they found in a corner. The winds were over 40 mph and seemed to be getting worse.

Sometime during the night, Bill and Arnold, who were in the guard shack began to wonder about their safety.

"Bill, I don't think this guard shack will survive this wind, we need to get inside one of the main buildings."

"Right, let's go!"

He opened the door, it crashed open, torn off its hinges, pulling Bill out with it.

The next gust of wind picked up the whole shack, with Arnold still inside and swept it into the water. The waves were high, even close to shore. Arnold came to the surface, coughing and spitting out salt water.

"Bill, can you hear me?" he shouted.

But nothing could be heard over the howling wind and six-foot surf. Suddenly, from the top of a wave, Arnold saw Bill clinging to the guard shack door only fifty feet away, so he swam to him. After a while, some of the railroad cross ties almost crashed into them. They both grabbed on to one of them as it offered more buoyancy than the door. Without much conversation, they were blown out to sea, pounded by the wind and waves, coughing gasping for air and spitting.

Back on shore, their log house, being on low ground, began to flood. As a result, along about noon, the furniture began to float so the men got up on tables and chairs. Anything above the water level became a make-shift raft.

"There goes the roof," a voice cried out.

"No, it held, only turned a little and set back down," someone else yelled above the howling winds.

The cabin leaked a little but remained intact. After the eye of the hurricane went over the island and the winds shifted, the roof almost righted itself. Towards the end of the day, the winds began to subside and the rain stopped. The men stepped outside.

"Hey Jim, weren't there two men guarding the railroad ties and tools outside in the little shack?"

"What shack?"

"I hope they got inside somewhere before the shack blew away.

"Look Thomas, we could walk across fifty acres of downed trees on the west side of this island."

Meanwhile, Bill and Arnold drifted north with the Gulf Stream and winds. For two days, they clung to the wooden cross tie, almost giving up hope.

"Look, Bill," Arnold whispered. There is a ship, I think they see us."

The men were picked up by a freighter off Palm Beach bound for Charleston, where they were put ashore.

Back in Islamorada, the building of the railroad came to a standstill for a while, as there were more men than work. Instead, cleanup was the order of the day.

The Maribel

Across the state in Punta Rasa, just south of Tampa, two men sat huddled over a table in the corner of a rough bar. The fiddle player in the corner was fiddling the house down, but the two men couldn't care less. One was long and lanky, with a very short haircut, the other young and seemingly very intense. The younger man was Zeke Blakie. Money was exchanged.

"So, let me get this straight," said the long lanky man.

"You bought my boat, but you are letting me keep it to do a job. And, you're giving me money for the job you want done."

That's right, Mr. White. Should you consider not doing the job after you have been paid, the next contract will be on you. Know that there will be no place you can hide within a thousand miles." Zeke said sharply.

"I'll keep my end of the bargain, and I appreciate my end of the deal very much. I won't let you down."

The next day, a thirty-foot sailboat, with MARIBEL painted on her stern and Mr. White at the tiller, set sail for the Florida Keys and around to the east coast. It would take the better part of a month for the trip around the tip of Florida, but time of was no consequence, or so it seemed.

Back in Marathon, it had taken almost two months to clean up after the hurricane. So, Jim and Thomas took some time off and began to formulate a plan.

"Thomas, I was talking to some people at the wholesale market and they confirmed tomatoes are planted in the Bahamas year-round. Most of the larger farms are on Andros Island, and they ship them direct to New York via freighters."

"I remember you mentioned that earlier. Should we plan to go to Andros Island in the immediate future?"

"Well, let's at least talk about it. I figure we will have to sell my wagon and the two horses so we can buy a boat. Then we can sail to Andros for a fresh start.

"Let's kick that round a few days. Meanwhile I will investigate what supplies we would need," Thomas said.

"Okay, meanwhile, I will go and look for a boat and someone to show us how to sail it."

Jim explored the docks in Miami, looking at boats and asking lots of questions. Finally, he saw an old sailor, sitting in a chair outside a bar. He was dressed in a sailor's jacket and wore a captain's hat. His skin was as grizzled and hard as a weathered dock post.

"Howdy, my name is Jim O'Berry, sir and I was wondering if I could ask you a few questions?"

"Well young feller, I'm Captain William Henry. What can I do for you, son?"

"My friend and I are planning to sail to Andros Island in the Bahamas," Jim explained. "We were wondering if you could tell us what size boat, would a crew of two be okay to make the trip to Andros Island?"

"Well, that depends," said the old sailor.

"You see, I think better with a little grog in my hand, young feller," William Henry said with a semi toothless smile.

"Well sure, come on inside and I'll buy you a drink."

Inside, the dingy dimly lit bar had only a few people, a dozen booths and about six tables. There were only a handful of people in the place. They sat down and drinks were poured.

"Just leave the bottle," Jim told the bartender.

"Okay young feller, if you are thinking about sailing to Andros Island, you have picked a good time to try it. These

March winds could give you all the blow you would need, and you don't have to worry about big storms this time of year either. You should only expect a thunder storm or two at the very worst."

The afternoon wore on, and Jim got a hat-full of tricks of the trade and a list of what provisions they might need, including items to trade to the natives on the Island, such as black-eyed peas, clothing, and farm implements.

"One thing more, young man, Andros Island is south east of where you will jump off from here in Miami, so you will have to steer further south, as the Gulf Stream moves north and could push you up on one of the smaller islands or worse yet, past all the islands into open sea," William Henry warned. When the bottle was empty, Jim thanked William Henry and left the bar. Outside, he mounted his horse and headed back down to the boarding house to find Thomas and tell him about his adventure.

Back in the bar, a long lanky man in the next booth who had been listening to the conversation between Jim and William Henry moved over to William Henry's table. He introduced himself and bought William Henry another bottle.

As Jim approached the boarding house, he saw Thomas coming out to meet him.

"Hey, Jim, boy do I have news for you, I found where we can buy or trade for all the supplies we would need for a two week stay on the water. The only problem is, they take up a lot of room and we'll need a big boat," Thomas exclaimed.

"Then you think it's a good idea we should pursue?"

"I have thought about it and it seems like a good idea and great adventure."

"That's terrific, and I found an old sailor that gave me lessons about the high seas, so now all we need is a boat.

The horses and buggy will not bring enough money to buy a boat, but we should have enough money to pull it off," Jim explained.

"Yes, and we already have some farming implements and seed," Thomas added.

"Tomorrow we'll both go up to the docks in Miami and look around again," Jim proposed.

It took a day to ride the twenty-five miles from the railroad jumping off place to the Miami docks. They slept on the ground that night. They walked the docks for most of the next morning without finding a boat big enough that was for sale. They were just about ready to leave when a voice called out.

"I understand you boys looking to buy a boat?"

"That depends," Jim said as he turned to face a tall lanky fella dressed in sailor's clothes with a close-cropped haircut.

Howdy, I'm Clarence White and I have decided to sell my boat and go home, and by the way where are planning to sail to?"

"Howdy, I'm Jim O'Berry and this is Thomas Atlee. We plan to sail her to the Bahamas, actually to Andros Island."

"Well, how about that. I'm from Abaco Island in the Bahamas."

"Now, what do you know about that. This is a great coincidence. And where is your boat, Mr. White?" Jim queried.

"Oh, she's moored on the third dock down from here. Let's go and I'll give you the grand tour."

They approached a boat, which was a good thirty feet long, with Maribel painted on her stern.

"Oh, my goodness. She's a beauty," Thomas exclaimed.

The boat was a typical small sailboat of the day, with a mainsail and a jib, and a small cabin. The deck was about three or four feet above the water line.

"Yes, she's thirty feet and can sleep four," Clarence White said.

"What are you asking for the boat?"

"Well, boys, I'll make you an offer you won't be able to turn down. Remember I told you I was from the Bahamas? Here's the deal. I need to get home to Abaco as soon as possible but I need some cash when I get there. If you can come up with $300 and take me with you to wherever you are going in the Bahamas, the boat is yours.

"Hmmm, I don't know, that sounds pretty good, but I don't know. Why can't you just sail the boat home yourself?"

"Well, I would, but if I don't have the money to pay off a debt, I might not live through the first day I get there without the money I need. That boat is the only asset I have to raise the money."

"I assume you will teach us how to handle the boat on the way over? Jim asked.

"Okay boys, I've already figured that out. I sell you the boat, and I'll even sail it for you over to Andros, teaching you on the way. When we get to Andros Island, I have a friend that will take me to Abaco Island. What do you think? I really need the money."

Jim and Thomas looked at each other, and smiling Jim said, "You got a deal. When can you leave?"

"Can you get your gear together in a couple of days?"

"You bet."

"Then it's settled. I'll see you back here in two days. Thursday morning bright and early," Mr. White said smiling.

They parted ways and walked back towards the old bar.

"Let's see if we can find William Henry and tell him the news," Jim related.

"There he is in his chair outside the bar," Jim said.

As they approached the bar, the bartender threw a man out of the bar and into the street.

"Hello there, William Henry. This is Thomas Atlee, my partner."

"Nice to meet you, Mr. Atlee, let's have a drink."

Jim bought William Henry a bottle and they sat down.

"William, just wait until you hear our news; we bought a boat and she is thirty feet plus the bow sprit and it's the deal of a lifetime."

They explained about meeting Clarence White and the deal they got. William Henry pulled on his beard and was very quiet.

"If I was you fellers, I'd watch my back, that deal seems too good to be real, besides, that man volunteering to sail you over is a bit unusual. Now you boys seem like straight shooters off the farm, but some sailors are always looking for an angle, be careful. I'd hate to read about you two in the papers," William Henry said.

Jim and Thomas left William Henry, mounted their horses, and headed back to the boarding house, talking all the way.

"I'm not sure, but I think we'll be okay, Thomas. Here is how we will play it, just to be safe, we both have small pistols that won't be noticed on our person and a good fish knife as well. As I understand it, we'll only be one night on the water. If any shenanigans start, we'll be able to deal with it. In the meantime, we will learn to sail the boat, and one of us will be on watch anyway. With the two of us we should be just fine. Besides, his story sounds pretty good. Remember, while he is sailing the boat, he can't do much anyway. That would come if we were asleep or if he catches one of us alone," Jim surmised.

"Let's go first thing in the morning and pick up our supplies and bid farewell to the boarding house bunch," Jim said.

The next morning, they travel up to the dry goods store. It was a big place with everything imaginable stacked, hung, and piled all over. They bought some trading items, pork belly, coffee, water in jugs, corn on the cob, lemons, salt beef in a barrel, extra salt, eggs and grits, and a few more odds and ends including fishing hand lines. They had also seen that the boat was equipped with a small kerosene stove in one corner of the cabin.

Jim paid the clerk, who was the owner of the store.

"Can we keep all this here until in the morning?" Jim asked.

"Sure-thing fellers, looks as if you boys are going on a trip?"

"Yes sir, we are headed to Andros Island to grow tomatoes," Thomas replied.

"I wish you boys luck, I understand there are a lot of tomatoes being grown over there that go direct by ship to New York City," the clerk remarked.

Early Thursday morning, Jim and Thomas retrieved their wagon, hitched a horse to it and picked up their supplies. It took a couple hours to stow their items and get the boat ready to sail.

Clarence was very helpful, and it wasn't long before they were sailing south into the Gulf Stream, heading for Andros Island. Jim didn't expect Clarence to make any trouble, but if he was a bad actor he would probably wait until the second day, or when they were tired or sleepy.

"Hey Jim, grab the tiller and I'll give you a few sailing tips," Clarence offered.

Jim climbed off the bow, moved back to the stern and grabbed the tiller.

"You see the wind is coming from the north west, which is perfect. You just steer a south-eastern direction and the sails will stay full. You can also sail west under these conditions too. Go ahead, give it a try," Clarence urged.

"Okay, here we go."

Jim eased the tiller over and turned westerly while Clarence took in the mainsheet and then handed it to Jim. The boat heeled over a bit to port.

"Let the mainsheet out a little and the boat will right its self," Clarence instructed.

Jim did and the boat settled toward the west.

"Now we are going to jibe. Turn to port and steer south and then east. The mainsail will automatically swing over to the starboard side and require retrimming. Also, it is important to take up the slack in the main sheet while the main is swinging from one side to the other otherwise it can build up too much momentum and cause damage. The stronger the wind the greater the damage.

Jim steered south, then east and handled the mainsheet handily. The jib moved on its own and the boat sailed easterly with ease. Then Jim resumed their original course.

The rest of the day was uneventful as the sun went down in the west behind them. The steaks of pink, gray, and yellow bounced off the clouds on horizon.

"Okay boys, at night the steering is a little different. We pick a star in the direction we were going and steer toward it, but for only a short while as it will move. However, I do have a compass if we need one. See that star low on the horizon way over there?" Clarence pointed to a bright, low star.

"Thomas, if it's okay, we'll take the first watch?' Jim asked. "Why don't you get a little shut eye, Clarence. If we have a problem we'll wake you."

"Sounds fine to me," Clarence replied.

"I'm gonna stay up a little longer," Thomas said.

Thomas snoozed sitting up across from Jim, who manned the tiller.

About midnight, the wind freshened somewhat, so Jim, as a precaution, let a rope trail out behind the boat. If someone fell overboard, he'd have something to grab hold of. Then he woke Clarence.

"What's the trouble, Jim? Oh, I see. Okay, let's reef the mainsail."

You see those little ropes about four feet up the sail. We're going to drop the mainsail down to the tabs and then tie them off. That will show less sail to the wind," Clarence explained.

All three went to work, Clarence dropped the sail to the tabs and then he and Thomas tied the reef knots.

"Thomas, you take over now and if you would Clarence, you could keep him company while I get forty winks," Jim suggested.

"Sure," Clarence agreed as he stepped back in the cabin for his jacket.

"Keep a sharp eye, Thomas," Jim cautioned.

The first couple of hours went well; then Thomas, leaning over the tiller, dozed off a few times. The boat was sailing smoothly with just enough roll to keep a person awake. The mainsheet appeared to be tied, but Thomas had it wrapped loosely, holding it with one hand.

In the gloom of the dark before dawn, Thomas could make out Clarence moving toward him.

"What are you doing with that knife, Clarence?" Thomas shouted.

"Why don't you just back off the boat, Thomas? And then I won't have to stick you?"

"Why would you want to do that?"

Out of the corner of his eye, Thomas saw Jim in the cabin doorway behind Clarence.

"I was hired to kill your partner; you're just a bonus."

"What? No one has anything against Jim"

"Well that's between me and him I suspect."

Thomas let go of the mainsheet with his left hand, loosed the tiller, and pulled his short-barreled pistol out of his pocket as the boat righted from the slack sail, forcing Clarence to stagger to stay upright.

"Now, Clarence, you have been a help up until now, but it looks like you brought a knife to a gunfight. It doesn't seem fair you should get shot, but I will shoot you where you stand if you don't put that knife down and tell us who hired you."

"Ha, you blasted dirt buster, Kissimmee hick," Clarence uttered between his teeth as he lunged toward Thomas.

Before Clarence could reach Thomas, Jim was on him and pushed him overboard about the same time Thomas fired his pistol. Clarence bobbed to the surface behind the boat that was moving slowly through the water.

"Grab the rope Clarence! Grab the rope!"

Clarence flailed in the water and finally found the rope about fifty feet behind the boat. His hand closed around the rope as it slipped through his fingers, but the knot in the end of the rope saved him.

"Help me pull him in, Thomas."

"I'm not too happy about bringing him back on board, but I guess we should."

"Let's see what he has to say."

"I'm shot, you shot me," Clarence wailed.

"What did you expect? Do you want back in the boat?" Jim asked.

Dawn was breaking to the east, as shafts of sunlight broke from behind a huge dark cloud, so they could see him plainly now. The pinks and blues of the morning sun on the water made everything much clearer.

"Who hired you, tell us and we'll let get you back in the boat and fix you up," Jim said.

"It was Zeke Blakie; he coughed and sputtered. Zeke gave me $600 for my boat and another $200 to kill you."

"You thought you would end up with $800 plus the $250 we gave you for over a $1000 and your boat back too if you had succeeded."

"Well, I suppose. Now pull me in," he sputtered.

"Just a little minute old saw, while we figure this out," Thomas said.

"That explains a lot," Jim said.

Zeke has been after my father for a long time. I guess he picked this way and you would have to share in my fate. I'm sorry, Thomas.

"It ain't your fault, and anyway you warned me, remember? Don't give it another thought. We have it under control now.

"Clarence is about thirty feet from the boat, when we get him to the boat it will take both of us to pull him in, and that would be a dangerous time. We don't know if he still has his knife," Thomas explained to Jim.

"I'll pull him in, you keep him covered with your pistol."

"What in the world is that?" Thomas asked excitedly to no one in particular.

Behind Clarence there were three fins moving through the water in the morning light.

"Sharks, help! Pull me in," Clarence shouted, as one brushed against his legs.

"For all that's holey, look Thomas, those sharks are over six feet long. Quick, pull the rope, we'll take our chances; I don't want to be the cause of anybody to be eaten by a shark."

"Pull Thomas!"

The largest shark hit him about 10 feet from the boat.

His blood curdling scream chilled the two as he let go of the rope, and the sharks began their frenzy.

This went on for several minutes, with blood in the water until the sea grew calm again.

"Oh my, oh my, that was horrible," Thomas exclaimed.

"I guess it was the bullet wound made him bleed and they smelled it, don't fret none Thomas, it wasn't your fault. He brought it on himself, and I guess God gave him his just reward."

During the fray, with the mainsheet loosed, the boat was rocking at a standstill, drifting with the current. It was a good half hour before the two even thought of sailing again.

"We'd better get this boat under control, or we'll be shark bait too," Jim said.

He pulled in the mainsheet and got the boat underway. However, during all the excitement, the winds had shifted from north east, to south east and the seas had changed direction.

"I'm not sure if our heading is right Thomas, but I'll keep going southeast. Where's that chart Clarence had?"

Thomas produced the chart, but that didn't seem to help at this point.

"Shouldn't we be approaching Andros this morning, Thomas? Clarence said it was a tall island which should be easy to see, but of course he was not to be trusted and we both know Andros is low and flat."

"Yes, and I don't see anything on the horizon. You know, Thomas, if we miss this whole island chain, we could be in really big trouble."

During the night, Clarence had misled the two, giving them a heading more to the east. This along with the northerly Gulf Stream had put them miles to the north of Andros Island.

"Well, according to this map, even if we miss Andros, we should find some kind of an island soon," Jim said.

In the direction they had been sailing, the Gulf Stream almost canceled the boat's progress, making their actual progress very slow.

"Jim, I have bad news."

"Well we don't need any more of that."

We evidently have a leak, I went forward where the supplies are and most everything is wet, most of it is unusable. The coffee is the only thing that is still dry."

"You mean the meat, bread, and all the other food is wet?"

"Well, we do have a few potatoes the water didn't hurt. The meat might be salvageable as the barrel it's in is only wet up about a foot. That is provided we eat it soon."

"Well, we best find landfall soon or we might get very hungry."

"Oh Thomas, what about the seed, did it survive?"

"Tomato seeds are all sopping in salt water. However, there are some blacked eyed cowpea seed in the top of the sack that are still okay."

"We'd better safeguard them for trade goods or to eat," Jim said.

"I think we had better start fishing," replied Thomas with a big grin.

That night the southeast winds were the prelude to the cold front working its way across Florida toward the Bahamas. When 30 mph winds hit the boat, the two men lowered the mainsail and relied on the jib to keep them quartering into the seas.

"Good grief, Jim, where in the world are we?"

"I'd say we are a good bit to the north. I am going to steer further southeast and pray to find dry land."

"Hey, I haven't had a cup of coffee since we started, do you suppose you could rustle us up a good hot pot of coffee?"

"Coming up, Captain O'Berry, coming right up."

They steered southeast all day, and toward night fall, they saw dim lights on the horizon.

"Look Jim, lights, how will we handle this?"

"We can't afford to run aground, so let's see how deep she gets when we get closer and maybe we can anchor for the night and make a plan in the morning."

"I'll see if I can find the anchor.

"I'm going to come around into the wind, within about a quarter mile from the island, or when it is still deep enough for the boat. You drop the anchor overboard and see how deep the water is."

Thomas had found the anchor and rope and dropped it overboard playing out the rope until the anchor hit bottom. It was about forty feet deep.

"We haven't stopped moving, I think the anchors dragging,"

"Okay, let out some more line, about twice as much and see what happens."

The boat was swinging broadside to the seas, but finally the anchor caught and the boat swung around into the wind.

"How many fish you caught, Thomas?"

"Bout as many as you did, Jimmy boy,"

"I guess its coffee for dinner then. Anyhow, we need to keep watch all night in case the anchor comes loose or something worse happens."

"You've been working this boat for several days now. You take the first shut-eye shift and I'll keep watch."

North Bimini Cay

A s dawn broke gloriously over the island, they readied the boat to move in closer.

"We may have to anchor out and swim in," Thomas mused.

"I wish I knew what the bottom of the boat was like, so we could know if we could beach the boat safely, but we'd best be safe than sorry," Jim responded.

"Okay the anchor is up, and the mainsail is reefed and working. I'll sound the bottom with this lead line I found this morning, to see how shallow it gets," Thomas called out.

"At about ten feet we had better anchor again, the wind is from the northeast, so the boat will swing inshore a bit. Maybe we could run another line with the other anchor to the beach to keep the boat in place," Jim thought out loud.

"Good thinking, we are at twenty feet," Thomas called out.

Jim had the boat headed towards shore. On the beach, he could see people beginning to gather, watching them intently.

"Looks like we have an audience," Jim said as he nosed the boat a little more to the north.

"Fifteen feet and coming up fast," Thomas called.

"Ten feet and I'm dropping the anchor," Thomas relayed.

Jim swung the boat around and the anchor caught immediately. He lowered the mainsail while Thomas brought down the jib.

"Whew, that was tight, but looks like we are anchored," Jim thought out loud. "I'll swim the stern line out: it looks like we can tie it off to that downed tree trunk on the beach."

"Sounds good, and give some nice words to those people on the beach and tell them how lost we are."

On the beach, one of the islanders took the line from Thomas and attached it to the beached tree trunk. "You fellows lost mon?" one man asked.

"Yes sir, we certainly are. We were headed for Andros, but here we are. Where are we anyway?" Thomas asked.

The whole crowd broke out in laughter, as Jim arrived on the beach.

"This is North Bimini Cay, and we welcome our new visitors," one man said.

"Howdy, I'm Jim O'Berry and my friend is Thomas Atlee."

"How about that," the man replied smiling.

"My name is Thomas too," Thomas Jones and the crowd laughed again.

"We have been without food for a couple days. Can you spare us a bite to eat? We can trade with what we have left," Jim explained.

"Don't worry about de trade now, we need to fatten you boys up a little. Come on up to de town and we'll get some food stuffed into you," Thomas Jones promised.

Jim and Thomas told the story of how they were farmers, new at sailing and that was the reason they got lost—there was no mention of Clarence White.

The crowd took them to a small settlement in the middle of the cay, which, oddly enough, had an open-air restaurant of sorts.

"Folks, we brought an extra hand plow, some black-eyed pea seed and a few other items you folks are welcome to. All we ask is a bit of food to get us back across the Gulf Stream and directions back to Miami," Jim explained.

"Oh Mon, this be our lucky day, black eyed pea seed is always needed. If you have a hoe, it might fit my hand just right," Thomas Jones exclaimed, as the crowd laughed.

The festival atmosphere continued into the afternoon and the people offered a place for them to stay for the night. Then they could be on their way in the morning. They slept well.

"Good morning gentlemen, I have already checked your boat and it is riding fine. We have put together some food and water for your trip back to Florida, and also, we got you a couple coconut shell, without the coconut, so you can bail de water out de boat."

"That's mighty nice of you, please thank everyone for everything you have done for us," Jim said.

"Since it is a couple days sailing, we have some live lobsters, dried conch, some rice already cooked with black eyed peas in it and a jug of our home-made rum," Thomas Jones replied.

The wind was from the north, so it was easy to weigh anchor and set sail and on the second day they sighted the coast of Florida.

"That is definitely some kind of marker Jim. It has a number two on it,"

It took the better part of three more hours before they tied up to one of the docking areas they had left from.

"It's early, Thomas, so why don't we go see if we can find William Henry?"

It was only about a quarter mile to the bar where William Henry hung out and they were there in about a half hour.

"There he is, sitting in his chair," Thomas pointed.

"Well, look what the sea spit out," William Henry said.

They went inside and bought a bottle of William Henry's favorite liquor.

"Good to see you William Henry."

"Jim and Thomas, you fellers made it over and back okay, please, tell me all about it."

It took about an hour for the two of them to tell him the story from start to finish.

"You boys was very lucky," William Henry said.

"Not lucky, as it was you who gave us a heads-up or the story might have gone another way. We owe you a lot, William Henry," Jim said.

"Well, my payback is seeing the both of you boys, fat and sassy as usual. What are your plans?"

"We ain't talked much about it, but I was thinking we might sell the boat and work for the railroad a little longer, until we can buy some farmland," Jim replied.

They spent the night on the boat, bought some paint and changed the name of the boat to ANDROS and put it up for sale. They got $500 for the boat, retrieved the horses and buggy and headed south to the boarding house where they continued to work on Flagler's Railroad for another couple of months, and also farmed tomatoes on the side.

"Jim, we got a good crop of tomatoes ready to pick. What are you gonna do when we finish here?"

"Well, I think it's time for me to buy some land and get married, if Elizabeth will still have me."

"Doesn't she have a sister?"

"Yes, Thomas, she does."

"I think I'll take my part and go back to Kissimmee for a spell," Thomas said.

"On another subject, can I hire you for a few weeks to get my place started?"

"You got a deal, I'll be glad to help for room and board."

In the next six weeks, Jim bought a piece of farm land with a house and a well. Although they had to plant between the coral and in holes, they got a good 40 acres planted. After everything was finished, Thomas went back to Kissimmee.

Jim stayed a little longer to clean up the house and make it habitable for a woman. Then it was June and time to head up to Kissimmee to marry Elizabeth.

Elizabeth Lanier

As Jim stepped up on the porch of the Lanier home he heard, "Well look what the cat dragged up onto my porch. Ma, come see," Elizabeth called into the house.

Her mother stepped out on the porch. "Why Mr. O'Berry, I thought you fell in a gopher hole or something."

"Well, I have been sailing the high seas in the Atlantic Ocean, and farming tomatoes, and it took eight days on horseback for me to make the trip to Kissimmee."

"Goodness, that sounds like a good story, you'll have to stay for supper and tell us about it."

Jim and Elizabeth sat together on the porch swing and he asked, "Where is your brother? Where's Robert?"

"Now Jim O'Berry, you did not come all the way up here to ask about my brother, did you?"

"You know better than that; I do have one question though."

"Elizabeth, did you have you another man courting you while I was gone?"

Elizabeth decided to cut to the chase. She leaned over and kissed Jim squarely, long and hard.

"I guess that means no?"

"Jim O'Berry, did you come to get me?"

"Well, I don't know, I guess I'll have to ask your pa."

With that she jumped up and waged her finger in Jim's face.

"You, Mister O'Berry, had best ask me proper," she said with finality.

"Well, oh, err, I thought I'd already done that."

"That was over two years ago, and I have been waiting for you to get here and ask me for real," she almost cried.

"Well, Elizabeth, I too have been waiting for the proper time to ask you. I wanted to make sure you still felt the same way. I tell you what: I'll come back tomorrow and do this properly. Let's just have supper and a nice evening, and I promise I will do everything you want and I'll leave nothing out. After all, this is a very serious and wonderful event we are planning," Jim placated.

"You promise?"

"I do promise; I love you Elizabeth. I've loved you since the first time we spent time together three years back. That's why I rode for eight days to come and get you to take you home with me."

She flew into his arms and they held each other close for a long time, and she giggled.

"Elizabeth, I need you in here to help me set the table," her mother called out.

She went inside and Mr. Lanier came out on the porch.

"Don't get up, Jim, let's talk a minute," he said as he sat down next to Jim, on the swing.

"I understand you left your pa and went out on your own?"

"Yes sir, as you no doubt know, Pa sold much of his holdings and retired to town. I stayed until he started the sell off."

"How'd that go?"

Jim knew where this was headed, so he decided to lay his cards on the table.

"A while back, when I went to college, I sold my cattle holdings. I used very little of my holdings, which were in the five-figure range. I took 500 dollars, as did my partner, when we decided to go to Andros Island in the Bahamas to grow tomatoes. Unfortunately, the Andros Island trip was not successful, so we came back to south Florida with as much money as we had left with. Part of that was from tomatoes we had grown while working on the railroad in south Florida. We worked for the railroad a couple of times to augment our expenses almost doubling our money when we sold the boat we had bought. So, I used some of the money to buy an eighty acre farm with a house on it below Miami and I currently have forty acres in tomatoes coming on."

"As best I can understand it, you seem to have had some good fortune in the past three years. However, I have learned a few things in my lifetime that are not in keeping with our style of life. There are some very bad people out there, and I've met a few."

"Yes sir, there sure is. And without going in to great detail. I too have met some and survived."

"That's mighty interesting Jim."

"Well sir, I have one more thing to speak to you about Mr. Lanier. As you know, I have been courting your daughter for some time now, and I want to ask you for permission to marry Elizabeth, if she will have me."

"Her mother and I were ready to concede to a marriage between you and our daughter before you gave me a rundown of your worth. You see, I have talked to many folks who know you and they all agree that you are the kind of man I would be happy to call my son-in-law. Yes, you have my permission along with Mrs. Lanier's"

"Oh, then I have another favor to ask, Mr. Lanier. Elizabeth feels very strongly about being asked to marry properly. If it is alright with you, could we wait until tomorrow night to let her know we have your blessings?" Jim said.

"I understand and that would be fine, but from now on, you can call me Bob."

"Thank you, sir, uh Bob."

"Supper is on the table," Elizabeth called out from the dining room.

Supper went well and lasted a couple hours as Jim went over in detail their adventure in the Bahamas—leaving out the part about Clarence White, of course.

After supper, the women went to the kitchen and left the men to talk.

"Folks, I need to get going as it will be dark soon and I need to get to father's place before it gets too late."

"Please come back to supper tomorrow night and we can talk some more."

"Thank you, Mr. uh, Bob. I will see you then. I have some business to take care of in the morning."

The next day, Jim bought a wedding ring for himself and a wedding and engagement ring for Elizabeth. He also bought luggage for both of them, since they would be traveling by train for most of the trip. They would go by horse and buggy to Orlando, take the train to Jacksonville, and then transfer to the Florida East Coast railway to Miami. There they would hire a buggy to get to the farm.

He also bought a new suit and all the proper clothes to be married in and took all the things home to his father's house to store for the day they would be needed. Both his parents were very supportive about the impending marriage.

Supper went well, and afterwards Mrs. Lanier suggested that Jim and Elizabeth go to the porch for some quiet time. Before they could sit down in the swing, Jim stopped Elizabeth.

"Elizabeth, I have to ask you a question," he said as he reached in his coat pocket. He produced the engagement ring, knelt on one knee and , "Elizabeth, will you marry me?"

"Oh, Jim, oh yes, yes, I will marry you," she said as she hugged him and they kissed.

He placed the ring on her finger.

About that time, Mr. and Mrs. Lanier walked out.

"I have just asked your daughter to marry me and we would like your blessings.

"You have them, son. We both wish you two the best."

"Mama, daddy, you were both listening, weren't you?"

"Now daughter, do you think your parents are deaf, dumb, and blind?"

"Well, okay, I forgive you," Elizabeth replied in her excitement.

"One other thing," Jim said, "I have a farm to tend, so I suggest we have the wedding as soon as possible if that's okay with you Elizabeth. Otherwise, I will have to go back to the farm and come back in a month or so," Jim continued.

"Oh, I see, and I understand. Can we discuss this tomorrow?" Elizabeth asked.

"Certainly, I know you have plans to make and people to notify."

"Jim," Mr. Lanier asked, "Where exactly is your farm?"

"It is near the little town of Perrine, just about fifty miles south of Miami.

Jim and Elizabeth spent the rest of the evening talking and making plans. Elizabeth had a hundred questions about the house. Before Jim left Elizabeth and her mother got together and came up with a wedding date of two weeks from Sunday.

The wedding attracted many people, not just the families. It was held in the morning, so they could have time to take the buggy ride to Orlando while there was still daylight. Jim's mother and father, as well as Wolf Johnson, most of the cow hands, and Thomas were there. Jim and his father's relationship were a bit strained, since Jim wanted to farm instead of run cattle, but Frank gave the couple a nice tidy sum to help them along. Thomas Atlee had agreed to drive them to Orlando, so he could return the buggy back to Kissimmee.

The first half mile of their buggy ride to Orlando, was with a rowdy bunch of men on horseback shouting and cajoling the newly-weds, made up of the cowhands, Thomas, and a few others.

As they rounded a bend in the road, there was a wide cypress swamp and a narrow water covered area they had to drive through. This is where the rowdy group turned back. As they started across the creek, they could see a large gator swimming toward them in the water.

"Jim, isn't that a gator headed for us?" Elizabeth asked, as she looked up the creek.

"It sure looks like it darlin', I wonder just what he is a thinking. He can't eat the wagon."

"Well, he looks like he wants to," Elizabeth said.

"Now, Elizabeth, don't you fret none, we can outrun that critter if need be."

The gator intercepted the wagon and at the last moment clamped on to one of the spokes on the buggy wheel as it came out of the water. The momentum of the moving wheel raised the eight-foot gator up almost even with the seat, as Elizabeth squirmed over to the left of the wagon seat toward Jim before the gator let go and splashed back into the water.

"Wow, I hope the rest of this adventure isn't as exciting as that was, husband."

"Well, I did promise you a good time. I'll see what else I can drum up," Jim answered, smiling.

The happy couple spent the night at a hotel in Orlando, where they caught the train bound for Jacksonville the next morning, while Thomas headed back to Kissimmee. The trip to Jacksonville was uneventful, but necessary in order to transfer to the Florida East Coast Railway, bound for south Florida and home. Several days later, they arrived in Miami where they rented a horse and buggy for the trip to the farm.

The Miccosukee Indians

The buggy trip from town to the homestead took about six hours. As they approached the property Elizabeth exclaimed,

"Jim, it is beautiful, and it's larger than I imagined."

The house was set upon concrete stanchions and was painted white, which made it shine in the south Florida sun.

"I hoped you would like it. Wait until you see the kitchen."

They approached from the east and much of the tomato acreage was hidden by the house and tall pines.

"But the best thing about the place, Elizabeth, is the farmable acreage. I can't wait to see what percentage of tomatoes will be full and ready for market."

They rounded the house to the barn when they saw about two dozen Indians, camped in the middle of the tomato field.

"What in the world are they doing in your field, Jim?"

"Our field darlin'. I will find out soon enough, they look like Miccosukees,"

"I don't suppose the Indian welcoming party is another part of the adventure you promised wouldn't happen, is it?"

Now, Lizzy, it wasn't planned, but don't you think this does step things up a notch or two?"

"Aw shaw. This trip doesn't need any stepping up notches, as you stepped up my notches just fine, Jim O 'Berry."

"Well I'm glad to hear that, and don't bother yourself a bit about the tomato field, Lizzy, I'll take care of everything."

They unhitched the horse, put him in the barn and went inside.

"Oh my, you have outdone yourself. The house is so clean and looks like we can just move right in without even having to sweep. Oh, and look, a pump inside the kitchen, thank you," Elizabeth exclaimed, as she hugged him vigorously.

"Well, it's not every day I bring home a bride."

"Now I need to go to the field and see what's going on."

A band of sixteen Indians were camped in the middle of the field. As Jim approached them, he could see they had trampled a good twenty square yards of tomato plants and eaten a good number around the edges.

"Good morning, Cenuntamo," Jim said in Miccosukee tongue," raising his hand.

"Do you speak English?"

"I do," one male about forty years of age volunteered.

"I'm Jim O'Berry. Welcome to the O'Berry Tomato Farm," he said nicely.

"I am known as Lifi (Dog) Claw, the hunter. These are my people and he turned waving his arm at the others. We are traveling from a tribe in the lower saw grass back to our home in Big Cypress."

"Ah, I have heard good things about the Big Cypress. I have heard the hunting is very good there."

Yes, plenty of deer, some bear, sand hill cranes, turkeys, curlews, and lots of alligators."

"Is your tribe Cree or Miccosukee?" Jim asked.

"Oh, you know Miccosukee?"

"Yes, my father has a vegetable farm north of the Big Cypress Reservation and some Miccosukee work for him, and I got to know them well."

"You know my language?"

"Just a little, Dog Claw. Do you need ooki (water)?"

"Yes, we could use some ooki."

"Well, have two women come to the house. I have ooki pump out back."

"How long will you be camped as my neighbors?" Jim asked.

"We plan to move north tomorrow."

"I have been gone for a long time and just came back today, so I don't have food to give you, but you can take all the ripe red tomatoes you can carry when you leave," Jim offered.

"But I would like to make a trade with you. I would like to come to Big Cypress and learn to hunt with your people and see if there is any farmland for sale to the west of the reservation. Could I do that?"

"We would be pleased to have you visit our home, Jim O'Berry."

"I will come in ostaakan (four) weeks. I know where your home is."

"This is good, but if you hunt with my people, you will need an Indian name."

He thought for a moment and said, "You will be known as Tomato Jim, and I will tell the people to expect you. You have been kind and you understand our ways, but why not come with us now?"

"I would like to, but I have a new wife, and this is my first day back, so I need to settle her in so she will be comfortable before I go."

"Ah . . ." He translated to the others and they all laughed.

"I see they understand."

"Yes, and I wish you well with your new woman," Dog Claw said with a grin.

"I'll let you know when I see you and your people again, and perhaps you will teach me more of your language."

Jim and Elizabeth moved in that night and went to bed.

The next morning the small band of Indians left for the Big Cypress.

The newlyweds got accustomed to each other and their new home, and in the next four weeks Jim and Elizabeth packed most of the nearly ripe tomatoes and Jim took them to Miami, where they brought a decent price, bound for New York. However, it was apparent he was about 10 percent short due to the destruction the Indians caused. While in Miami, Jim met a tomato dealer who seemed interested in working out a deal with Jim on his next crop. He wanted to finance the planting and fertilizing for half the profits. He would accompany the tomatoes on the train to get the best price in New York. Jim told him he was interested and would contact him at the proper time.

The next few weeks were devoted to stocking the house with food and getting Elizabeth settled in their new place. She took to the area and could hitch the horse and buggy if she needed to go someplace. The nearest neighbors were Annabelle and Lawrence Cornelius who lived about four miles down the road. Jim and Elizabeth paid them a visit so Elizabeth could have someone to be neighborly with. They invited the Cornelius's and their three children to dinner.

Soon, Elizabeth thought she might be pregnant. Then it was time for Jim to make his way north to the reservation of the Miccosukee tribe in Big Cypress. He set out on horseback, leading another horse loaded with a sack of flour, sugar, and the last of the tomatoes for the tribe.

Big Cypress Swamp

I t took Jim three days to get to the Big Cypress Swamp and Dog Claw's home. Some of the travel was very difficult, as the everglades were covered with water, later to be known as "The River of Grass". Travel through the open areas was easier except for the vines. In certain areas, a bright orange colored vine covered the grass like a net, and the horse had to walk very carefully. Twice, Jim had to step down and lead the horse through the vines. Wide stretches of open glade, with a marl mud covering lime rocks stood with six inches of water on top. Every quarter mile or so, a stand of cypress trees would dot the wide expanse of the Everglades. Pigmy rattlesnakes, deer, panther, and a few bears inhabited this area. Along the coast, Florida crocodiles could also be found.

Jim avoided the huge saw grass expanses as both he and his horse would be cut to pieces by the long, tall saw edged grasses. Herons, egrets, hawks, curlews by the hundreds were disturbed as he traveled through the area. Overhead, huge numbers of birds would glide in unison, all changing direction at the same time, as if by a magic signal. Finally, the topography changed to palmettos, long leaf pine, and cypress stands. It wasn't long before Jim came to his destination.

He entered the cluster of Chickee homes, which were four posts, covered with thatched palm fronds as roofs, about ten feet square. They were fitted with a sleeping table, about three feet off the ground and many had plank floors. Some were open, and part was used for cooking—usually with a huge cooking pot. Others had log sides and were quite large. A gaunt, older man was staring at Jim, and a few other people began to move over to where he had stopped the horses.

"Hello, Tomato Jim," the old man shouted, waving. He was wearing the traditional multicolored Seminole shirt.

"I didn't think anyone would recognize me," Jim replied.

"Oh, the songs of Tomato Jim have been sung in our chickees and will be sung again tonight. We all know who you are, I am Tom Moon Cloud, and we welcome you."

Jim was amazed, as he didn't think he made that much of an impression on the group camped in his tomato field.

"Well, Tom, I have brought some things for the people," Jim announced.

"You are welcome in our camp and we thank you."

"Is Dog Claw the hunter here?" Jim asked.

"Dog Claw will be back later in the day. He is scouting in anticipation of a hunting trip with you tomorrow," he replied.

"How did he know I was coming today?" Jim asked.

"Oh, we are Miccosukee Indian," Tom Moon Cloud responded with a grin.

The men gathered round and unloaded the goods off the pack horse.

"Hello, John Tall Horse," Jim said greeting one of the men he knew from his father's farm. They shook hands and talked about Jim's father's farm he had worked on.

"Well, Tomato Jim, we will put your horses in the pen over there and feed them for you," John Tall Horse said, pointing to the pen.

"That is mighty nice of you."

"You were good to our people. Not many are these days." *The members of this tribe were descendants of the original five hundred Indians left after the last Seminole War, but it would be many years later, in nineteen hundred*

and forty-four that the federal government officially recog-
nized the Seminole Indians as a tribe.

They walked through the camp where there must have been fifty chickee's.

"Here is the chickee you will use during your stay; you can put your things in there," Tom Moon Cloud said pointing to a chickee.

"Tonight, we will feast on garfish, koonti bread, bananas, and sofkee."

"Can I help to do anything?"

"The women will fix the meal, but I was about to skin a deer, if you would like to assist me?"

"I would be happy to help. Lead the way."

Tom led the way through about a dozen hogs that roamed free in the camp to where the deer was hanging.

It only took about a half an hour to skin and cut the deer up. With no refrigeration, the meat would be dried, smoked, and salted, or eaten immediately.

"Tomato Jim," a voice called out behind him.

"Ah, Dog Claw the hunter," Jim exclaimed.

"It looks like Tom Moon Cloud has already put you to work."

"Not work, Dog Claw. It is a privilege, and skinning a deer is always a pleasure."

"Do you mind if I see how the meal is prepared?" Jim asked.

"Not at all, the women will be honored. Come and meet Lucy Water Flower. She will tell you all about it."

"Lucy Water Flower, this is Tomato Jim."

"Yes, I know. We have been expecting him," she replied.

"He wants to see how you women cook the food."

She and the other two older women in the chickee giggled, for this was not the way their men would do it. There were two fires; one for the fish, and one under a huge iron pot for the fried bread. This was duplicated several times throughout the village, as there were over a hundred people to feed.

The four huge garfish must have weighed twenty pounds apiece or more. Lucy Water Flower deftly cut off the heads and the tails with an axe, carefully cut down the belly with a short saw blade and pulled out the entrails. Then she laid the fish on the coals where they would cook for about 20 minutes in the hard-shell skin and then be turned over.

One of the women molded the koonti root (cassava) flour, mixing it with water in the shape of a large hamburger and dropped them in the bubbling oil. There was one for each of the people who were to eat with them. In later years, when koonti was not available, and a general store was, the people would use store bought flour.

Before the meal, the garfish was taken off the coals and let cool. Then the rock-hard scale of the fish needed to be removed, revealing the white meat inside. It was all laid out on banana leaves, cut into pieces, eaten with their fingers, and enjoyed by everyone.

The garfish often required the use of a knife, as it was a bit tough, but excellent table fare. The sofkee drink made from corn was the only thing Jim didn't take a liking too, but he drank it anyway.

Jim followed suit from the others, cut the bread open and inserted a piece of the fish.

"Jim, you can also take one of the breads, open it up and put some of this guava in it and see what you think." Tom advised.

"Oh boy, that is a really good desert," Jim replied, as they all laughed.

The next morning, before daylight, Dog Claw the hunter, woke Jim up. He had his rifle and a brace of poles. He also brought fried bread with leftover fish.

"We will be leaving soon, we will eat on the way, bring your rifle."

They ate and walked about thirty minutes to a creek, where they boarded a dugout canoe about eighteen feet long made from a huge cypress tree. Jim sat in front with the lever action rifle his mother had given him. They moved upstream with Dog Claw standing in the stern, silently poling them through the swamp.

After a while, Dog Claw stopped and whispered. *"Jim, up ahead is where a big gator stays most of the time. I will shine the light and you shoot him in the eye. Shoot quickly or the gator will disappear under the water."*

They poled along the creek, hunting the gator. In about fifteen minutes the gator was spotted. *"I see him,"* Jim said quietly as he raised the rifle and fired.

"Good shot, Tomato Jim."

The gator rolled over and started to sink.

"Now we must get him into the boat before he sinks," Dog Claw said as he slipped over the side into waist deep water.

Jim did the same and they pulled and pushed the gator to the shoreline of a one-foot high bank. Together they rolled the gator up onto the bank.

"It's a good thing this critter is dead," Jim exclaimed and Dog Claw chuckled.

"Okay Jim, help me bring the boat up to the bank and lower the side so we can roll the gator into the boat," Dog Claw explained. It took about twenty minutes to get everything just right. Jim held the boat up on its side, while Dog Claw rolled the gator over into the boat. The gator's head was facing to the rear of the canoe where Dog Claw would be.

"Our boat is riding low and is really tipsy," Jim exclaimed.

"Yes, we must be careful," Dog Claw said as he poled the boat back down the creek towards toward the village.

It was still dark, with only a streak of light in the east. After about twenty minutes, with Jim facing forward, in the stillness of the early hours Jim heard a loud hiss, from the gator and a big splash. The gator's tail thumped Jim's legs against the side of the boat. Jim turned but he could not see Dog Claw. The gator was awake. This huge prehistoric monster rose up on his feet, opened his jaws and hissed another warning, but Dog claw had leaped out of the boat.

He came up dripping, shoulder deep in the creek, clutching the pole he used to push the boat with.

"Jim, be careful, the gator was only stunned and now he is awake. I'm in the water and the boat is drifting, don't rock the boat, I'm coming to you."

"Dog Claw, both rifles are in the bottom of the dugout, under the gator."

"I'm holding on to the boat behind you. You take the pole and turn us around."

Jim stood shakily and used the pole to push the boat around so he was in the back. He realized he must stand to pole the boat. This was no time to tip the boat over as the gator would be in the water with them. "I hadn't planned to learn to pole the dugout under these conditions."

"I think you would call this 'on the job training,'" Dog Claw said grinning.

"Good, now Tomato Jim, we can just drift downstream and you keep us in the middle. If the gator tries to get out of the boat, grab your rifle, jump in and just move to the opposite side of the creek and stand very still," Dog Claw instructed.

"Why don't I try for my rifle and just shoot the gator again?" Jim asked.

"You could, but if the bullet goes through the boat the added water might destabilize the boat and make it uncontrollable. Hopefully we will get to the landing and shoot him again there, and then it won't matter," Dog Claw explained.

This went on for another forty-five minutes, and finally, Dog Claw said.

"Okay, Tomato Jim, we are at the landing. Is the gator still alive?"

"Yes, he is still up on his legs, with his jaws open and I don't think this 25/20 bullet will go through both his skull and the boat,"

"Okay, shoot him again."

About that time, as Dog Claw moved up on the left side of the boat, pushing it sideways towards the shore, the gator smacked his huge tail against the boat, almost tipping it over. This gave Jim just enough time to grab his rifle from beneath the huge beast. It was then that the gator decided to get out of the boat, just as Jim shot him again, as the gator and the boat rolled out over Dog Claw. Jim was thrown backwards into the water on the other side of the boat.

The shot echoed off the cypress trees and in the early light, three great blue herons, startled by the shot, jumped and flew off. Dog Claw stood very still until he realized that Jim's shot had finally killed the beast. The gators mouth was relaxed and his legs would not move.

"I think he is dead now," Jim said.

The shot imbedded in the alligator without puncturing the dugout. Besides, the gator was half out of it when it was shot. The shot drew a crowd from the camp, and six men jumped down to the boat and pulled the gator up on the bank and prepared to butcher it.

"That was some shot Jim, the gator was moving and you were being thrown backward and you still killed him," Dog Claw said.

Jim waded through the water towards the gator to help, but Dog Claw stopped him.

"They will take care of the gator now, Tomato Jim; we have other things to do for the rest of the day. Have you ever eaten curlews or sand hill cranes?"

"No, I never have," Jim said as they talked and walked through the camp.

"The breast meat is very good eating. Perhaps we will find one for you to try. We will be afoot; I see you wear tall leather boots. That is a good thing."

They walked through the woods, headed toward a pond Dog Claw knew about. This area was filled with flat pinewoods. Without warning, a covey of roughly forty quail burst from the brush just ahead of them. Both men were surprised by the sudden action, even though this was a fairly common occurrence in those days.

Jim, with his attention momentarily diverted to the birds took a misstep and suddenly felt a thump on the side of his left boot. Looking down he saw a rattlesnake with a fang fixed in the side of his boot.

"Dog Claw, can you help me get this thing off my boot," Jim yelled.

"Oh-ho, Tomato Jim, you have found lunch, you may also turn out to be a hunter after all." With a grin he raked the snake off Jim's boot with his knife.

Jim raised his rifle to shoot the snake.

"No Jim, do not shoot him," Dog Claw then stepped on his head, and cut it off.

"Good thing for your boots, Tomato Jim, I guess I should have warned you about the snakes in this area."

"No need, I was just careless, Dog Claw. It won't happen again or I might have a heart attack," Jim said grinning.

Dog Claw hung the snake up to bleed. After a few minutes, he gutted it, made a cut around the tail that was tied to the tree, and peeled the skin off the snake in three quick moves, like peeling off a sock. Then he put the snake in his carry sack, tossed the snake's rattles to Jim and they moved on. Lunch was assured; complete with souvenir.

Although lunch wasn't something the Miccosukee tribe took seriously, as two meals a day was normal. Dog Claw thought his guest might like a mid-day snack. He gathered some sticks and built a fire, roasting the snake over the coals.

"You eat much snake, Tomato Jim?"

"Not a lot, but I have eaten rattler before and find it alright if you have nothing else."

It wasn't long before the meat was ready. They both ate heartily and continued on their way looking for curlews or sand hill cranes. After a while, Dog Claw stopped abruptly holding up his hand whispering,

"Do you see the deer at the edge of the cypress?"

"Yes, he is about a hundred and fifty yards out."

"Can you break his neck with that rifle of yours instead of ruining the heart?"

"Well, I only have a couple inches for error, but let's see."

He moved up about ten feet to a stump. He sat down on the ground behind the stump and rested the gun on the stump.

"Oh, you shortened the distance and require a rest?" Dog Claw whispered with a smile.

"Nothing I'm sure you wouldn't do if you were shooting."

"True, but I thought you were an exceptional hunter, it took two bullets for the gator," Dog Claw laughed quietly.

"Want to bet a bear claw on it?"

"I don't have a bear claw to bet."

James Brian Lee, hunter

"Oh, and I thought you were a hunter." Jim said with a grin.

"Okay, you shoot and we'll see who the hunter is."

The shot rang out across the sawgrass and the deer dropped where he stood.

Birds flew everywhere out of the swamp, and another covey of quail jumped not far away.

"Nice shot, we might have to rename you after all Tomato Jim and learn from you about preparing the deer to carry back."

"Learn from me? I came here to learn from you." They both laughed.

Jim gutted the deer to lighten the load and propped it open with a stick to allow the carcass to cool so as not to spoil.

While Jim was doing this, Dog Claw cut a small cypress and made a carrying pole. They tied the deer to the pole, hefted it to their shoulders and began the walk back with Dog Claw in the lead. When reaching camp, the smiling women took the deer and began skinning it.

"I am going to have to go west tomorrow, Dog Claw, and look for farmland."

"I think you will find some near a place called Immokalee, about two days ride from here. I will show you the way in the morning."

"Is there anything about Immokalee I should know?"

"Immokalee is the Miccosukee name for 'his home' and was the home of a white religious man who helped the Miccosukee people. He died there."

"Is there a town?"

"No, there are only the rocky ruins of his home, which we leave as it is in remembrance of him. When you leave, I will give you something to leave at his home for us if you would not mind?"

"Are there any game or inhabitants there?

"Well, there are many panthers. There are also turkeys, a few bears, gators, and maybe a few wild horses to test your skills on."

"Immokalee sounds interesting. When will you be traveling south again?"

"Next spring a few of us will make the journey."

Be sure and stop by my place and camp, even if we are not there. Camp by the pump so you will have water handy," Jim invited.

That night they feasted on gator tail seasoned with sour orange, koon-ti bread, sofkee and bananas. The next morning Dog Claw the Hunter came to Jim's chickee with a group of men.

"Good morning, Tomato Jim, we have come to say good-bye. Since we now know you better, while you have been with us, we are giving you a new name. You are now to be called Tomato Jim the Hunter, a name of honor among us."

"Well, gentlemen, I don't know what to say except thank you. I will be known as Tomato Jim the Hunter and will always keep you and your people in my prayers. I do have one word of caution for your people. Beware of your borders and safeguard your people, as there are those that are not as wise as you and would do you harm or try to take or use your land." Jim warned.

"This we know but thank you for your words. Please take this eagle feather to Immokalee and place it on the ruins when you find them," Dog Claw said.

"I will, with pleasure, may your chickees stay dry and your bellies full."

"I hope your new wife gives you many sons," Dog Claw called out as Jim rode away.

It was the second day out when Jim happened upon a small band of Indians.

"Hello, are you Miccosukee? I am need of directions."

The group of horsemen seemed suspicious of this rider but moved closer.

"We are Miccosukee and Creek, where are you going?"

"I am looking for Immokalee, to place a sacred feather at the ruins for the people of Big Cypress and Chumuklita (bow head to the ground or prayer)."

The group, very curious, but wary, spoke among themselves for a few moments and then one of the men said, "This is very good, who are you?"

"I am Tomato Jim the Hunter from the Big Cypress people and I bid you good fortune."

One of the older men rode his horse to the front of the group and pointed northeast.

"If you ride nearly half a day, and look for the creek, Immokalee will be on this side."

"I thank you and so do the people of the Big Cypress," Jim replied.

"If you are from the Big Cypress people, who are our friends, then you are our friend as well," the man spoke.

Three hours later Jim found the creek and a half hour more he found the ruins. He tied the feather to the tallest part of the ruins, which were only about five feet high. Realizing this was a holy place and had once been the home of a white holy man, Jim said a prayer.

"Lord, bless these people who live in this sparse land and deliver them from harm and exploitation. Lord, fill their chickees with food, happiness, children, and warmth. Amen!"

Punta Rassa

Later that day, Jim rounded a cypress swamp and ahead through the pines. In the distance, he could see a neat, white farmhouse. He arrived at the farm of about 40 acres and approached the house.

"Hello the house, anybody home?" Jim shouted.

A voice came from around the house toward the barn.

"Who's calling?"

"I'm Jim O'Berry, a tomato farmer looking for land."

A big man over six feet six inches and about 250 pounds moved quickly around the house carrying a shovel. He was dark haired, had on overalls, a faded blue shirt and a big smile.

"Howdy, Jim O'Berry, would you be the son of Frank O'Berry?"

"Yes sir, that I am."

"Well, Jim, I know your father. I used to sell him bell peppers. I'm Donald Webb and pleased to meet you. You say you are looking for land?"

"Well, actually I'm trying to find out if a farm over here would be more profitable that one in the south Miami area where I am currently located."

"Maybe I can be of some help then, let's go sit the porch and have a cool glass of water."

"That sound mighty good."

"Mother, would you please bring us a couple of glasses of water to the porch?"

Mrs. Webb came out with the water. She was a healthy-looking woman of about thirty-five, apparently adapted to farm life.

"Emma, this is Jim O'Berry, son of Frank.

"My, my, Mr. O'Berry, what brings you to this out-of-the-way place?"

"Howdy ma'am," Jim said smiling, as he rose and removed his hat.

Jim thought," *Seems as if she might like to be closer to a town. I'll bet I get an offer of sale before I leave.*"

"Well ma'am, my wife and I have a farm over south Miami way, but the cost of farming is rising. So, I thought I would investigate this side of the state. My father did well over here, but a little further north.

"Do tell? Well I declare, how does your wife take to farm life, Mr. O'Berry?"

"We have only been married a few weeks, but I think she likes it quite well. She grew up on a ranch, like I did, so our backgrounds are similar."

"Now, Emma, I know you'd like to visit, but let's see if we can help Jim first. While Jim and I talk, why don't you set another plate for supper?

"Well I'd be happy to, and we can visit at supper," Emma said as she went into the house.

"Thank you kindly, ma'am, Jim said as he turned to Donald.

"Mr. Webb."

"Call me Donald, all my friends do."

"Say Donald, where do you take your crops to sell?"

I take them on a wagon over to Fort Meyers and sell them to a wholesaler. He puts them on a boat to New Orleans.

"Have you sold any tomatoes like that?"

"Yes, I use it as an alternate crop to the bell peppers. Last year I sold 150 bushels and got a fair price for the market."

"What do you mean 'for the market'?"

"Well the wholesaler is the problem. I know he gets a lot more than he paid me, but I never figured out how much."

"Seems to me a trip to New Orleans would be in order to see if it would be worth sailing the crop to New Orleans yourself?"

"You mean on my own boat . . . that I would have buy?"

"Eventually, but you need to know the market up in New Orleans first."

"Well, Mr. O'Berry, you have certainly put a bee in my bonnet. You know, the Tampa market is increasing too, as the town grows," Donald thought out loud.

"Tell you what Donald; I think I can find out about the Tampa market easy enough as that would be only a letter to my father. He knows that market very well, even though he is retired now. Or take a trip of a little over a hundred miles up the coast if necessary. Would that help you to figure out an alternate way to market?"

"Boy howdy, it sure would. Goodness, you have given me a lot to think about, but I haven't helped you ."

"Okay, Donald, do you know the price per acre for farm land or where the land office is located?

"I can do both. A few miles down the road, a friend just bought eighty acres at $32 an acre, and the land office is on the trail into Punta Rassa, near Fort Myers. That's about a day and a half's ride from here."

"Thanks, you've been a great help."

"No problem, Jim, but let me be just a bit more help. I could accompany you to Punta Rassa, show you the way, and I can learn a little more about shipping via boat, and perhaps even price boats to see what it would take."

"I sure would like the company. However, you need to know that I could possibly run into a certain scoundrel in Punta Rassa that tried to have me killed over something my father was forced into. That meeting could be a bit dangerous because he most likely thinks I'm dead.

"Say no more Jim O'Berry; I'm the best man you ever saw when times get hard, either with fists or guns.

"You sure you want to run the chance of a gunfight? I'm sure he won't be alone. Now just so you will know, I am going to the sheriff's office first and let him know the story, so if anything happens it will not be because we started it. I believe the sheriff is familiar with the person in question too."

Jim relayed the story of how Zeke's dad was killed by the rattlesnake, Jim's trip to find Andros Island, and the Alapattah Flats assassination attempt, keeping Donald on the edge of his chair the whole time.

"I have heard of Zeke Blakie, as he stole a cow herd from a friend of mine several months back. He was seen and recognized, but the person that recognized him died from a gunshot wound he got in the scuffle before he could identify him to the sheriff."

"We got a room you can stay in tonight after supper and we can start out in the morning if that's okay with you?"

"Ya'll come to supper, Emma called from inside the house."

Supper was pork chops, collard greens, and baked sweet potatoes. The sweet potatoes had been smeared with pork fat, so the skins would bake out soft and edible.

"So, Jim, tell me about your wife?" Emma asked.

"Her name is Elizabeth. She is a happy, healthy woman who loves to laugh, and we are on an adventure of a lifetime," Jim replied.

As the conversation went on, Donald explained to Emma how he was going to accompany Jim to Punta Rassa and would be gone a couple of days, keeping out the part about Zeke Blakie.

The next morning, after a breakfast of fried chicken, biscuits, and buttermilk, Jim stood up, the chair scraping across the wood floor. "Emma, that was one of the best breakfasts ever."

Donald gathered his belongings, keeping his saddle gun in the saddle bag along with an extra shirt and pair of pants.

Jim and Donald saddled the horses and set out for Punta Rassa. It was easy to see that there was plenty of unimproved land that would take little to make into a farm—if he decided to farm here. But, that depended on a lot of things falling into place which might not ever happen.

In the distance, they could see a flock of wild turkeys feeding this side of a cypress stand.

"You ever run a turkey down on a horse Donald?"

"Can't say I ever did, but I shoot one about every two or three months. We have a lot of them around the place."

"Well, running over one on a horse is easy if you get the jump on them before they fly, but getting close enough and accurate enough to snap his neck with a cow whip, separates the men from the boys, I've only done it once, when I was a younger man during a round up, but I tried it several times.

"That sounds like good cowboy fun, but I'll stick to my shotgun."

Punta Rassa was located in Lee County and the Sheriff's office was in Fort Myers.

Donald led the way and it wasn't long before they arrived at their destination.

The Sheriff's office was a typical wood building with a jail in back. Jim and Donald had their saddle guns stuffed in their waist bands so the sheriff would understand they were serious.

"Good afternoon sir, are you Sheriff Bowers?"

"Yes gentlemen, what can I do for you?"

"This is a courtesy call Sheriff. I'm Jim O'Berry, son of Frank O'Berry over to Kissimmee way. This is Donald Webb, a friend. My purpose here is to find Zeke Blakie and see if we can come to some kind of truce. We don't want any trouble, but if it comes we will meet it head on."

Jim relayed the whole story, from the beginning, ending with the death of the assassin Clarence White.

The sheriff sat back in his chair thinking before saying anything.

"You sure you ain't aiming to shoot Zeke down in the streets?"

"No sir. Not unless Blakie starts trouble first."

"Okay gentlemen, here is how this will go. I will accompany you and help you find this scoundrel. He is a very cagey feller, barely keeping out of jail, so I have an interest in this man as well."

"That is a mighty fine plan Sheriff, and we're glad you are coming along," Jim said.

"I'll just go get my horse, as the bars where he may be hanging out, are a couple miles away," Sheriff Bowers said.

"Okay Sheriff, we'll wait outside."

Outside, Jim and Donald had a little time to talk.

"Now Donald, when we spot him, if he bolts, draws, or does anything radical, let's let the sheriff do most of the work, if possible."

"That sounds like a good plan; perhaps the sheriff can do what we can't legally do ourselves."

It didn't take the trio long to get to the docks and bar area the sheriff spoke about. There were about six bars and various shacks along the waterfront. They stopped at the first one, called the "Bar None", with two horses tied outside and dismounted. The sheriff took the lead.

There were two men, a lady of the evening, and the bartender in the bar.

"Gentlemen," the sheriff addressed the men.

"Could I have your names please?"

The first man to speak was short and about 40, wearing a tattered old Stetson hat.

"Well Sheriff, I'm Tom Davis, from over Kissimmee way, and this here is Bobby Brown who used to ride with the O.B. Brand."

"Well I'll be a gopher in a swamp if it ain't Jim O'Berry," Bobby Brown exclaimed.

"Hello, Bobby. He's okay Sheriff, I can vouch for this man. He is as good as they come. Bobby, have you by chance seen Zeke Blakie?"

"No sir, I haven't, but I've only been here about an hour, looking for work."

"Well, Bobby, I do want to talk to you, but right now we're in the middle of trying to find that scoundrel Zeke Blakie. Will you be here for a spell?

"Yes sir, Mister Jim. I'll be here when you come back."

The trio turned and left the bar, making their way another 50 feet to the next bar, named the "The Best Bar and Grill". As they approached the door, a man came out the door, counting his money.

"You there, Blakie," the sheriff called out.

Blakie looked up; saw the sheriff, then Jim and the big fella Donald.

He stopped in his tracks, frantically threw the money into the air and ducked back into the bar, before anyone could react.

"Hold on there Blakie, we just want to talk to you," Sheriff Bowers shouted.

He went to the left of the door and carefully looked into the gloom of the bar. He could see three people, the bartender, a piano player, and a lady of the evening.

"Blakie, I'm coming in alone."

"Donald, I'll go around back, you watch the sheriff's back." Jim whispered.

"*Sheriff, I'm right behind you,*" Donald spoke in a low voice.

Before they could move, a shot rang out, hitting the sheriff in the shoulder. He spun around and hit the ground. Donald fired three shots over everyone's head, trying to draw fire from Zeke, while Jim ran around to the back door.

Inside, the three bar patrons ducked out of the line of fire.

Donald pulled the sheriff up and out of gunshot range to the left side of the door.

"Dad burn fool," Sheriff Bowers muttered.

I guess he was scared seeing me with you and Jim; thinking we were coming to arrest him I guess."

"That makes perfect sense," Donald agreed. *Jim's plan worked,* he thought.

The shots began to draw a few people. Meanwhile, Donald got the sheriff to his feet.

"Sheriff, where can we find a doctor?"

"The closest doc is over at Fort Myers, which is near an hour's ride. Did the bullet go clean through?"

"Yes, it did and looks like it missed the bone."

"Okay then, let's stop the bleeding with something. The barkeep most likely has plenty of rags," Sheriff Bowers said.

"Hey inside; bar keep, can you hear me?" Donald called out.

"I can hear you. That feller went out the back," the barkeep said.

About that time, Jim rounded the corner out back.

A shot rang out and wood splintered just above Jim's head.

Zeke, already mounted on his horse, threw a shot toward Jim when he saw him. Jim ducked back behind the corner of the building. Then looked around the corner and shouted. "Hold it, Zeke."

But Zeke's horse was already at a dead run, partially screened by some trees and bushes out back. Jim went back to the front where the Sheriff and Donald were.

"He beat me out back and jumped on his horse. He threw a shot at me but missed, when I looked around the corner again there was no way I could hit him at that range," Jim explained.

The three of them entered the bar.

"Barkeep, the Sheriff is shot, we need some rags to stop the bleeding," Donald instructed the barkeep.

"Coming right up Sheriff and they'll be clean." the barkeep said.

"I'm sorry he got away Sheriff," Jim said.

"Don't worry boys. He won't get far, cause now lawmen all over Florida will have a poster on him for resisting arrest and assault on a lawman," Sheriff Bowers explained.

The sheriff winced when they poured whisky on the wound, then patched him up.

A deputy showed up and then went for the doctor over in Fort Myers.

"Well now that's done, let's go back to the first bar, I need to talk to Bobby Brown," Jim said.

They walked back to the Bar None bar, where everyone was standing outside talking about the ruckus over at The Best Bar & Grill.

"Okay, Bobby," Jim spoke so the crowd would hear, "Zeke shot the sheriff in the shoulder but got away. Let's go sit down a spell. I want to ask you a question."

The three of them went into the bar. They sat at a table and Jim bought a drink for the other two.

"Bobby, you say you are looking for a job over here? What happens if you don't get one?"

"I suppose I will go back to Kissimmee or even Orlando to see what I can find."

"What about the east coast of south Florida?"

"I never thought about it, but I guess that would be alright. Do you know of anything down that way?

"I have an 80 acre tomato farm that's half planted and a new wife. You know Elizabeth Lanier, don't you?"

"Yes, I rode for her father before I went to the O.B brand to work for your father."

Okay, Bobby. Well, I married Elizabeth, and I need a good man to help me with the farm. Would that be something you would be interested in?"

"Well, it would be kind a like moving back to the O.B. brand but with tomatoes instead of cows. I like the idea, Jim."

"Good, then it's settled. You'll get room and board and a monthly salary starting now, if that's alright with you."

"I'd work for less since it's you. You have made my day!"

"Donald and I are on the way to the docks to look at boats. We'll be back this way and pick you up soon."

"Boats?" Bobby said under his breath, as Jim and Donald left the bar.

They mounted up and rode a few minutes to the docks.

"That Zeke confrontation went pretty well didn't it, Donald?"

"It sure did, Jim. We didn't' have to lift a finger, the sheriff did it all."

I might have had a shot at Zeke, but he was moving too fast, so I thought better of it," Jim explained.

"I think I get your drift, now he may even have to vacate Florida instead of a year in jail, which wouldn't be enough."

"Well, if I could have hit him, it would have had to be a back shot, which I won't do. If I ever get the chance at gunplay, I want him looking at me."

They tied off the horses and walked down the main dock where lots of boats were moored where they found a small shack with a man in it. Jim figured he was in charge of the docks.

"Howdy mister, do you run this dock?"

"Sure do, what can I help you with, a fishing trip? Or passage to somewhere?"

"No, not today, I'm Jim O'Berry and this is Donald Webb. Are there any boats for sale here?"

"Yes sir, there are three boats for sale. I'm Mark Sawyer. Glad to meet you folks. Are you interested in a look at them?"

Mark was in his early twenties, blonde, about 150 pounds with a smile to match. He was sharp and seemed easy going. At about five feet ten inches, he was about the same height as Jim, but much broader. He looked like he could handle himself.

"Yes sir, that would be a good thing to do," Donald remarked.

"Okay, what kind of boat are you thinking about gentlemen?"

"Something that would have the best carrying capacity that two men could handle, I suppose," Jim answered.

"Okay, gentlemen, just give me a minute to pull in my fishing line and we'll get started.

For the next hour, they looked at the three boats. Finally, determining that a thirty-five foot sloop would do nicely and the price was within reach, as they could pay for it in two trips, with some profit to boot.

"I was thinking about hiring someone to help me with the farm, so maybe I could kill two birds with one stone," Donald said.

"I'll speak to Bobby about Tom Davis if you like?"

"That would be great."

Both Bobby and Tom Davis were sitting in the bar talking about the shooting and jumped up when Jim and Donald came through the door.

"So, is Zeke on the run?" asked Tom.

"Yep, and that means he will not be in our area any more if he is smart," Donald replied.

"Bobby, can I speak to you outside a minute?"

"Sure," Bobby walked out the door with Jim.

Once outside, Jim asked, "How long have you known Tom?"

"About a year, I guess."

"How does he fit in the overall scheme of things?"

"Oh, he's a good worker, never known him to tell anything but the truth, and I trust him."

"Okay, Bobby, I assume Tom is also looking for work. Donald has a farm a few hours from here and is planning on running his own boat up to New Orleans to sell his crops and needs a man that can do most anything. Do you think Tom would go for that?"

"I do know that he is a cow puncher, worked the cattle boats at Punta Rassa, so he might just do."

They both went back inside the bar, where Donald and Tom were talking. Donald turned when Jim walked in. Jim nodded and turned back to Tom.

"Tom, if you are looking for work, I have a farm not far from here. I am considering buying a sailing sloop and taking my crops up the coast, maybe as far as New Orleans. Is that something you might be interested in? It pays room and board and a monthly salary."

"I assume you have been working the farm by yourself so far."

"Yes, and my wife keeps the books. You and I would be doing the work together."

"I ain't no sailor, but between the two of us I reckon we could deliver your crops, once we grow them," Tom replied with a wide grin.

They agreed on the salary and shook hands.

Well, Jim, I suppose we should move on. I am going to have to hurry and build a room on for Tom," Donald explained.

"That makes sense and we can be at your place by dark. The three of us will camp and tomorrow we'll help you build that room. Do you have everything we will need?"

"I'm going to run down the street to the general store and buy some more nails and that would about do it."

New York Tomatoes

A week later, Jim and Bobby arrived back at the tomato farm. They stopped the horses at the front gate and Jim called to Elizabeth.

"Lizzy, we're home."

Elizabeth came running out, and seeing Bobby, she exclaimed, "Why, Bobby, where in the world did you come from?"

"Jim found me over on the west coast," Bobby replied.

"Why, Jim, Bobby used to punch cows for my daddy before he went to the O.B. brand. Good to see you again Bobby," Elizabeth said, turning and grabbing Jim's arm. She all but pulled Jim down off the horse and gave him a big hug.

"Why Lizzy you must have missed me," Jim said with a smile.

"Yes, and these tomatoes are missing you too," she said pointing at the field.

She was pregnant, but not showing yet and Jim didn't know it. The house had a back room with its own door, so Bobby settled in and the planting began as they expanded the field from forty to eighty acres of tomatoes, which was about all two men could handle.

The next few years went well, and the farm was a success. Jim continued to make improvements around the farm, and they had money in the bank. It was 1914 and the New York

Tomato Market was the hottest place to ship tomatoes. The only problem was that the tomatoes rarely got to New York where the top price was. Jim was discussing this with Bobby one day at the market where he sold his tomatoes when he was approached by a man in a suit.

"Pardon me, I couldn't help overhearing you say you would like to market your tomatoes in the New York market? My name is Clyde Boykin, I'm a truck farming agent with offices in New York. May I be of service?"

"Well, you have heard correctly, Mr. Boykin. That New York market seems more difficult to get to than I ever thought it would be."

"Oh, Mr. Boykin, this is Mr. Bobby Brown, an associate of mine, and I am Jim O'Berry."

"Well, growers who have dealt with me in the past have increased their bottom line by twenty percent after paying my fee of three percent. But for five percent I work even harder. I actually accompany the shipment all the way from Miami to New York by rail, paying my own expenses," Boykin said.

"Really? That is quite a service," Jim said.

"Well, there is a catch. I can't do that for a small shipment. That's why the New York market is so difficult to grasp by small growers. Just how large is your field?"

"We just planted eighty acres and using the new ammonia Haber-Besch fertilizer process that came out just last year, we expect to get roughly forty bushels per acre, or about 3200 bushels that should be ready in November."

"Hmmm, that is 200 bushels above my minimum. But there is still a slight glitch. One of my other clients will also have a good crop about that time, although I am not committed just yet."

"I assume you have references I can speak to." Jim questioned.

"Of course, my last customer this spring was Claude Monroe of Monroe farms east of Orlando. Before that, last fall I moved potatoes for William Clinton up north of Orlando around Sanford city. If you go talk to them, I will give you a letter of introduction. Should that route not be something you could do, I will have them write to you," Mr. Boykin explained.

"Go ahead and have the growers write me, then I will follow up."

Two weeks went by and two letters came to Jim O'Berry from the two growers, with good recommendations for Clyde Boykin's services. One was leaving the next day for north Georgia, but the other in Sanford City would be available. Jim thought about traveling to Sanford, but that would take a week or more to go and return, so he decided to take their word and see if Mr. Boykin could handle his shipment. Boykin's response was two weeks in coming, but he stated his other customer's crop would be three weeks later and he would be back by that time, so he would gladly handle Jim's shipment and would be in touch soon to finalize the agreement.

In the meantime, the farm work went on for Jim, Elizabeth, and Bobby as the eighty acres was planted. It took all their savings and then some to plant this crop. In November the harvest began. One day a letter came from Mr. Boykin with a contract. Jim and Elizabeth went over the contract in detail. Basically, it said that Mr. Boykin would be in charge of the shipment, selling it on the New York market, accepting the payment, and forwarding a bank note for the full amount less his fee of five percent within two weeks of delivery. Since Boykin had evidently performed this service with others before, they decided to take him up on the agreement.

Jim and Elizabeth sat on their front porch that evening talking about the tomato crop. "Jim, just how well do you trust this man Boykin?"

"A mighty good question Lizzy. He looks good on paper, sounds good, but I have yet to speak to anyone who has known him. I would like to send Bobby up to one of the growers he spoke of, but that's 275 miles and would take up to fifteen days just to get there. The crop has to be picked in about twenty to twenty-five days. There just isn't time," Jim explained.

"I'm very concerned Jim, since we could be risking roughly $16,000. That's a good-sized investment.

The next morning, Jim and Bobby got together and worked out a plan, where Bobby would travel to New York along with Mr. Boykin to assure everything went as planned.

"I should be back in about two weeks or so, best I can figure," Bobby said.

They all felt better about the situation, but still something haunted Elizabeth.

"Jim, I think you should go. Giving Bobby that responsibility is not fair to him, and who best to look out for our money than you? Bobby and I can run this place and get the field ready for the spring crop," Elizabeth explained.

"I suppose you are right, Lizzy.

The tomatoes ripened and they began to pick them. It wasn't long before they started to haul the tomatoes to Miami in ten wagons they had rented, which amounted to four trips to Miami, and someone would have to stay in Miami to safeguard the tomatoes for the four days it would take. Bobby was elected for that job, while the other drivers took the loads. On the last day, Jim took his overnight bag with a change of clothes. He took a room in a hotel, as the train was set to leave the next morning. He bought a round-trip ticket that afternoon and settled in for the night as the train was to leave at eight a.m. the next morning. At a different hotel, Clyde Boykin got a note delivered around seven that night. Boykin, annoyed at the content of the note, grabbed his coat and left his room.

The next morning, Jim was up early to get some breakfast before the train pulled out. He had about a block to walk. Outside, he approached a couple who were arguing. Jim couldn't help but see that the woman was in a very bad position with the man. He thought quickly, I had better let this man know he is being seen.

"Excuse me sir, can you direct me to the local restaurant?"

Just then, the man back handed the woman, with his back to Jim as Jim touched him.

"Excuse me, but I would hope you would treat this woman with a little more respect."

The man wheeled around with a pipe in his left hand and smashed it against Jim's head and he crumpled to the ground.

"Get his wallet," the man said to the woman.

"Is he the right one?" she said as she went through his pockets.

"Yeah, his loss."

The man was big and powerful and kicked Jim in the ribs a couple of time to make sure he was not going anywhere soon.

"Someone's coming," the woman said.

"We're gone my love," he replied, and they ran down the nearest alley.

The man that was coming saw the man on the ground get kicked the last time and hurried toward them. When he got to Jim the couple were nowhere to be seen.

"Sir, are you alright?"

"Stole my wallet," Jim mumbled, his left eye swollen shut.

"I'll get a law man, but first let's get you somewhere you can rest."

"I'll be alright," Jim said as he tried to stand up and passed out.

The man caught him and saw some more people and called out, "Get the sheriff and a doctor." The next morning, Jim woke up in a hospital bed, wondering where he was.

"How long have I been here?" Jim asked a nurse standing near his bed.

"Well, Mr. O'Berry, you came in yesterday morning, so not too long."

"Well, I need to get going, where's my britches?"

"I see you feel better, Mr. O'Berry," the doctor said.

"Yes sir, I need to get back to my farm."

"Okay, but you sustained a concussion and it could still affect what you do. "What are your plans?"

"I plan to rent a buggy and drive it to my home near homestead."

"I suggest you not only rent a buggy, but a driver too. That way you won't' have to drive or bring it back."

"Perhaps you are right, I still feel a little woozy," Jim admitted.

On the drive home, Jim was quiet and there was not much conversation with the driver. Jim speculated to himself on the events of the last couple of days.

"No one knew he was going to get on the train, so why suspect Boykin of anything as dastardly as having him put out of commission. The result is I missed the train and could not watch the tomatoes like he intended. I suppose I will just have to trust Mr. Boykin to send the money," Jim thought to himself.

The wagon pulled into the yard and Elizabeth had seen it coming and was outside to see who it was.

"Jim? What are you doing here? What's the matter with your head, it's all bandaged?"

"Now, Lizzy, don't fret none. It's all over now. I got ambushed, robbed and spent the night in the hospital. Doctor says I got a concussion, so I hired this man to bring me home. Run fetch $3."

"But, what about the tomatoes?"

They went as scheduled, I just didn't' get to go with them, please pay this good man," Jim answered.

Elizabeth went inside and was out in a couple of minutes. She paid the driver and he went on his way.

In the house, Jim explained how he missed the train and his stay at the hospital.

"Do you think Mr. Boykin had anything to do with your missing the train?" Elizabeth asked.

"I doubt it, as the only thing I did in that respect was to buy a round-trip ticket."

"Then the only person to know was the man at the ticket window?"

"Well, yes I suppose so. If Boykin was really a crook to begin with, I suppose he would have taken steps to see that his plan went through as planned."

"I think you need to speak to that ticket man, Jim."

"Hmmm, I think you may have something, but he would have to admit he was in cahoots with Boykin. To do that he would need a reason."

"What if you set a trap for him? Say, go buy another ticket and then go to your room with some help and wait for them to show. It has only been two days, so there may still be time to catch Boykin. If he is in with Boykin, he would not want you to get on that train, right?" Elizabeth explained.

"That makes sense, and he would most likely know who the couple that robbed me were and would contact them for a replay. If I stay in the hotel, they would have to come to me. That way Bobby and me could handle them."

"The only hole in that plan is if Boykin was the only one that knew the people that robbed you."

"Well, in that case I would just get on the train and try to track down Boykin in New York anyway."

"Jim, are you well enough to do this?"

"I am feeling better, so I believe I could do it. I'll go get Bobby and tell him what we are going to do."

Bobby was out in the field and saw Jim coming as he walked down a row of tomato plants.

"What happened to New York?" Bobby asked.

Jim explained and told him of the new plan.

"Do you think the sheriff should be involved in this mess?" Bobby asked.

"Might be a good idea, we'll go talk to him. Why don't you get things together as we will just have time to get to

Miami before the ticket booth closes. And Bobby, bring your saddle gun."

One hour later they were in the buggy headed for Miami. They reached the train station just before five p.m.

"Bobby, you meet me at the back door of the hotel in about 30 minutes. I'll get the ticket and give you the room number, so you can come up the back way."

Jim made his way to the ticket counter.

"Howdy, I think I'll try this again," Jim said to the ticket clerk.

"Oh yes, you missed the train day before yesterday with the tomatoes?" the clerk answered.

"Yes, I was attacked and they stole my wallet and ticket, so I will need another. I don't suppose anyone turned the ticket in for cash, did they?"

"Well, no, not that I know of, but I will be glad to replace the ticket for you sir, I assume you will be staying at the hotel?"

"Why yes, and that would be extremely nice of you to replace the ticket. Thank you very much."

Jim left and went straight the Sheriff's office.

"Good afternoon, Sheriff."

"Why, aren't you that feller that got bushwhacked a couple days ago?"

"Yes sir, I am. I suspect my business partner may have had something to do with that, so I am setting a trap. I just wanted you, as the law, to know what we are doing."

"What kind of trap, may I ask," the sheriff asked, standing up behind his desk. The sheriff was well over six feet and looked hard and competent.

"I have started the plan in motion, by purchasing a ticket to New York to aid my partner in selling the crop. Roughly $16,000 is at stake. I also suspect the ticket clerk, as a part if it all. If I am correct, I will have visitors to my hotel room tonight, as they couldn't pull the same trick on me in the morning. My man and I will be waiting for any intruders.

If there are none, I will just board the train tomorrow," Jim explained.

"I see. And you would want me to keep my eyes open tonight I suppose?"

"Hopefully we will not need you, but yes, I expect I may have a visitor or two around midnight or so. They will think I am alone, but I will have a man with me."

"Well, this could be a long night. I doubt either of us will get much sleep," the sheriff quipped.

Jim left the sheriff's office and went to the hotel, noting no one seemed to be watching him. He registered and got a key. There was no one in the lobby, so he went to the back door and let Bobby in. They went up the back stairs to get settled for the night.

"Bobby, I think I'm right. No one I spoke to the other day knew I was connected to the tomatoes, but the clerk did."

"Yes, that seems suspect, don't it, Mr. O'Berry?"

They made up the bed with a rug rolled up in it with the covers made to look like a person asleep.

"Bobby, you get inside that big chifforobe closet with your saddle gun, I'll lay down behind the curtains with my double barrel shotgun on the other side of the room and we will have them in a cross fire."

They got situated, and both dozed off and on, whispering now and then. About one o'clock a.m. there were footsteps outside in the hall. Three men approached Jim's room. One had a rope, another had a feed sack, while the third, apparently the ticket clerk, who was the leader, held a gun. He also had a key. Since all the rooms had the same locks and keys, getting a key was the easy part. The clerk whispered, "I'll knock him out, you put the sack over his head, and you (speaking the third man) tie his hands behind him, then we'll take him for a ride."

At the door, the leader turned the key in the lock. Inside both Jim and Bobby were dozing. They surrounded the bed, the leader pulled the blanket down with his arm raised, intending to hit Jim in the head with it.

"What the hell?" The gunman said aloud.

"Drop that gun and nobody move," Jim commanded.

After about three seconds, the gun thumped onto the floor.

At this point, Jim fired into the ceiling, to attract the sheriff and all three men froze.

"Don't move, or you're next," Bobby chimed in from the other side of the room.

"Move if you wish to die here and now," Jim threatened.

"I got 'em covered, Jim. Light the lamp."

Jim struck a match and lit the kerosene lamp. The leader who had the gun was the ticket man at the train station.

"Well, mister ticket man, it seems you are the one that is responsible for my beating last week," Jim said as he hit him with his shotgun barrel, knocking him down.

"How does that feel? I just thought I'd let you know how it feels. I think you will get the feel of it for the next few days."

The ticket man stayed on the floor in a sitting position at which time, the sheriff came into the room as Jim continued his questioning.

"What did Boykin promise you?" Jim asked.

He was to give me twenty-five percent of the anticipated sale of the tomatoes," the ticket man said.

"Looks like you were right, Mr. O'Berry," the sheriff remarked.

"They are all yours, Sheriff. They were intending to knock me out, put a bag over my head, and who knows what else," Jim said.

"We were not intending to do permanent harm, Sheriff, just delay him long enough," the ticket agent said.

"Long enough for what?" The sheriff asked.

"Well, Mr. Boykin was to sell the crop and I would get the twenty-five percent which he paid me in advance."

"How much did he pay you?" Jim asked.

"Five hundred dollars," was the reply.

"Boy, did you get taken, just like I did. That crop is worth a lot more. You left a lot of money on the table," Jim said.

The ticket clerk hung his head, realizing he had been hoodwinked and now caught.

"Sheriff, I believe that $500 less the fine this feller owes you should be held in an account for me when I return," Jim said.

"His fine is $100, Mr. O'Berry, so you will have $400 coming to you when you get back.

"Thank you, Sheriff."

"Mr. O'Berry, Boykin intends to conclude the sale the day after tomorrow, you might be able to get there in time to catch him," the ticket man confessed.

"I intend to do just that."

"Sheriff, there was also a woman involved in my beating, I'm sure you can find out who that was from one of these three. I would appreciate it if you would stop by the ticket counter and have this ticket man to make out another round-trip ticket for Bobby here, as he will be going with me," Jim told the sheriff.

The sheriff took the three criminals in tow and Jim began to get ready for the trip north on the morning train.

"Bobby, in the morning we'll go by the general store and get you a change of clothes and a bag for the trip. For now, let's get us a little shut eye."

"Wow, Mr. O'Berry, I ain't never been on a train, much less to New York City."

The next 24 hours the two travelers dozed a little on the train but didn't get much sleep. They were not in the birthing area, so sitting on the wooden seats did not accommodate restful sleep. Bumpy dozing was the best they could expect. The train arrived mid-afternoon of the next day. The day the sale was to have been concluded. Jim and Bobby found their way to the truck farming unloading platform and inquired about the tomatoes sitting on the dock.

New York greeted the two with 40-degree weather, but at least there was no snow or ice. Most of the dock was empty, except for one door marked produce. They made their way through the door and spoke to an attendant sitting at a desk.

"Oh, I'm sorry sir, Mr. Boykin settled with us early this morning, about three hours ago," the attendant replied.

"Did he mention where he was staying?" Jim asked.

"No, but most people delivering produce usually stay at the Mayfair Hotel, just around the corner on State Street," the attendant replied.

Jim and Bobby made their way to the Mayfair Hotel. They walked across a marble floor to the desk. A uniformed gentleman behind the desk looked at them like they did not belong in this auspicious hotel.

"We'd like Mr. Boykin's room please," Jim asked.

"I'm sorry sir, but Mr. Boykin has checked out and left no forwarding address."

"Well you'd better be careful who you check into your hotel, as Mr. Boykin is a thief and swindler, and he paid your bill with my money . . ."

The clerk looked disturbed with his mouth gaping open, as Jim and Bobby turned and left the hotel.

At the door, they stopped.

"This means he had somewhere else to go. Bobby, I doubt if it would be back to Kissimmee, although he might be headed for Jacksonville. Let's go back to the station and see when the next train is scheduled for Florida."

They tried searching and watching on three trains to no avail. Finally, they boarded their train back to Florida.

Well, you realize what this means Bobby?

"Don't worry about me, Mr. O'Berry, I'll be okay, you got a wife to take care of."

"Yes, that's true, Bobby, and I do appreciate your concern. However, the debt comes first. Lizzy and I will make out okay. I have one more chore for you if you are willing and you will get paid for it too. I want you to accompany Lizzy by train to Jacksonville and back to Kissimmee."

Worn out, they both slept soundly in spite of the clickity-clack of the train over the tracks on the way home. The next morning, after stopping by the sheriff's office for Jim's $400, they picked up a buckboard at the livery and headed back to the farm.

Elizabeth saw them coming down the road and ran out to meet them. It was about 4 p.m. and the grass was wet from a rainstorm a couple of hours before. The sky was overcast and looked like a beautiful sunset might be coming that evening.

Jim stopped the wagon as Elizabeth approached. She was dressed in a blue gingham dress with her hair down to her shoulders.

"How was the trip?"

"Could-a-been better."

"Oh, I see," Elizabeth said as she reached up and took Jim's hand.

"Well, come on in, I have a pitcher of lemonade for the both of you men."

They put up the horses and then washed up for supper at the pitcher pump attached to a three-foot long table on the back porch.

That evening after a supper of fried chicken, collard greens, and mashed potatoes, Jim and Elizabeth remained seated at the dining table to plan what to do next, while Bobby turned in for the night.

"Lizzy, you know we don't have the money to plant a new crop. I'm going to have to move around a bit and see what options are out there. I'll leave in a day or two, after I tidy up the place a little."

"Depending upon what I find, you should go and visit your folks a while until I get things straightened out. And if you can, while in Kissimmee, please visit my mother and father."

"I surely will," Elizabeth replied.

Meanwhile, Jim's father and mother, who were living in Kissimmee, were getting back in the cattle business according to the letters he received from his mother. Jim had not heard from his parents in several months. A couple of days later, Jim left for town on his horse bound for the general store. Most of the gossip was found there, so it was a good place to start.

Job Quest

J im stepped off his gray quarter horse, adjusted his light grey felt Stetson and tied his horse to the hitching post. His boots clomped on the board sidewalk as he went inside the Perrine General Store. Jim was a well-known figure as he often bought things here over the past several years. He was wearing a nice checkered shirt and work pants and suspenders.

"Well, look what the dog dragged in fellers," the store manager bellowed.

Several men were grouped around the old potbellied stove, situated near the counter.

"Howdy Lonnie, Eugene, Marc, brother Glen, Josie and hello to you too Howard. How's everybody doing?" Jim said greeting the crowd.

"Have a cracker or two, Jim," Howard said pointing to the cracker barrel as he handed Jim a blue and white tin cup for the coffee pot sitting on the potbellied stove.

"We are all about the same here, but I hear you had a streak of bad luck," Howard, the store manager said. Howard looked like a store manager, dressed in his pants, white shirt, and apron. His thinning hair neatly combed over to cover the bald spot.

"Oh, I suppose so, but it's my own dang fault."

"Why'd you think that, Jim?"

"I trusted a stranger," he said as he poured himself a cup of coffee.

"What are you going to do now? Can you replant?" Henry Bradford asked.

Henry had done quite well out in Louisiana, moved here, lock stock and barrel, built a house with gas lighting and a windmill that pumped water to the porch.

"No, it took all my cash to work that eighty acres of ground. I'm gonna have to find something else to take up my time until next year.

"So, you're looking for work I suppose?" Herman Milton asked.

"Now boys, don't be too hard on ole Jim here, cause he ain't afraid of work at all, why he'd lay right down beside of it," Howard quipped and they all laughed.

I suppose I'm open to suggestions if anyone knows of anything this side of Jacksonville," Jim replied.

Arnie Beckworth slid off the stool he had been sitting on and stood up.

"You know, Jim, there was a feller stopped by my place and asked me if I knew of anyone that could farm and provide meat for a real estate company that was going to sell farm-land in the everglades. They plan to put up a tent city, plow up some land for truck farming and sell that land to fellers they intend to bring in from the north on the railroad spur they are planning to build. They have started building a spur track from Miami to the west, out near the loop road where the farmland is," Arnie relayed.

"Well don't that sound interesting, Arnie. Just how would I go about finding these gentlemen?

"I reckon that's the easy part, Jim, you just go north up alongside the railroad and you will run into these fellers as they are camped at where the spur will start at a place called the Miami Junction," Arnie explained.

"I sure am beholden to you for that piece of information," Jim said shaking Arnie's hand.

Jim rode home, arriving around dark that evening, to gather some of his things and tell Elizabeth what he intended to do. They ate a dinner of venison, mashed potatoes, and green beans, plus a dish of guava cobbler with cream. Afterwards, they sat at the dining table to talk.

"Elizabeth, I will most likely be gone for a while if I get this job. But, in the meantime, I want you to write your parents and explain what we are doing and tell them you are on the way and will stay with them until this job ends. This place here is not going to be a place for a woman and to stay alone for several months with no one to watch out for you. That would be ill advised."

"I suppose so, Jim, so just how would I get to Kissimmee?"

I have sandbagged a few dollars, Lizzy; you and Bobby will take a train to Jacksonville and then back to Orlando and then by buggy to Kissimmee. We'll plan it out tonight, so you can put your schedule in the letter to your folks. In the meantime, I will be on the lookout for other work I can do to include you in the plan, as I will surely miss you."

"Oh, Jim, I will surely miss you too."

"You be very careful what you do since we have another baby on the way. No heavy lifting, or anything like that, okay?"

"Looks like our fourth child is beginning to show," as he rubbed Elizabeth's tummy.

Have you thought about a name if it's a boy?

Why yes, I thought about Frank James O'Berry, after your father," Elizabeth said smiling.

"What about if it is a girl?"

How do you feel about calling her Kathleen?"

"That sounds just fine." Jim leaned over hugging and kissing Elizabeth.

For the next few days, Jim and Bobby closed down the barn, boarded up the house windows and the three of them took the buggy to Miami where Jim put Elizabeth and Bobby on a train to Jacksonville. Jim had paid Bobby in advance, and since Bobby was at home in

Kissimmee, this trip was actually a blessing for him. When the train arrived in Orlando, Bobby rented a buggy and took Elizabeth to her parents' home in Kissimmee. Elizabeth jumped off the wagon and ran up the steps to hug her mother and father.

"Step down, Bobby! It's might good to see you again, and thank you kindly for escorting Elizabeth home," John Lanier said.

"Thank you kindly, Mr. Lanier, Jim wouldn't have it any other way. Since Jim O'Berry has no need of my services for a spell, I thought I'd ask if you knew of anything going on that I might saddle up with," Bobby replied.

"Well, wait just a minute, Bobby, I just had a whopping idea," Mr. Lanier exclaimed.

"Why, Bobby, bless my soul! I sure could use some help with my cows, and since you once worked around here that would be a natural for you. I know you are a valuable tomato farmer, but I also know that you know cows."

"What do you have in mind?"

Remember when you worked here a couple of years ago? Well, we have grown a bit and I need more help." Mr. Lanier and Bobby made their deal for Bobby to start work the next day. Bobby was to bunk in a spare room off the back of the house with its own entrance.

Jim had met with the farm people at the railroad spur site and was advised to head out to the farm site and meet with his supervisor and get the lay of the land. The camp was located 40 miles to the west, which meant most of two days to get there. The spur was starting to be built and the right of way for the track was clear. That would be easy going for not only the railroad builders, but also Jim's horse.

Jim rode past some cabbage palms and pulled up when he spotted a little four-point buck deer about a hundred yards

ahead. It was early, but the big puffy clouds were already
overhead. A buzzard lazily made wide circles against the blue
sky. Jim pulled his rifle out of its scabbard, aimed and shot
and killed the deer. A flock of Curlews rose up from the grass
like a huge sheet of white and flew away, wings whistling.

*I'd best be cleaning this deer quick, so I can be on my
way,* Jim thought to himself.

He hung the deer up with a stick between the hind legs,
bled, cleaned and propped open the cavity with a couple of
sticks so it would cool below body temperature. He threw
the deer over the saddle in front of him figuring to make it a
present to the farm camp. In about an hour, Jim rode up to
the main tent at the site.

"Hello the camp," Jim shouted.

A short stocky man with a trimmed beard stepped out
wearing a black summer waist coat and a black bowler hat.

He wore a colt .45 high on his waist and had elastic bands around each arm to keep his sleeves up, like card dealers would do.

"Nice deer," the man said.

"I'm Jim O'Berry and you must be the gentleman I'm to speak to about a job."

"Welcome Mr. O'Berry, please step down and come set a spell."

Jim dismounted and tied his horse to a post where another horse was hitched, he shook hands with the man. They sat on a bench outside the tent.

"I thought your camp could use some meat," Jim continued, indicating the deer on his horse.

"That is mighty nice of you, Mr. O'Berry, mighty nice. I'm Bob Adams." Bob was round-faced and appeared to be used to giving orders.

"Jim, I run things around here and I want to make you at home. As for the job, if we come to an agreement, that would be a very important piece of our puzzle out here. You see, the South Florida Farm district we represent bought some very nice bottom land, mostly marl with a little rock thrown in that we intend to sell to farmers brought in by railway from the north. Your job would be to set up a model farm."

Jim handed Bob a letter from the camp where he had inquired.

"From this letter, Mr. O'Berry, I understand from the boys you met with at the spur that you are accustomed to that kind of farming."

"Yes sir, marl is a mixture of dirt, ground rock, and sand, making sort of a clay that does grow things pretty well. I have farmed tomatoes in rocky pot hole marl soil before. It wasn't the best to work with, but it is doable. Suppose I like what I see and hear. Just what would be my responsibilities?"

"I'm glad you asked that Jim, let's take a little ride and let me show you around while we talk."

"Currently, Jim, we are on horseback, but when the farmers arrive, we will have a motor car to show them around in."

"I'm sure they will like that."

"Barney," Mr. Adams shouted into the tent, "Bring another man and come take this deer off the man's horse and butcher it, Mr. Adams ordered. Cut off half the back strap on one side and wrap it so Mr. O'Berry can have it for dinner."

Two men came out of the tent and took the deer off Jim's horse. Jim and Mr. Adams mounted their horses and rode up to a single-strand barbed wire fence that enclosed about 40 acres.

"This will be the sample farm site you would cultivate, Jim. Your job would be simply to farm this 40-acre site and raise some hogs, a few steers and some chickens, provide meat and vegetables to our potential clients. You will have two extra hands to help you. We are also building a small hotel for the clients to bunk in. They will be here, in roughly 60 days and then another batch will be railroaded in when they leave. This will happen as long as it takes to sell all of our property. You will be paid $2 a day, plus room and board, with a $50 bonus if everything is ready on time. Payday is Saturday afternoon. You will have 4 months to get the farm going. Fail and you will be terminated with money earned. However, keep in mind we want you to succeed and will help in any way we can."

"Who will pay my help?"

Oh, we will of course."

"What about mules, plows, discs, seed and fertilizer and anything else I will need? Oh, another thing. Is there already a plan of what crops I will farm?"

"We will provide everything. What you grow is mostly up to you. I would like to see some corn, black-eyed peas, collards and tomatoes, but you will make that determination. I would suspect you will pick what will grow best here."

Jim looked out over the land. He could see about 10 to 12 miles across a wide flat savannah, before strands of cypress trees broke the horizon. The cool, clear spring day was pleasant as a red-tailed hawk flew overhead calling to his mate.

"Fair enough, when will I start?"

"You be back here in about 10 days or so, say Monday week. By that time all the equipment should be here. The bunk house should be built and some of the stock pens we will build this week."

Barney came from around the main tent, and Mr. Adams nodded in concurrence to him.

"Mr. O'Berry, here is a piece of back-strap from the deer you kilt. You might like it for supper tonight."

"That's might neighborly of you folks, I do appreciate it."

Jim took the meat wrapped in a clean cloth and placed it in his saddlebag.

"One more thing, Mr. O'Berry. I don't know you very well, so how would I know you ain't running from the law and won't even show up next Monday?"

"That's an easy question to answer, Mr. Adams. As a young man, my daddy, Frank O'Berry, you may have heard of him, sat me down one day and told me that I had one thing that no one could ever take away from me, but that I could lose in a heartbeat. He said that once you lie, steal, or cheat, you will forever be known as a liar, a thief, or a cheat.

"I am an O'Berry, Mr. Adams. When I shake your hand in agreement, you can bank on it, as long as things are true, legal, and open."

They shook hands, and Jim climbed on his horse, wheeled around and jumped his horse into a slow lope and headed back to Perrine, South of Miami.

"Well I'll be," Bob Adams mumbled. He shoved his hat back on his head and watched Jim as he looped off to the east.

"I might have me a 'do-gooder' boy on my hands. Perhaps a tough one at that. That might not be the best thing ever. I may have to give that some thought," Adams mused.

That night, Jim enjoyed that piece of deer back-strap, the tenderloin of a deer, along with some hard tack.

Four days later, Jim went to the general store in Perrine. He walked in and was greeted by the usual group sitting around the pot of coffee on the stove.

"Howdy, Jim," Howard the store manager greeted Jim.

"Howdy boys, Jerry, Ham, and I ain't seen you for a spell, Grover," Jim said.

"Well, don't keep us all in suspense, Jim, did you take that job or not?" Howard asked.

"Just hold your tater, Howard. I haven't had any coffee in two days. What kind of a host are you anyway?" Jim answered back, as he sat down near the stove.

Jim took his time pouring the coffee. Everyone was sitting on the edge of their seats leaning forward, waiting for the story. Jim took a sip, enjoying the heat of the coffee and said. "Yes!"

"Yes? Is that all there is to it?" Howard croaked. Silence filled the room.

Jim started to laugh and so did all the other boys, almost spilling their coffee, as they knew Jim was funning ole Howard. As the laughter died down, Jim told them the whole story, since that was most likely the only gossip they would get that day.

"Sounds like a pretty good job for a good farmer like yourself, Jim," Horace commented.

"Yes, it should give me enough money to start another tomato crop, with a little to live on. When I leave here I'm going up to the Lanier place in Kissimmee to see Elizabeth and tell her the news. I assume you boys knew I sent her home for a spell."

"Sure, we know, Jim. You know how news travels around here," Howard chimed in.

"What are you going to need for the next four months or so?"

"Here's a list Howard, just put it in a couple of burlap bags, please,"

"Oh yeah, Jim, there is a letter here for you from Elizabeth."

Jim opened the letter read it and then said, "Okay boys, I know you all are anxious to hear the news from Kissimmee, so here she is."

Jim,

Here is some news you may want to consider.

You remember ole Johnny Belle, Captain of the paddle wheel boat Tinker Belle? Well he docked here at Lake Tohopekaliga last week. He came to Kissimmee for provisions and said that the people that ran that hotel on the Kissimmee River midway to Lake Okeechobee were leaving, moving to Tampa, and did I know anyone that would like to run that hotel? It pays roughly $80 a month. It would start about four months from now. I'm sure we could run that hotel if need be. *Jim left out the personal part of the letter.*

"Sounds interesting doesn't it boys, but I hope I make enough at the demonstration farm to go back to the tomato farm. Howard, thank you kindly for remembering the letter."

Jim bought what things he figured he would need, like gloves, brogan boots, a couple pair of overalls, and everything he might need for the next four months, including plenty of hard tack, Pemmican, venison jerky, coffee, and grits, to use until the hotel restaurant at the demonstration farm got started. Then he remounted and rode northwest towards the Lanier home in Kissimmee and Elizabeth. He was chewing on a hardtack biscuit and a square of Pemmican made from dried meat, ground up and mixed with beef tallow squeezed into a hard square.

"These hardtack biscuits could keep for fifty years and were meant to make you think you ate something, it's a good

thing I have some pemmican to go with it," Jim thought to himself.

Three days later, Elizabeth saw him riding his pale gray mare coming up the road and ran out to meet him, almost pulling him off his horse.

"Jiminy Crickets, Lizzy, I'm shore glad to see you too. But let me get off this mare first," Jim laughed and she giggled as he jumped down, picked her up off her feet, spun her around and gave her a big hug.

"You got news, husband?"

"Yep, I should make enough money by Christmas for us to put in a new tomato crop at the homestead, but if not, we can consider that hotel job. All this should take place before its time for the baby to come. What do you think of that?"

"Well, that's just great, but just how long will you be here, Jim O'Berry?"

"It will take me about four days to get back to the demonstration farm, so I got a couple days here I suppose."

"Well just suppose we make the best of that little bitty time you have for me Jim O'Berry, husband of mine."

"I will, I will," Jim promised as he smacked her on her bottom.

"Ooh, watch it mister, Somebody might see us."

"Remember wife of mine, now we have a license," he said grinning as he chased her up to the house.

At supper that night, Jim outlined his new job to the Lanier family.

"Jim, do these fellers you will be working for seem to be on the up and up to you?" Elizabeth's father John Lanier asked.

"I suspect they do have the land to sell and will bring in settler farmers to buy it. I don't know how much they know about the area or what they might tell the new people. I do know that every three or four years a hurricane comes and floods a lot of that everglades flat land. I also know I will be paid weekly my daily wage, so the only thing they might hedge on would be the bonus. I plan to arrive a day early and survey the operation before going in. Just to see how their plans are working out," Jim explained.

"That sounds wise, Jim."

"However, before I would like to go visit my parents across town. Elizabeth, I would like you to go with me too."

"You know I would."

"Jim why don't you and Elizabeth take my buggy instead of going horseback?"

"That would be mighty gracious of you, I appreciate that very much Mr. Lanier."

They arrived at the house and knocked on the door. No one answered, so they walked around to the back and found his mother tending her garden.

"Mother, you have company," Jim called out.

"Glory be, look at you two. What a picture, let me put this hoe down and come on in. I'll fix you some lunch," Martha said.

She put the hoe away and hugged first her son and then Elizabeth.

"Where's Pa, mother?"

Your Pa is off buying cattle, land, and leasing more land. Son, we are back in the cattle business."

"Why, mother, what happened?"

"Well, let's sit down in the kitchen and I'll tell you all about it while I fix us lunch."

Martha poured some sweet tea for the two of them.

"It came as a complete shock to me," she said.

"I was in the kitchen and I heard his motor car come flying around the corner and screeched to a halt in front of our place. I was putting a cake in the oven, so I couldn't run out front immediately to see what was going on. Frank came busting in the house shouting "Martha, Martha, where are you?"

"Well, I was so startled, I let the oven door slam and the cake fell. I went running from the kitchen asking what was the matter? I didn't know if I should get the shotgun, or what."

"What did he say, Mother?" Jim asked. "It's war Martha, war." Your father said almost out of breath.

"War? War with who?" I said.

"A big war in Europe. And Martha and you know what that means?"

"No Frank, I honestly don't know, not really," I said.

"Beef, Martha, beef, that is what war means. The government will need beef and lots of it for a war this big, and anyone in the cattle business will get rich."

"So, I said, Frank, we don't have any cattle, and for that matter, we don't have any pasture land." "And he said, 'No, we don't, but if I have my way, we will. Especially if America gets involved, and that, I believe, will happen very soon.' "

"And then he said, 'You know Red, I've been bored to death with this city we've been living for the past few years. If it weren't for you, I would have gone crazy. But now I have a chance to get back in the cattle business. Looking back, I guess I just quit too soon,' he admitted to me."

"Now people, that's the first time he has called me Red in years. That's why I knew he was serious."

"So, that's the story. He'll be back in a week or two to rest up for a day, then he will be at it all over again. He has an old shack he stays in sometimes around Buckles Bend. This has been going on for about six months now, and he almost has the seed stock with enough pasture to work for the next three years. He has a base crew of six people helping him.

"Frank had read in the newspapers that this world war would be the war to end all wars if the United States entered. That's when Frank started in earnest to build a herd. I asked him how many head of cattle we have and he told me around 6000 and if the war lasted another six years we would be in high cotton."

They ate lunch and talked for another hour before Jim and Elizabeth left for Elizabeth's parents place. A few minutes into the ride back, Elizabeth asked Jim a question.

"Jim, what if the war doesn't last another six, or even four years?"

"Pa would be in big trouble I suspect."

The Demonstration Farm

The next day, Jim set out for south Florida and the demonstration farm. It took four days to get there from Kissimmee. Jim rode through the swamp noticing that the pale pink air plants were in full bloom on the cypress trees. The swamp was almost dry, so snakes were scarce. It was a nice fall day, with big puffy clouds and buzzards gliding around high in the sky.

He peered through the trees and saw that most everything Adams had told him was on schedule. The barn was up, the hotel was under construction, and he could see one set of harrows at the barn. As he rode into the settlement, he also noticed a brace of mules, two milk cows, and a few more horses in the corral. Jim rode up to the main tent and stepped down off his horse, tying it to the new whitewashed post.

"Hello the tent," Jim shouted.

Mr. Adams and two other men came out.

"Hello Mr. O'Berry, I see you are a day early, ready to get started I suspect," Adams said.

"The sooner the better, as it will take three or four months to get the crops up."

"Come in and let's talk before I get you settled in." Adams said and led the way to a table with chairs inside the front part of the tent.

"We have everything you need to get started."

They talked a while ironing out the details of the operation. Finally, Jim said, "I thought I would plant the corn on
the back side of the rows, then tier down by height in order
to show off the whole acreage to its full potential."

"That sounds good. Let's get you settled in so you can get
started. Oh, listen for the dinner bell and come claim a seat
at the table." Adams said as he led the way to the bunkhouse.

"Jim, this is John Barley, Jake Lanier, Tommy Hostetler,
Jim Manson, Bob Cutter, and that big feller over there (pointing) is Barney McBride. Now all these boys have had a hand
at farming, so get to know them and use any two you like,"
Adams said.

"Boys, nice to meet you, which of you men really like
farming?"

Jim watched carefully as two of the men volunteered
without hesitation, and the others followed suit a step later.
The first was Jake Lonnie.

"Okay, now who has really farmed on a large scale before?

Jake Lonnie stood up. "I worked on a tomato farm down
around Fort Myers for a man named Donald Webb, Mr.
O'Berry."

"Really? How'd that turn out?" Jim asked, well-knowing
that was referring to his friend.

"Fine and dandy, but Mr. Webb's boat sank that he was
transporting tomatoes to New Orleans on, and he had to cut
me loose."

"Were you with him when the boat sank?"

"No sir, I was tending the farm, Tom Davis was on the
boat with him, but he drowned. Mr. Webb was rescued by a
sponge boat."

"Did he say how the boat sank?" Jim asked.

"Yes sir, he said his boat was sabotaged most likely by the
tomato wholesale people but couldn't prove it."

"Interesting," Jim said, as he had spent some time with
Donald Webb and was largely responsible for Donald getting
into the boating business of hauling tomatoes to New Orleans.

"I'm sure sorry to hear of Tom's death and Donald's problems as I knew Tom and Donald as friends."

Jim picked Jake and one other farm boy, Ned, to be his helpers and they began to work the farm.

It took less than a month to prepare the soil and get the seeds in the ground. The soil was moist and it rained at least once a week. Everything was coming along fine as the seedlings were doing well. The few that didn't do well were quickly replaced.

Demonstration Farm

Clyde Boykin

One day while walking along the side of the big tent, the one Bob Adams had his office in, Jim heard voices inside the tent, one was Bob Adams and he stiffened as he thought he recognized the other one. He eased up to the entrance of the tent and peeked around the corner of the opening. Sure enough, he was right. It was non-other than Clyde Boykin the tomato money thief. Boykin was talking to Adams about buying some of the property they intended to sell to farmers from the north. "Now why, Mr. Boykin would you want to buy up several acres of farmland down here? You said yourself you are not a farmer," Adams exclaimed.

"It's really very simple, Mr. Adams," Boykin responded.

"I plan to hold on to that land for another year and resell it after the value increases, you don't have any problem with that do you, Mr. Adams?"

"I never have any problem with cash money, Mr. Boykin. Did you come here prepared to do business?"

Well, Mr. Adams, I obviously wouldn't carry that kind of cash with me, you understand, and I was not aware if you still have enough land to sell," Boykin replied.

Jim realized the Boykin was talking about his own tomato money that Boykin has stolen in New York.

"I understand sir, and I can tell you now, we can look over the plots and I can reserve what you want for a period of, say, ten days?"

"That sounds fair, but I'll be back as soon as humanly possible."

Jim noticed a black horse he had not seen before, so that must have been Boykin's horse. The horse was tethered on Jim's side of the door. Quickly, Jim stepped over to the horse and cut the cinch belt almost through, leaving enough for walking the horse, but any strain and it would break. Then he reached down into the saddle bag and came out with a bundle of money, about eight hundred dollars, which he was about to replace, but he thought better of it. After all, that is my money.

Jim then worked his way back to the corral, saddled his horse and then grabbed his rifle and saddle gun from the bunkhouse. He mounted his horse and exited the property through the palmettos where he had come into the property before without being seen.

Jim thought to himself, *"I'll just go around and get in front of Boykin, then ambush him after he gets down the trail a while."*

From a distance, Jim could see Boykin as he stepped up on his horse. He spent the next hour getting far enough ahead of Boykin so the camp would not hear gun shots if they happened. Jim positioned himself on the far side of a narrow trail through a cypress swamp. He tied his horse out of sight and got behind a big pine tree for cover on the far side.

Jim could hear Boykin's horse as he splashed through the cypress swamp water.

From behind the tree he shouted, "Stand where you are and put your hands in the air."

"What's this? I've got no money stranger, if you mean to rob me," Boykin offered.

Jim stepped out from behind the tree with a rifle pointed at him.

"Now why would I attempt to rob a thieving robber like you?" Jim asked.

"O'Berry?

"That's right, now step down easy, both hands up.

"Drop that waist gun on the ground first," Jim commanded.

Boykin knew he had only one chance, and that was to try and run. He threw the gun on the ground toward Jim, which attracted Jim's attention for a second. He kicked his horse, crouched low in the saddle and rode like the wind, leaning to the left behind the horse away from sight. He was amazed he heard no gunshot. About that time, the saddle's cinch belt broke and he hit the ground hard at full gallop. He lay on the ground, still in the saddle and dazed.

Jim rode up to where Boykin lay.

"Now is that anyway to get off your horse?"

"Oh, my shoulder, I think it's out of joint."

"I'm not surprised, the way you dismounted."

"Now stand up."

"Okay, okay, I'm up."

"Now tie your hands together."

"Now look here, O'Berry, you . . ."

Jim interrupted him. "You want to argue? I'll just kill you where you stand." Jim's cold tone was perfectly understood. Jim handed him a picking string he kept in his saddle bag. Normally these short pieces of rope were meant to tie up three legs of a calf that had been roped. "Step back," Jim ordered and picked up Boykins saddle and threw it on the horse. He tied another piece of rope to the chinch strap to repair it and buckled it tight.

As a safety precaution, Jim went through Boykins saddle bags and came up with another pistol and an advertisement for the property sale company Jim was working for at the demonstration farm.

FARMERS WANTED

BIG FARMLAND SALE IN SOUTH FLORIDA
RICH FARMLAND ONLY NEEDS A PLOW AND SEED
TRANSPORTATION BY RAIL WILL BE PROVIDED TO ALL
WHO QUALIFY.
PLEASE REPLY TO P.O. BOX 3567 KANSAS CITY, MO.
FURTHER INFORMATION WILL FOLLOW.

SOUTH FLORIDA FARM LAND ASSOCIATION

"Now stand facing your horse at the saddle and put your arms over the saddle."

Jim went to the other side of the horse and inspected his tied hands, putting a finishing knot on the rope. Then he took Boykin's rifle out of his saddle scabbard.

"Now mount up," Jim said holding the horse's reins.

Jim mounted his horse pulling Boykin on his horse and headed south through the woods and around the cypress stands, keeping in the flatwoods. After about an hour Jim stopped. He saw a lone pine tree about 12 inches in diameter, rode over and stopped. Boykin's horse stopped at the tree.

"Get down," Jim ordered.

"Why are we stopping here?" Boykin asked.

Jim ignored the question, dismounted and led Boykin over to the pine tree.

"Lay down on your back, with your feet towards the tree." Jim ordered.

Jim took out a big bandanna handkerchief and temporarily tied Boykin's feet and helped him get up facing the tree.

"I'm going untie your hands, do not make a move."

"Not much I could do with my feet tied."

"Not much. "Put your hands around the tree." Jim tied Boykin's hands together as Boykin hugged the tree, and then untied his feet.

"Look, O'Berry, I still have about $1,500 of your tomato money. I'll get it for you," Boykin entreated.

"Where is it?"

"It's in the bank at Jacksonville."

"That's too bad."

What do you mean?"

That's too far for me to go and get it and get back here to untie you. The wolves or the ants would have had their way with you by then."

"No, no, you can have it telegraphed from Miami."

"Well that's better, I can be back in four days that way."

"Four days? Are you mad? I could die by then!"

"Yes, I see you only have only one canteen on your horse. Enough water for about two days"

Jim went over to Boykins horse, got the canteen and put it beside Boykin on the ground.

"Now you can stand or sit, it doesn't matter none to me. I'm not sure just how you will get to your water though. Tell you what, you'd better just drink it all now, that will last a day and a half or so."

Jim picked up the canteen and held it to Boykins mouth as he drank it dry. He recapped the canteen, putting it back on Boykins horse. Then he mounted his horse, taking Boykins horse in tow.

"What do you intend to do, O'Berry?"

"Why, I intend to leave."

"When will you be back?"

"Oh two, three days maybe."

"You can't do this," Boykin shouted.

"Well, Mr. Boykin, here's the thing. We had a deal. You broke the deal and stole my money, so I am making a new deal. You die out here alone and you can keep my money."

"What? You mean you would let me die out here, tied to a pine tree?"

"Well, I thought about it, and killin' you with a pistol would give me no real satisfaction. But knowing you died, tied to a pine tree, would give me a great deal of satisfaction,"

"Look, O'Berry, I understand you are put out with me, what if I could get you, say $800 quickly, and then I could get you the rest when we go to Miami. Would that satisfy you?"

"You mean the $800 that was in your saddle bags, Mr. Boykin? Well, I believe I already have control of that money, assuming of course it's in your saddlebags.

The stare that came from Boykin could have cracked ice.

"Well, Boykin, this is your lucky day."

"You are letting me go?"

Jim laughed and said,

"No, this is your lucky day because in the past, when someone deserves to be tied to a tree, I usually pour honey on him so the ants or perhaps a bear will enjoy the event better. But I'm all out of honey today. That's why this is your lucky day Boykin,"

"Look, O'Berry, if you'll turn me lose, I'll sign a bank note you can cash it for the full amount, less the money I've spent."

"Hmm, I'll consider that. We'll discuss it when I get back, you might be a little more motivated by then."

Jim mounted his horse, spun him around trailing Boykins horse and headed south towards the east-west trail. Before he got to the trail, he stopped, stepped off his horse, and adjusted Boykins saddle so if rode hard the saddle would just slip around under the horse, throwing the rider. Then he tied it to a tree.

Two hours later, he arrived at the Demonstration Farm and found Adams.

"Mr. Adams, things are going well with the farm, but I need to attend to some business in Miami. The two boys working for him could keep things under control until he got back.

"I understand, Mr. O'Berry, but you understand I will have to dock you for the days you are gone."

"Fair enough, Mr. Adams, and I appreciate your consideration, I'll go and get the boys prepared for my short absence. I'll check in with you in about three days if all goes well."

He mounted his horse and headed east toward where Boykin was waiting, tied to a pine tree.

As he neared the tree where the horse was tied, it was getting dark. Then he rode on to where Boykin was tied.

"That you Boykin? I almost missed finding your tree, I see you decided to sit a spell, if you can stand, I'll cut you lose and we can head east."

Boykin scrambled to get up on his feet, which was not easy. "Where in tarnation do you plan to take me?"

Well, that depends on you. If I get my money in a reasonable fashion, we might skip the sheriff's office and you can crawl back under whatever rock you came from. Get that bank draft out of your saddle bag, sign it all legal-like and we will see how she goes."

Boykin took out the bank draft, made it out to Jim and signed it. It was on the National bank of Jacksonville and had to be presented in person.

They rode half the night and finally stopped around midnight and made a cold camp. Facing a cypress stand, with palmettos at their back, and a small pine tree at the edge of the palmettos, Jim took out some hard tack and a couple pieces of venison jerky and gave Boykin half of it. Boykin with his hands still tied, ate the food.

When they finished eating, Jim said, "Go sit by that pine tree and I'll re-tie your hands for the night. I can't have you pussy-footin around, now can I? We'll settle in until daylight."

Boykin slept sitting and leaning against the tree. Jim rousted him as daylight broke. He re-tied Boykin's hands and helped him into the saddle.

Jim turned to step up on his horse. Boykin kicked his horse, running over Jim. In the melee, Boykin's horse stepped on Jim's left arm, injuring it badly. One hoof struck the back of Jim's head, dazing him. On the ground, Jim drew his pistol that was tucked into his belt, but his horse was in the way of a quick shot and he was seeing double anyway. In moments, Boykin was out of range. Jim scrambled to his feet, and attempted to mount his horse, but his shoulder hurt so bad he fell back on the ground. His shoulder may have been dislocated. It took another few minutes for Jim's head to clear and he made a makeshift sling for his left arm. He mounted his horse and attempted to trail Boykin. He might catch Boykin if he stayed on the trail due to the fix he did on Boykins saddle, but chances of that were 50/50. Boykin was not dumb.

"I know he will try to get to Jacksonville ahead of me and take out all the money in that account, or telegraph ahead to stop my bank draft, like I would have done," Jim thought.

Jim had one advantage. He might find Boykin laying on the round due to the saddle slipping. Also, if that didn't work, he could go directly to the telegraph office in Miami as fast as his horse would get there, with intermittent walking his horse so he would not wear him out.

Ahead, about a quarter mile, as Boykin was looping along, the saddle began to slip.

"Oh no, not again," Boykin yelled.

He slowed the horse and leaped off the saddle before it got totally under his horse and landed with a roll, not hurting himself any worse. Damn that O'Berry, he got me again, but this time I won't be so easy to catch. The horse not liking the saddle under his belly, bucked a few times and then stopped. Boykin caught up with his horse, fixed the saddle and continued on, but at a creek, he turned downstream to hide his direction and then walked his horse about a hundred yards off the right of the trail. It wasn't long before he saw, through the trees, Jim looping along the trail in hot pursuit of where he thought Boykin was going.

Jim walked into the telegraph office around 4 p.m. and addressed the clerk.

"Good afternoon, have you seen a big man about 45 years old come in to send a telegram to Jacksonville today?"

"No sir, not today," the clerk answered.

"Okay, send this to the Jacksonville National Bank, I have a bank draft in the amount of $15,000 signed by Clyde Boykin, STOP. Can you hold that amount until I can get to Jacksonville in three days' time STOP."

The clerk sent the telegram. Jim put his horse behind the adjoining building in case Boykin came to the telegraph office while Jim was there. Jim sat down to wait and in about an hour and a half a reply came back from the Jacksonville National Bank.

"Here is your reply, Mr. O'Berry," the clerk said with no smile on his face.

Jim read the telegram. "Mr. O'Berry, we cannot honor your request STOP. Mr. Boykin does not have an account with this bank STOP."

Jim sat back down in the chair staring at the telegram.

"He got me again," Jim said under his breath. Jim stood up and left the telegraph office. He headed towards the sheriff's office and relayed the story that he had caught Boykin and was bringing him in when he got away, by running over him with his horse.

"I'd be much obliged, Sheriff if you would keep an eye out for him. He needs to be behind bars.

"I will keep an eye out for him, but I noticed you are still carrying your saddle gun in your belt. Be careful what you do with it, Mr. O'Berry," the sheriff admonished.

I will Sheriff. I'm headed to the closest hotel, so I can get a good night's sleep.

The next day Jim rode back to the demonstration farm. The next few months went well and the week before the first train full of farmers who would be the potential buyers arrived, Mr. Adams called Jim into the main tent. Jim sat at Adam's desk, while Adams counted out Jim's final week's salary and added a $50 bonus to the envelope and handed it to Jim.

"I guess this means I've done as expected and you want me out of here before the buyers come in." Jim said.

"Yes, you're a good man, Jim, and we have appreciated your work. Adams handed Jim a letter of commendation."

"You know that either in the first or second year, this 'farm' land will flood?"

"There is that possibility, that is why in our advertisement we included a paragraph about that possibility," Adams said as he handed Jim a copy of the ad.

FARMERS WANTED

BIG FARM LAND SALE IN SOUTH FLORIDA.
RICH FARMLAND ONLY NEEDS A PLOW AND SEED,
THE HEAVY RAINS EVERY TWO OR THREE YEARS KEEPS
THE LAND FERTILE AND REFURBISHES IT FOR THE
FOLLOWING YEAR.
TRANSPORTATION TO FLORIDA WILL BE PROVIDED FOR
ALL QUALIFIED PARTIES. PLEASE REPLY TO P.O. BOX 6537,
KANSAS CITY, MO.
FURTHER INFORMATION WILL BE PROVIDED.

SOUTH FLORIDA FARM LAND ASSOCIATION

"Pretty slick, Mr. Adams. I guess I can't find fault with this ad, and I wish you well with the sale of the property. Jim rose and shook Adams hand. He gathered his things, mounted, and rode off to the east. As he rode out of sight of the land sales office, Jim reached back into his saddlebag and pulled out the original advertisement, saying nothing about heavy rains.

"So, I was right, he was hustling me away from the farm for fear I would tell the truth about the Everglades farmland. Adams had lied. That's too bad. I was just planning to just walk away.

After all, I have the eight hundred dollars from Boykin.

Jim arrived in Miami and went to the telegraph office.

"Can you find out the name of the leading newspaper in Kansas City, Missouri?" Jim asked the clerk.

"I suppose I could, Mr. O'Berry, if you're willing to pay the price. It could take a couple of messages."

"Feel free to find that name for me and I will have another lengthy message to send."

Jim got the address and sent a message to the newspaper.

ATTENTION FARMERS BUYING
FARMLAND IN SOUTH FLORIDA!

BE SURE TO BRING YOUR RAINCOATS, AS IT OFTEN RAINS FOR DAYS EVERY OTHER YEAR OR TWO AND TAKES MONTHS TO DRY OUT. THE SOUTH FLORIDA FARMLAND SALES COMPANY IS SELLING THE FARMLAND.

THEY SHOULDN'T HAVE LIED TO ME. SIGNED:
AN EVERGLADES FARMER

Meanwhile, back in Tampa, Zeke Blakie was furious. He knew his mercenary did not make it back and did not kill Jim O'Berry and now Jim is back in Kissimmee where his father lives, so he devised a plan.

"Time to take this problem on myself," Zeke said to himself.

The Riverview Hotel

Jim spent a week with Elizabeth in Kissimmee while they decided to go ahead and take the hotel job. It was the wrong time to plant anyway, and the farm would keep. They relaxed, took long walks, even fished some in Lake Tohopekaliga. In short, they rekindled their romance and got ready to move to the hotel on the Kissimmee River. Elizabeth and her father had collected all the information and notified the owners when they would take over the hotel. They timed their move to the schedule of the paddle wheeler that docked at Kissimmee.

"My father wants me to take Sears, the bluetick hound, off his hands and I thought he would be an added attraction to our family at the hotel. Lizzy, what do you think?"

"Yes, with you off hunting some of the time he would be good company when you aren't there.

"Do you have all your things packed darlin'?" Jim asked.

"I sure do, but you have all the baggage, a horse, a milk cow, guns, a plow and who knows what all in those boxes you have stacked up there."

"It's a good thing we are traveling by the big ole paddle wheeler boat, otherwise we'd need three wagons to get all this stuff moved."

The boat came the next afternoon after Jim and Lizzy had said their goodbyes to both Elizabeth's family and Jim's father and mother in Kissimmee. Jim and Elizabeth were greeted at the boat Tinker Bell, by Captain Johnny Belle.

The former operators of the hotel were to be picked up by the same paddlewheel boat Jim and Elizabeth were arriving on, so the transition would be a smooth one. There were only three people on the boat that would stay the night at the hotel. The trip from Kissimmee to the hotel on the Kissimmee River didn't take but about a half day.

The boat arrived at the hotel and slid up on the beach, the bow cutting a 'V' in the sand. They all left the boat and walked up to the house where the caretakers were waiting. It was just a little past noon, so Jim and Elizabeth had plenty of time to look around and get to know the former operators. The caretakers, Joe Brown, and his wife, Kim, brought them up to speed, leaving enough staples and groceries to last a few days and, of course they took care of the three people on the boat as their last night at the hotel.

The next morning Jim and Elizabeth saw the former operators, Captain Johnny Belle, his crew of one, and passengers off, bidding them farewell as the paddle wheels splashed in and out of the water, propelling the boat down the river. A backdrop of dark green hyacinths, pale green cypress trees and white billowy clouds made a beautiful picture. Jim and Elizabeth waved goodbye as the boat headed down river towards Lake Okeechobee. The big boat moved along, scaring great blue herons and white pond birds as they chugged along. Jim went to his arsenal of rifles and shotguns and put one by the front door, behind a curtain.

"Elizabeth, after I check out the barn and pens where animals are, I plan to take a ride starting about two miles north of here and ride west in a half circle, back around to the east, and back here. I want to take a look at the country around us. I'll be back before dark. You keep that shotgun of yours handy while I'm gone," Jim cautioned. The dog will stay with you.

Elizabeth had started to get moved in and to get familiar with the workings of the hotel. She changed the sheets on the beds. After, Jim took a survey of the hog pen and barn area. He noticed that the barn and attached stalls were pretty small, but large enough for the milk cow and, of course, his horse. The pig pen looked secure enough, and there was also a small smokehouse behind the barn.

Jim thought the chicken pen didn't seem sturdy enough for this wild part of the country, so he set out to reinforce it. You never know when a bobcat, coyote, or even a wolf or bear might appear; especially in the night.

"You got the chickens all settled?

"Sure-do, Lizzy, you should have eggs in a few days, I expect."

"Oh good, I plan to bake you a cake as soon as the eggs are ready and we have flour and the milk from the cow."

Meanwhile, Elizabeth moved them into the caretaker's room, which was a little larger than the rest of the rooms. She actually had a full-length, oblong mirror on a swivel stand. She stood in front of it and liked what she saw, smiling and singing under her breath as she went about her chores.

Okay, Lizzy, I'm going on my ride-about now. See you before dark. Jim rode for about four hours taking note of the Oak hammocks, cypress heads, and flat pinewoods, the east the end of the Alapattah Flats he had ridden through a few years prior, on the way to the east coast when he sailed to the Bahamas. He saw several deer from a distance—too far to shoot—noticed a large flock of turkeys, and was back to the hotel around 6 p.m.

The day had gone quickly as Jim worked on the pens and stalls. First thing Jim knew, Elizabeth was calling him to supper. Elizabeth had made a stew out some of the things they brought with them—potatoes, carrots, onions and a little smoked beef.

"It's stew tonight husband."

"That sounds mighty fine," Jim said as he stood up and moved his plate and silverware from the table by the pump.

"Isn't that nice Jim, a pump inside the house, instead of on the back porch. What will they think of next?"

"Sure is, and while you clean up the kitchen, I'll go down to the beach and start us a fire and we can sit for a spell and watch the stars."

"Just you make sure that's all you have planned, Mr. O'Berry."

"Why Elizabeth, what else could I have in mind?"

"You know very well what I mean, no tuggin at my drawers, Mister O'Berry."

Jim smiled and headed to the wood pile, moving some of the wood to the edge of the beach where the grass ended. He also brought a blanket they could sit on. The bank was about six feet higher than the river and afforded a good view of it.

He got the fire started and called Elizabeth. She came out to the fire, and asked, "What's that shining out in the river?"

Jim turned and watched as a parade of alligators floated down the river. "Why Lizzy those are our friends the alligators, I count about six going by right now. That's their eyes reflecting from the light of the fire. They move around after dark to find fish, turtles, garfish, or whatever they can find to eat."

"I knew there were gators in the river, but I never thought there would be so many. Remember when we drove the buggy to Orlando to catch the train to Jacksonville? That gator grabbed a spoke in the wheel and almost jumped into my lap."

"Now, Lizzy, I remember that, but he let go when he saw you."

Elizabeth, still standing shoved Jim over and pounded on him playfully. They enjoyed the rest of the night, as well as each other.

About 4 a.m. the next morning, Sears, the dog, began to bark. The growls and noises coming from out back sounded serious. Jim grabbed his double-barreled shotgun and rushed down the stairs to the back door. There was a little moonlight, enough to barely make out Sears barking and growling at what looked like a wolf. He fired at the wolf and got a solid hit, but in the background, he saw more than one shape disappear into the darkness. He fired the other barrel at the last shape he saw and got a loud yip, indicating another hit. Evidently some of the buckshot found another wolf, but not an immediate kill.

"What was it, Jim?" Elizabeth asked from the back door.

"A pack of wolves, Lizzy. I got the one that Sears had at bay. It looks like ole Sears earned his dinner today."

The rest of the week went without incident, then about 11 a.m. one morning, they were both out in the barn, when they heard the boat's horn, signaling the arrival of the paddle wheel boat. Jim walked around the house and saw the boat about a half mile away down the river. He also saw something else.

"Lizzy, bring my shotgun please," Jim shouted out.

In the grass above the beach lay an eight-foot gator, apparently sleeping in the morning sun, lying there with his mouth wide open. Elizabeth came out with the shotgun.

"Oh my," Elizabeth exclaimed.

"We need to get this critter out of the way before the boat docks. You might want to back up a little since I don't know which way he might jump."

"I'll ease up to him just behind his front foot and see if I can scare him into the water."

Jim moved up stomping the ground with his boots, thinking the gator would feel him walking and would flee. That did not happen. Jim tapped the gator on the foot and got nothing, then he tapped his snout, with the shotgun barrel, expecting him to react, and react he did.

With a snap of his jaws, the big reptile came alive. His head turned and his teeth snapped shut in the blink of an eye around the barrels of the shotgun in a death grip. Jim froze, and Lizzy stepped further back. The paddle wheeler had approached much closer and everyone on the boat was watching the action. Elizabeth stepped back toward the wood pile and picked up the axe. Jim pulled and the gator dug his feet in, half facing Jim, but refusing to let go of the barrel of the shotgun.

"Shoot him, shoot him," voices from the boat shouted.

Jim was holding his own but was beginning to worry about what would happen if he won. Gradually, the steel barrels began to slip between the teeth of the gator. As the barrels slipped free, the gators teeth snapped shut. The beast half ran, half jumped off the grass onto sand below, and ran toward the water. He splashed into the river and disappeared. The passengers and crew all cheered. Lizzy, with the axe, stood behind Jim to help if necessary.

The big paddle wheeler's bow slid up on the sand and grounded at an angle. The gangplank went down, and six passengers walked down the gangplank. They all huddled around Jim and Elizabeth, shaking their hands and remarking how brave they both were. Captain Johnny Belle and his crew man joined them after anchoring the boat both bow and stern.

"Now, Elizabeth," Capt. Johnny Bell joked, "you know you scared that gator away, waving that axe at him, don't you?" They all laughed.

At the table that night the conversation went from the gator episode to the wolf hide they saw hanging out back. The city folk from the north in the crowd were awed by everything they saw. The next morning, all the passengers boarded the paddle wheeler, and headed south towards Lake Okeechobee.

Jim and Elizabeth set about cleaning the hotel, and then Jim got ready to hunt, as meat was scarce and they needed a deer to round out their stores. Fall was coming as the black-jack turkey oaks were turning color. Last year's turkey chicks were half grown by now, and the gobblers were running together in the fall, but next spring, they would be strutting their stuff for the hens, gobbling to attract them. The clouds were black toward the northeast and the winds had picked up indicating a possible cold front was on the way. It rained for the better part of two days, so Jim had postponed his hunt until things dried out. The temperature dropped well below 40°, and there was even some frost.

Jim left the hotel at about 4 a.m. on his horse, headed for an oak grove he had seen in his ride around the country-side a few days before. That was also where the turkeys had been. His goal was to try to find out where the turkeys were roosting. Jim tied his horse to a small oak tree, pulled his shotgun out of the saddle scabbard, and started the quarter mile or so walk to the oak hammock.

His breath was visible in the blackness of the early morning hours. It was a cold, black, overcast morning, with no moon or stars.

Jim felt his way along a deer trail until he almost bumped into an oak limb. Apparently, he was on the edge of the oak hammock and decided to stay here until it began to get light.

Turkeys are both smart and dumb. They have the best survival skills of most any animal. Their eyesight is fantastic. They can run like a racehorse and when jumped, can reach the treetops almost as fast as you can get your gun up. Yet, with Jim's wing bone turkey call, Jim had even called turkeys back in that he had previously shot at. They were smart, but dumb. The wing bone turkey call was the dried hollow wing-bone of a turkey. You cupped the front side with your hands and with your lips together, sucked the end closest to you. The sound resembled the perk, perk, perk of a turkey.

Disorientated, Jim moved a little too far to the right, brushing against a palmetto fan, making a loud foreign sound in the stillness. He knew he was in trouble when out of the dark, he heard the frantic flop, flop, flop, of turkey wings as they abandoned their roost. The turkeys were in the trees roughly twenty yards in front of Jim, but it was still pitch black. Thinking he would get a little closer, he moved forward, but the crunch of the brittle, frosted oak leaves gave him away. The crunch was magnified by the black stillness of the early morning. Two more turkeys left the roost. Jim wondered if there were any turkeys left. He sat down on the ground, leaned up against a small oak tree, and waited.

It was a half hour before the light began to filter through the trees. In the half-light he looked hard in the trees for the tell-tale form of a turkey. He sat there until full light, when off to his left about fifty yards he heard more turkeys beginning to talk to each other as they do just before leaving the roost. Then they started to fly down, one at a time like they had a string tied from one to the next. However, they landed about 150 yards off to Jim's left in an opening in the hammock.

Thinking it was over, Jim stood up and leaned forward to look around the trunk of a large tree on his right. There he was. One loan turkey gobbler was still there, stretching his neck out to see what the ruckus was on the ground below him. They locked eyes at the same time and the turkey jumped. Jim, however, was quick and at about thirty yards, shot the flying turkey and big bird tumbled to the ground, stone dead. It was a young gobbler about fifteen pounds and they would eat well at dinner time.

Laying the bird down, he thought he would use the wing-bone caller, just in case. He perked like a lost hen and got a gobble-gobble back from a bird way off to the left. The bird moved around behind him, but then disappeared.

Jim tied the bird off the ground to a tree limb and decided to explore this hammock for deer sign. He followed the trail he came in on, as it wound its way through the hammock. Finding a downed tree, he sat on the trunk, near the uprooted roots which shielded him to one side. He cut a couple of cabbage palm fronds, which he stuck in the ground in front of him to shield his form. About two hours went by, when he saw a big buck coming down the trail. When the deer got within range, Jim shot the deer, a six-point buck. Now the work began. With both the deer and turkey gutted, he retrieved his horse and carefully lay the deer over the horse in front of the saddle and tied the turkey on the right side behind the saddle so he could easily mount from the left. In about an hour he was back at the hotel.

"What you got there, husband?" Elizabeth called out as she saw him coming.

"Just a little meat for the pot," he replied with a grin.

He let the deer slip off the horse onto the ground and untied the turkey, as Elizabeth took it in hand.

"You got all the beds made up, Lizzy?"

"I sure do, husband, and it's time to take a rest."

"Well, let me clean up a bit. Why don't we go upstairs and rumple up one of those beds before you get too big with that child for us to play around?"

"Absolutely not. We have that deer and turkey to take care of now you rascal. Maybe later. Besides, that's for making babies, not for having fun."

She snickered and began work on the turkey. In about an hour, the turkey was plucked.

"Jim, it's taken me a while, but I finally got all the feathers off this bird. I'm about to go put it in the oven. *With no refrigeration, the turkey had to be baked soon after it was killed.*

"Are you about through with that deer?" Elizabeth shouted over toward where Jim was working.

"Yes, I'm about finished, Lizzy. I've skinned the varmint and about got him butchered and I've cut some of the deer meat in thin strips for venison jerky and I will hang it in the little smoke house later. Some I'll pack in the salt barrel. One hindquarter to be roasted and the rest hung in the smoke-house. We'll have backstrap fried up for tonight and tomorrow," Jim explained. They would eat a lot of turkey and deer this week."

The next two months went well, with the exception of losing a couple of chickens to a small red fox that managed to get into the hen house. Jim intended to order some more chickens through the ferry boat captain.

"It's about time for the boat to arrive isn't it, Jim? Lizzy asked.

"I believe you are right, Lizzy, according to my pocket watch.

A few minutes later, the boat whistle sounded.

"It's only been about fifteen minutes, Lizzy, there goes that familiar toot, toot of the boat whistle."

They both stepped out on the porch, where Sears was sleeping.

Lizzy had her long blond hair down, cascading down around her left shoulder. She laughed and pointed.

"Look at that, there must be a full load today," she said smiling.

The boat's bow slid up on the sand, knifing its way up about ten feet before it came to a stop. The gangplank was about amid ships and it was dropped on the sandy beach. The captain shut off the engine and passengers began to walk down the gangplank. Two couples and three more men came off the boat, and they were walking up to the hotel, when another man appeared on the gangplank, he stopped, looked at Jim, pulled and a pistol and fired.

The bullet hit the door jamb next to Jim's face, exploding wood splinters in his cheek. Startled, Elizabeth jumped inside and went for her shotgun. The dog howled and jumped off the porch growling. The gunman fired another shot, which also missed.

"I'll kill you, O'Berry, the man shouted. Jim stepped just inside grabbing the rifle by the door. Jim peered out the door and fired a shot just as the man jumped inside the boat. Then he couldn't see anyone, except the other passengers, as they fled towards the back of the house.

The man with the gun disappeared inside the boat, opening his suitcase and pulling out a long-barreled Remington revolver, and he put his small derringer back into his pocket.

"That you, Boykin? Did you bring me the $16,000 dollars you owe me?" Jim shouted from inside the hotel. He had shifted to the left side of the door, so all that was exposed was his gun and his eye. The good thing was that he had the gunman cornered in the boat. The bad thing was that the captain and his first mate were still on the boat. Jim heard a big splash from the boat as Elizabeth came up behind Jim with her shotgun.

"Someone just jumped in the water on the other side of the boat, Lizzy, and that's Clyde Boykin doing the shooting, the scoundrel that stole our tomato crop. I supposed he is peeved at me for tying him to a tree for a spell.

"Look, Lizzy, the fella that jumped off the boat is the first mate. He's running for the back yard like the other folks did," Jim said as Elizabeth picked more splinters out of his cheek. Jim aimed his rifle at two shapes he could see in the wheel house.

"Dad gum it, I can't tell Boykin from the Captain inside the boat," Jim exclaimed.

"I'll see if I can flush him out, Lizzy," Jim said as he stepped out on the porch, keeping his rifle hidden behind him. And it worked.

Boykin appeared at the open window of the wheelhouse, with his long-barreled revolver. He fired about the same time as Jim did. He missed, but so did Jim. Jim's shot hit the bell in the wheelhouse as the clang rang long after the shots died. Realizing his position was deteriorating, Boykin turned to the Captain.

"Back this boat out of here and head down river," Boykin ordered.

"The ship' engines have been shut down too long. It will take time to get up steam," the Captain replied.

"Well get to it and be quick. I'll hold out up here until you do," Boykin shouted.

"Okay, but don't expect miracles, Captain Johnny Bell said sharply.

About that time, Jim shouted out to Boykin, distracting him.

"You know Boykin, you could have save all this if you had just been honest enough to pay me what you stole from me. Now I guess you've decided to kill me."

Meanwhile, the Captain went below, made sure the boat could not be started, took off his boots and eased out of the window, slipping noiselessly into the water. He swam downstream about 200 yards before coming on shore where he could see solid ground. He jumped up and ran for the back of the hotel.

Boykin, not hearing the engine start went down into the engine room only to find that the Captain had disappeared.

"Boykin cursed and stomped around for a couple of minutes. Then he headed back up to the wheel-house to figure out his next step.

"O'Berry, I got the captain here, and if you don't put the first mate back on this boat, I'll shoot the Captain."

"Well, that's a fine kettle of fish, I guess he wants a crew to take him down river," Jim said.

"Jim, look out the south window. Isn't that Captain Johnny Bell running barefoot around to the back?"

"Well bless my aching feet, it sure is. Ole Boykin is bluffing. Lizzy, go fetch the barefoot captain."

In a few minutes, the captain came sloshing through the hotel, all wet except for his captain's hat.

"Well, howdy Captain Johnny, I see you decided to go for a swim this chilly afternoon?"

Elizabeth was wrapping the captain up in a blanket about this time.

"Who is that fella, Jim?"

"He's the one that stole my tomato crop. I captured him once, but he got away. I really don't want to kill him, but it may come to that."

"You ain't fooling me none, Jim O'Berry, I think this man has put you out enough where you might like to end it here and now. I'd kind a like a piece of him too." Captain Johnny Bell exclaimed.

"Well yes, he has been a burden, but I had about gotten over it, or so I thought.

"Tell you what, Elizabeth will bring all but two of the people in here. We'll get two armed volunteers to watch the boat from each side of the house to make sure he doesn't come ashore and slip in the back door and gun us down. In the meantime, Lizzy, get the captain a rifle. Then we'll figure out what to do."

With the lookouts in place, Jim and the Captain sat down to hammer out a plan to get Boykin off the boat one way or another.

"What about starving him out," Elizabeth offered.

"The only problem with that Elizabeth, there is plenty of food on board to keep him for several days," Captain Johnny said.

"I think there is only one way to subdue the man, and I'll board the boat and do it. Lizzy, get me my saddle gun, I have a plan."

Elizabeth looked at her husband hard, knowing this could be the last time she saw him alive. She hugged him and then turned and headed upstairs to do what he had asked.

"How do you intend to handle it, Jim?" Captain Johnny Bell asked.

"I'll put Elizabeth upstairs with the rifle, she can shoot as well as anyone here. I'll take the double barrel shotgun and my saddle gun and try to flush him out. In an even fight, he will back down. I'll try not to corner him if possible, for he might fight back then."

"Sounds like you know him pretty good," Captain Johnny said.

"I was close to him on several occasions," Jim replied.

Elizabeth appeared with Jim's gun-belt and handed it to him.

"Don't worry, Lizzy, I have an edge, you take this rifle and go upstairs, if you see an opportunity, shoot him. However, I'll do my best to keep that from happening,"

Both Elizabeth and Captain Johnny wondered just what that plan was. Jim buckled his gun-belt, grabbed the double barrel, and started for the front door. From the porch, Jim shouted, "Boykin, I have three guns on you. If you show yourself with a gun, you will be shot. I'm coming to the boat and I intend to bring you out, dead or alive, it's up to you. We might still be able to come to a mutual agreement."

I know all about your agreements, O'Berry, Boykin mumbled under his breath. *He thinks he has me cornered, but I can play the same game the Captain and mate played. I'll just ease myself overboard and swim under water as far as I can and come up under those hyacinths over yonder near the shoreline, then I'll slip up on him when he least expects it.*

Boykin, took off his shoes and tied them around his neck. He thought the water would be a bit cold, but he could handle that. He emptied his Remington cap and ball revolver of powder and caps, knowing the water would ruin the powder. He had more in a waterproof powder container. He would reload near the shore. He looked out the window at the place he would come up at. The green hyacinths, some with purple flowers seem to move a little. Which could have been a big ole bass moving through the area. He slipped over the side of the after deck, took three deep breaths and eased under the water, swimming as fast as he could, and thought to himself, *Looks like I'm just inside the hyacinths, so I'll move over toward the shore.*

Everything was going well, he stopped and eased his head out of the water. He then drained the water out of his Remington long gun, getting it back into working condition. He had more powder in a small powder dispenser, so he primed the gun added caps, and cocked the gun.

Now it would shoot well, he thought. As he kept the gun out of the water and began to move toward the shore through the hyacinths, with just his head and pistol barely out of the water. He bumped into something. The water exploded. A big gator's jaws opened. In a flash, they snapped left toward what bumped him and snapped shut on Boykin's head and shoulders. The gun went off in a reflex action, attracting the attention of those on shore. Boykin tried to stand, but this was a large gator, pulling him down and rolling to drown him.

"Mr. O'Berry, Mr. O'Berry, he's over here," shouted the lookout to the south. All attention turned to the churning in the water, first the gator, then Boykin's body, then the gator again, as the beast rolled intending to drown his prize. Then all was quiet. Jim, halfway to the boat, froze.

They all came out and stood on the shore, staring in silence at the hyacinths where the ill-fated Boykin had met his end.

"Lord almighty, if I hadn't seen it I would not have believed it," the lookout broke the silence under his breath.

"Looks like you got your boat and your boots back Captain Johnny," Jim said walking back toward the hotel.

Needless to say, the topic of conversation at the dinner table that night was all about Boykin and how he came to his end. The next morning, everyone boarded the paddle wheeler and headed downriver for Okeechobee City, all with a story to tell.

"Well, Lizzy, I guess we can go back to our normal lives once again; the circus is over."

"Yes, Jim, and it's about time; and time to start the work day, but before we do, how about a piece of huckleberry pie?"

"Why, Lizzy. I thought you'd never ask. Do we have pie before or after we rumple up that bed of ours?"

"The only thing you'll rumple is in the garden with a hoe. Our garden needs tending. Huckleberry pie is all you get this morning."

The weeks and months passed without incident, until the rainy season came, but no rain.

One day a small sailboat slid onto the beach at the hotel with two men in it.

"Hello the house," one of the men called out.

Lizzy came out on the porch and could see two men, one with a long beard, work clothes and the other was younger with a new straw hat.

"You boys looking for a good meal to help you on your way?" Elizabeth called back.

"Well, that would be nice, but that is not our purpose to being here ma'am," the man with a long beard said.

The man with a beard was Emory Brown, dressed in work clothes and wearing no shoes. The other man was Tom Brown, Emory's son, dressed about the same, but with a clean-shaven face and high-top brogan shoes, easily seen as his pants were way too short.

"We are bringing bad news for you folks. The river is dried up in some spots so the paddle wheeler can't get through no more," He drawled, as he came up to the porch.

Jim came around the house, his saddle gun stuck in his belt as a caution.

"Captain Johnny Bell sent us to let you know," the younger man said.

"Well, come on in and set a spell, boys. How is the Captain anyway?"

"He's fit to be tied. He's floundering around town with no place to go. This drought could last for months they say."

Lizzy had put on a pot of coffee and soon served it with a piece of yellow cake.

Okay boys, it seems Lizzy and I are done here. It looks like we are going to have to vacate this hotel and go overland back to civilization. Do you think there is any way to get a buckboard downriver to us? If that is something you could do, we would hire you boys to do so. Just give me a price."

"Well, Jim, I seriously doubt it. However, we could bring it overland for about $20 plus the buckboard rental."

"Well, add another $5 to your fee and borrow a buckboard from my father in Kissimmee. Just explain the situation and that should be the best way to go."

"You got a deal Mister Jim, me and Tom here can most likely be back in about ten days. That would give you time to get things ready to travel."

"Well, Lizzy, looks as if we are going to south Florida sooner than expected."

"Just in time for the birth of our new baby," Elizabeth responded with a smile.

The buckboard arrived as planned. They had most of their belongings packed and ready to go. The hotel was boarded up as good as possible to be ready for new occupants next year. The man that brought the buckboard, had brought his own horse, so he left that afternoon. The horses were fed and put up for the night. Intending to leave the next day, they slept on a bed with no sheets, with just a blanket, so leaving the next day was quick and easy.

The cow and Jim's horse were tied to the back of the buckboard, with Sears, the hound, and the big black sow hog, Lula-Belle trailing along with them.

Three days later about 4 p.m., they reached Kissimmee. They used the pens at the ferry dock on the lake to house the cow and the pig. Jim dropped off Elizabeth at her parents and continued on through Kissimmee, before he went to his parent's house to return the buckboard.

Jim took his father's wagon and drove it over towards Frank and Martha's to visit. He went through Kissimmee town and stopped at the town hardware store.

John, the store owner greeted him at the door.

"Hello, John, I trust business is good these days?"

"Well, Jim, I can always use another customer, what can I help you with?"

"I haven't seen my father in a while and I would like to take him something nice that he wouldn't buy for himself."

"Well, Jim, I have some new Stetson hats, boots, or maybe a silver belt buckle from Mexico."

He walked through the store pointing out different things.

"Oh, here it is, a brand new .45 pistol with silver inlay and pearl grips. A beautiful piece, and it's as good to shoot as any other pistol."

"Well, you're right about one thing. Pa would never buy one of those himself. How much is it?"

"Not too bad, Jim, it sells for $27, and I'll throw in a box of .45 ammunition, so he can target practice a little."

"Okay, John, you got a box for it?"

"Sure do, the box it came in."

Jim took the gift along with the box of ammunition and put it in the wagon and headed towards his father and mother's place. When he arrived, he decided to take the buggy around back, where he saw another horse he didn't recognize. He stopped, tied up the team, and turned to go up the steps when he heard a crash, like a chair turning over and his mother scream, then silence. He started to run up the steps, then he remembered the gift. He opened the box of shells and loaded the gun, and put it back into the box.

Carefully he went up the steps, looked through the screen door but saw nothing. He walked into the house, through the kitchen and at the living room door, he could see his mother and father siting together on the sofa. His mother's face looked drawn and scared. His father sat stock still and apparently very angry on the sofa. They were both looking at the other side of the room that Jim could not see. Since he did not know what he was facing, he decided to take a chance.

Grandpa Frank and Grandma Martha O'Berry

"Hello mother, father, both of you look like you're sitting at the opera-house watching a scene you don't especially like," Jim said as he moved quickly over in front of his father, never looking to his left.

"Here Dad, remember I told you I would give you a present when I turned forty-five, well here it is. Please open it so mother can see," and he handed the box to Frank.

"Yes, Frank please open it so we can all see the box of rocks your son brought to you in this hour of need," Zeke Blakie said as he sat in a chair on the other side of the room holding a gun.

Jim whirled around, keeping in front of his father, who silently held the box, which was not his uppermost thought at this moment.

"Well, well, the infamous Mr. Blakie, do you plan to murder us all now? If I had a .45, I would see just how fast you are, how 'bout we step outside and see, while my parents enjoy my gift?"

"Well, Jim-Boy, that ain't exactly what I have in mind for you folks."

Martha, sensing that Jim was trying to tell them something, as he was not forty-five years old, leaned over and opened the box in Frank's hands. Seeing the gun, she reached in and took it as Jim was in front of her just enough.

"Now, Zeke, you remember when the sheriff and two of us walked into you coming out of a bar over on the west coast? Well, we were there to see if we could come to a truce, but you ruined that by shooting the sheriff. Not very wise don't you think? Ultimately, we thought you might have fled out of the state," Jim said realizing something was going on behind him.

"Well ain't that nice of you, Jim-boy. But, you see, I made a promise to your father there, and since my plan didn't work out, I decided to fulfill that promise myself. Nobody even knows I'm in town, but I will be seen in Gainesville with the help of a friend."

"Now, Mr. Blakie, if I can get Jim here to move over, I have something I would like to say to you," Martha said, as she silently pulled the hammer back on the .45 six-shooter.

"Before she does, Zeke, I have a question," Frank said.

"Why did your mother kill herself?"

"You keep out of my mother's business old man or I'll shut you up right now."

Zeke's attention turned to Frank.

"Wasn't it because you father was so mean and beat her, and all she had were the two kids. He left you three to fend for yourselves and when the cat dragged off your sister, it was the last straw. It was really your pa that caused all the ruckus, wasn't it?" Frank shouted, his face turning red.

"Zeke, you remember what I told you the day your daddy died? I told you if didn't mend your ways you would end up the same way your daddy did. Well, you just did." Frank said quietly.

Jim stepped in front of his father, as Zeke raised his gun. The explosion was deafening as Martha's shot blew Zeke backward in the chair, with a look of surprise on his face.

THE END

EPILOGUE

I am Kathleen O'Berry Lee, daughter of Jim and Elizabeth O'Berry. The name O'Berry evolved from the Irish O'Barry, which was mispronounced so much that my great-great-grandfather allowed it to be Americanized to O'Berry.

My grandfather Frank was an optimist and he also was very unhappy that he ever quit the cattle business. When World War I started, he went back into the cattle business, intending to sell cattle to the army, but the war ended too soon—before the herd matured. He was distraught at the loss of most of the money saved. However, Martha reminded him of when they had nothing but an ox cart, two oxen, two horses and a few farm animals and a rocking chair to their name.

He sold all the cattle he could. It took roughly 6 months to clean everything up, with enough left over to lead a good life. Frank and Martha went on to live out their lives in south Florida in a modern ranch style house. They both passed in the early 1940s.

My mother and father, Elizabeth and Jim O'Berry went to south Florida and farmed for many years. However, for Jim and Elizabeth, all did not go well. Their first-born son died three days later, leaving Elizabeth very despondent for the next six months. Child death at birth or soon thereafter was a common occurrence in those days. Eighteen months later, their second child, a daughter was born. Everything went well for the first six months, then she died in her crib, which devastated the couple. Two years later their third child, a daughter, was born. The next two years went smoothly until they realized she was autistic. They took her to Jacksonville to a specialist, but to no avail. At three years, she was eating tomatoes in the backyard and choked to death. It seemed that children were not to be in the O'Berry household. However, they had two more daughters, Rose and me. Poor Rose, at two years old was struck by a rattlesnake and died within minutes. That left them with me as their only child.

Unfortunately, mother and daddy grew apart, finally divorcing. Daddy remarried, after a while, to Annie, a retired school teacher. They stayed in south Florida for many years. My father, Jim, painted houses during those years and my son, James, spent two summers painting houses with him and hunting in the Everglades. When retiring from house painting, daddy farmed and had a roadside vegetable stand in Cutler Ridge below Miami.

When they began to fail physically, they moved to south Georgia to Annie's home town and family, where their lives ended naturally. Daddy left many anecdotes and notes on his life to my son, James, and they became the basis for much of this book.

Mother re-married, her second husband died of a heart attack after two years of marriage. She then married a well-known cattleman in the Kissimmee area. They had a good life together for many years but finally he also passed. Mother lived with us until she passed away. In the meantime, my son, James, lives in Tarpon Springs, Florida, near his son, James Brian, and we are all very close.

About the Author

J im Lee is a fourth-generation Floridian raised, in his early years, on a cattle ranch south of Kissimmee, Florida. As a boy, he spent considerable time hunting rabbits and running fish traps. His family moved to Orlando where he remained until he joined the U.S. Army. During his time in the service, he worked as a cryptographer in Japan.

Jim has hunted many areas of the state, fly fished many central Florida lakes, and salt water fished most of Florida's coastline and the Florida Keys. Turkey hunting and offshore fishing are his passions.

He was schooled at the University of Florida and at Alameda University. While making a living and raising his children, he was CEO of Florida Material Handling and Caster, Executive Director of the Florida League of Anglers, Sales Manager for Craft Equipment, Agent Manager for Allied Van Lines and Mayflower Van lines, owned a restaurant and finally a became mortgage broker. All the while, he wrote various articles for fun and profit.

Lee published *Seafood Legends* in 2008 and distributed them on both coasts of Florida and published a second edition in the summer of 2018.

He was a correspondent for the Tampa Tribune for 27 years, writing a weekly column on fishing and human-interest stories. His articles have been published in *Saltwater*

Fishing magazine, *Florida Sportsman* magazine and six other outdoor magazines. He also published *Florida Fishing* magazine, a newspaper give-away that was distributed on the Gulf Coast of Florida, and through J.C. Penny Co. where he wrote ad copy.

Lee wrote and produced several radio shows, and wrote ad copy and sold ads for three radio shows on three different radio stations, *The Getaway Show with Jim & Joe, The Getaway Show with Sergio,* and *The Getaway Fishing Show.* Lee also hosted a nationwide telephone fishing report for the Tampa Bay area, where northern anglers could get the current information to be able to plan their trips in advance.

Lee also served as a food critic for seafood restaurants on-line on a weekly basis and wrote a weekly column for the *Tampa Bay Area* website.

Home in Rockdale on A1 south of Miami

Hunting shanty

Mother O'Berry and Lillian

James A., Kathleen, and Elizabeth O'Berry

James A. O'Berry 39 years old, May 1925

James A. O'Berry, James W. Lee holding his son, James B. Lee

If you enjoyed reading this book
let others know!

Leave your personal review on
Amazon and Goodreads.

To meet Jim in person, at readings and speaking engagements, or to find out when he is scheduled for an appearance in your area, visit him on the web at www.JimLeeAuthor.com.

To book Jim to speak at your next event email him at: jleebetterrates@tampabay.rr.com.